WHAT A WAY TO GO

WHAT A WAY TO GO

Julia Forster

Atlantic Books

LONDON

First published in trade paperback in Great Britain in 2016
by Atlantic Books, an imprint of Atlantic Books Ltd.

This edition published in 2017 by Atlantic Books.

1 2 3 4 5 6 7 8 9

A CIP catalogue record for this book is available
from the British Library.

Paperback ISBN: 9781782397540
Ebook ISBN: 9781782397533

Printed in Great Britain

Atlantic Books
An Imprint of Atlantic Books Ltd
Ormond House
26–27 Boswell Street
London
WCIN 3JZ

www.atlantic-books.co.uk

To my mum and dad

Prologue

▼▼▼▼▼

Soon after my parents split up when I was five and I became one of the Lone Rangers, I asked Mum to record the credits of television programmes for me. I used to play back the videos, pressing my face close to the screen so that my nose was almost against it. My hair would stand on end with the static. I'd pause the rolling list of actors, producers, executives and directors, and in those frozen moments I'd search for my name – Harper – and those of my parents, Mary and Pete. I'd only just learnt how to spell them. If I ever spotted those three names together, it would be a special sign. A sign that one day, my parents would get back together. Here's the story of how they never did.

PART ONE

one

▼▼▼▼▼

I'm sitting at the top of the stairs with my legs dangling through the banister railings when Dad comes to pick me up one Friday after school. My copy of *Chambers*, the fat red dictionary, is by my side. I've been looking up the meaning of the word 'sheath': *a case for a sword; a tubular dress; a contraceptive device...*

At Lone Rangers parties I've heard tales of every kind of family break-up. From the ones where you can only visit your separated parent under supervision at Access Centres in cold church halls where the chess sets are missing pawns and the only cassette tape played is by The Beatles, to the ones where the ex-parents still go on family holidays together without a single argument. I've also compared notes on how to try to get your parents back together; I know kids of failed marriages who have faked everything from Valentine's cards to selective mutism.

On the whole, my folks can manage my fortnightly handovers without throwing cutlery or crying. Success is them having a conversation that lasts longer than two minutes.

At the front door, Mum says to Dad, 'Have you got time for a quick cuppa?'

I don't need a dictionary to understand that Mum inviting Dad in means one of two things. Either she wants a rise in her maintenance payments or an extra weekend off looking after me. Dad coughs then wipes his feet several times on the itchy doormat which says WELCOME TO THE MAD HOUSE!

They head into the kitchen where the kettle's filled. I think of going down to say hello, but would rather find out what Mum is after by earwigging their conversation. I grab my rucksack and creep downstairs, treading on the steps in the special way so that I don't make them squeak. Then, I dart across the hall into the lounge like a gerbil in headlights. I wedge myself between the radiator and the back of Mum's never-never sofa which is wrapped in plastic. Luckily the heating's off.

'Have a pew,' Mum says.

Dad sits on the sofa. The plastic cover crackles. I breathe as quietly as I can.

'How's things at British Steel?' Mum asks.

'Been better,' Dad says, then changes the subject. 'I guess this is about Harper? Is she up to her anti-capitalist tricks again?'

'She seems to be heralding free enterprise now, actually. She's setting up her own shop. Wants to contribute towards the fund.'

'What "fund"?' Dad asks, very slowly, as if he's selecting letters with which to make up a word from the dregs of a Scrabble bag when the game is nearly up.

'The house fund,' Mum says.

Seems Dad's Scrabble bag's empty.

'Interest rates are only going one way, Pete.'

'You're nowhere near having enough for a deposit, are you?' he asks.

'How would you know what I manage to save?'

'By your shoe collection?'

'Do you have any idea how expensive it is to bring a kid up alone?'

'You're *not* doing it alone.'

Although the radiator isn't on, I'm starting to feel toasty. Someone on our Kendal Road dead end is practising scales on the piano as if playing with their big toe. Far off, an ice-cream van tinkles its metallic lullaby.

Mum says, 'The landlord has been dropping hints that he wants to sell. If we don't buy this place then we'll have to move. Again. Harper'll have to go to a different middle school if I can't find another rental nearby.'

We've already moved three times in as many years. We struggle to find places to rent because most landlords in Blackbrake either don't believe a single mum could earn enough to pay the rent, electric and water, or they don't approve of divorce. I'm the only outcast in my class *and* on my street with separated parents. As far as school goes, my best mate Cassie reckons year eight will be crap whatever school you're in because the National Curriculum is starting under the GERBIL this September. I don't know what this means, but I think it has something to do with a flagpole and the school pet.

'So...' Dad says.

Mum says, 'I'm asking for a rise.'

'Another one?'

Mum's voice is an octave lower: 'You got Ivy Cottage, after all.'

Dad: 'You got the Mini!'

Mum: 'That rust bucket full of out-of-date baked beans? Which do you think is worth more?'

Dad: 'That's not the point. You got Harper.'

'But *you* didn't want her,' Mum says.

'Now, Mary...'

I block up my listening chimneys by pushing a thumb hard into each of my ears. My parents often sort through their scrapyard of arguments. They never find anything shiny or new, just the usual unwanted, broken, battery-flat crap which they pick over like a car scrap merchant looking to take something worthless and make it valuable again.

There's a car-breaker round the back of Louise's house in Coventry – she's one of the Lone Rangers parents. Excavators scrape through the heaps of totalled cars, their bumpers bent awkwardly after head-on collisions. Men in orange overalls salvage what they can from the write-offs then squash the wrecks into massive cubes to be liquidized. I imagine all the things the car metal could be made into: hospital beds; drip stands; wheelchairs; a record stylus; clasps on a jewellery box; cartridge pens; cheap wedding rings...

When I poke my head around the side of the sofa, both Mum and Dad have gone.

I sit on the pebbledash doorstep to wait for their return. Next door at number eleven, Edna's Rottweiler barks blue murder.

The Lone Rangers logo is a paper-chain family of three; there's a kid in the middle with arms which stretch out in both directions to keep hold of the mum in one hand and the dad in the other. You can tell that no child helped to design that logo because this is not how it feels when your parents separate.

Us kids left behind in the wreckage of a broken home cope by creating two cut-out versions of ourselves: one for each parent. At Mum's, I watch four hours of telly a day, read trashy novels and speak my mind. At Dad's, I watch my Ps and Qs, digest facts and toe the line.

After twenty minutes or so, Dad drives down Kendal Road, pretending that he's come straight from work when he hugs me, though I catch the malty smell of Blackbrake lager on his breath. Mum plays the same game and fakes meeting Dad for the first time that evening. I bet she went to check the bank balance.

While I'm putting my rucksack into the boot of Dad's car, Mum dumps five large boxes of baked-bean tins on to the pavement just outside our front door and disappears upstairs again without even saying goodbye.

Mum and Dad won a car full of a thousand tins of baked beans in a competition before the divorce. When they split up, Dad got custody of the cottage. Mum took me plus the X-reg Mini. The tins were split fifty-fifty. They're beyond their use-by date now but, Dad says, as he loads the car boot with the boxes, tinned food never goes off.

two

▼▼▼▼▼

On the outskirts of Blackbrake, Dad and I hit a traffic jam on the
ring road. Some people cheat by driving along the wide pavement
with their hazard lights flashing. Dad leans across my lap, winds
down my window, then sticks two fingers up in a V-sign at each
of the cars as they pass.

'I can do that for you, if you like?' I say.

Dad sinks back into his bead-covered car seat and sighs, 'It's all
right.' This is the sum-total of our conversation on our journey
to Ivy Cottage.

If you tried to spot the difference between life in a village
like Hardingstone compared with a town like Blackbrake, you'd
notice that in the countryside, people don't lock front doors, cars
or even bother putting on handbrakes. No one drinks lager in
the streets in Hardingstone and nor are there arson attacks down
the playground.

Before Mum and I left the cottage in Hardingstone, I used to
play with the village kids all the time. But when I started seeing

them just two days out of fourteen – on the weekends I was visiting Dad – they began to leave me out of their games. I made a real effort to join in, but within a few weeks they stopped talking to me altogether. It's like I have some kind of jinx.

My only friends now in Hardingstone, apart from Mrs Curtis, are down the graveyard. At least they don't answer back. Or call me a weirdo.

It's dusk when Dad and I arrive at Ivy Cottage, the street's so quiet I swear I can hear crocus bulbs cracking the soil, desperate for sunlight. A new blue Lada estate is parked right outside the cottage. It puts me in mind of a hearse with its polished bonnet and many large windows. I peer through one of them; instead of carrying a coffin, the car is littered with crumpled papers, empty takeaway cartons and cardboard boxes, as well as large plastic bottles of chemicals marked 'hazardous'. It must be Patrick's car; Mum's always said that Dad's best mate should come with a health warning.

I walk up the moss-covered garden path, trying not to get stung by the waist-high nettles growing at either side of the narrow pavement. The sharp smell of lemon juice wafts out of the gaps in the rotting window frames next door where Mrs Curtis lives. She'll be at her jam pans of lemon curd. Inside, an Italian LP is stuck on her gramophone. It's the only song I've ever known her play:

> Ma l'amore no,
> Ma l'amore no,
> Ma l'amore no,
> Ma l'amore no...

Inside Ivy Cottage, we find Patrick crouching in the kitchen next to the open door of the electric oven which he has switched on to the highest temperature setting. He's still wearing his raincoat, scarf and woolly hat. When he stands up to his full height to explain, the red bobble on the top of the hat scrunches up against the ceiling. 'I couldn't find the coal scuttle,' he says.

Grey mould shapes creep up the once-beige wallpaper in the cottage. The rising damp has left orange stains, too, as if tracking its plan of attack towards the ceiling. Outside, the ivy, which used to crawl up just one side of the house, chokes the whole cottage. It's so thick now that before I can open the window in my bedroom, I have to take a pair of scissors to the new growth and give it a good trim.

If I had to find an A-side to my dad having so many history books lining the walls it would be that they offer extra padding for the sounds and smells from next door, and soak up the dampness in the air like a yellow car sponge.

At the hearth, Dad ties sheets of newspaper into figures of eight, stacks the twists in the grate then places kindling on top; the fire has never drawn well, so next a large piece of newspaper is put over the fireplace to trap the oxygen, which makes it catch eventually. Once it has begun to roar, Dad tongs single lumps of coal on to it.

I nurse the fire while Patrick helps Dad to carry in the boxes of beans from the boot of the car. Dad unpacks them, stacking the tins in pyramid shapes in the puzzle cupboard under the stairs. Then the three of us sit by the fire and Patrick shares out the sherry trifle he brought with him. He makes sure I get the most glacé cherries.

'You *still* not got a new telly?' Patrick asks Dad. 'How d'you survive, Harper?'

'With difficulty,' I reply.

'She reads,' Dad says, without looking up from the fireplace.

Dad hasn't replaced the television since the cathode ray tube blew up. I can still picture the black and white telly we had: it was the size of a small cupboard, with a wooden frame and a screen that bulged outwards. Like when I wake up in the mornings, the telly took several minutes to come to its senses. While you were waiting for a picture to appear, a fuzzy mess of hissing white lines crossed the black screen.

'Why *don't* we get a new television?' I ask.

'Bubblegum for the eyes,' Dad replies. 'When I was teaching history, you could tell the kids who watched too much of it – they had fewer brain cells. It was depressing.'

'You up to anything exciting tomorrow?' Patrick asks.

'Village fête,' Dad says, prodding the fire with the brass poker.

'Sounds fascinating,' Patrick says, winking at me.

I leave the two of them by the fire to finish off the last of the trifle and I go to boil the kettle with enough water for my three hot-water bottles.

In my bedroom I draw the crushed-velvet curtains closed. The hems are two feet too long; when I was seven I tried to shorten them with a stapler, but the green velvet was much too thick. I could just cut off the extra material, but deep down I still imagine that Mum might come back to fix them.

Weekends in Hardingstone are low voltage, thanks to Maggie Thatcher. Dad explained to me recently that Hardingstone is

13

becoming 'dormitory' because of her policies. I discovered when I looked up 'dormitory' in *Chambers* that this means Hardingstone is becoming 'a large room in which people sleep'. It's true that Hardingstone's sleepy; people walk, without aim, as if the footpaths are covered in treacle; they speak as if their mouths are stuffed with caramel and their heads with feathers. Even the large bomb from the First World War which stands lopsided in the graveyard hasn't bothered to explode yet. The house where the bakery once was has long since had its oven sealed and the school closed its doors to pupils in 1982; last year it was converted into a house. There's nothing much to do here but carve up your quiet life into quarter hours each time the church bells toll.

Mornings, I usually wake up around ten and watch the white aeroplane writing of my breath as I call out for Dad to make sure he's still there. Once I'm up, I stand in front of the fridge in the kitchen, willing breakfast to suggest itself: difficult, given that the contents are often just a large bottle of mayonnaise, a block of butter and a couple of bowls of leftovers hidden under a layer of what I can only describe as cuckoo spit. Luckily, the village two miles down the road is big enough to have a convenience shop. While we're in civilization, Dad also buys us both a magazine to read during the weekend – his about history, mine about pop stars – two potatoes to bake and eat with out-of-date beans, a box of cereal and, if the mood strikes, a Viennetta.

Sundays, I do homework, piano practice and wish I could watch *The Waltons*. We walk around the dead village so that bang on one o'clock we're at the Spread Eagle – now up for sale with permission to convert – where Dad orders a roast dinner with all the trimmings for us both. We always sit on the same red velvet stools in the snug and Dad does the Sunday crossword while I make a list on the back of a beer mat: my fortnightly guess at who'll be in the top ten later that evening.

Every so often, Dad and I go on trips to places of historical interest – the kind of visits he used to go on with his students when he was a history teacher, I suppose. Last autumn we went to Flag Fen in Peterborough to see how Neolithic people lived in their roundhouses back in the Bronze Age. I bought a tiny piece of ancient wood, over three thousand years old, which I keep in its plastic box by my bed. And last summer we went on a day trip to Portsmouth to see the carcass of the *Mary Rose* which sank in 1545.

Dad may be able to remember the names of all the kings and queens of England going back centuries and important dates from the past thousand years like when the Magna Carta was signed, but he draws a blank whenever I ask him about our recent history and what my life was really like before the divorce.

three

▼▼▼▼▼

That Saturday morning I go on my every-other-weekend graveyard inspection. Hardingstone church is sandwiched between several towering trees. Underneath their evergreen branches, hundreds of gravestones are sinking crookedly into the soil. They're in a state of what's known as 'benign neglect' – something Mum says is only a good thing if it's to do with either graveyards or being a single parent.

Many of the gravestones are so old that you can't read the writing any more: years of hard rain and sad hands have rubbed the letters away. One grave has had the same plastic windmill next to it for years, whipping round in the breeze. The colours of the sails have faded to a pale, murky yellow. Scattered around the graves there are candles, damp and warped crucifixes, mouldy teddy bears and photos bleached by the sun in rusting frames.

My inspection always includes visiting my friends: Harry James Curtis (1915–1949), who was Mrs Curtis's husband, and Heaven Called a Little Child (March 16–30, 1888). I didn't know either of them, but as Heaven Called a Little Child died exactly a hundred years ago, her parents must be dead now too, so I always clear Heaven Called's grave of weeds and wind-fallen wellingtonia branches.

As I'm piling up the debris, the church bells toll like a waterfall; the bell-pullers must be practising for a wedding. I run up to the holly hedge surrounding the cemetery just in time to see a white Rolls-Royce driving right down the middle of the lane as if the chauffeur doesn't want to even *think* about scratching the sides. There are two thick, white ribbons tied on to the wing mirrors; they meet at the tip of the bonnet in a V-shape where a silver lady looks set to fly away. The back seats in the car are empty; I guess he's on his way to collect the bride.

I imagine Mum on her wedding day, breezing up the path to the church. Dad, as he waited at the altar with sweaty palms and armpits. I have a hazy memory of a framed photo from their wedding day, a close-up of them by the gates of Hardingstone church. It used to sit on the mantelpiece in Ivy Cottage; it disappeared as soon as Mum and I quit the village. If I concentrate, I can still picture the tiny white flowers that Mum wore in her hair.

When I arrive back at the cottage, I find Dad in the kitchen sniffing under the lid of a bulging carton of coleslaw.

'How do you fancy chips for lunch?' he says, chucking the coleslaw in the bin.

'Is the Pope Catholic?' I say, joining him in front of the fridge. Inside, what was once an onion bhaji now looks more like fossilized wood.

'There's the village fête first, though. Let's get something for breakfast there, shall we?' he says.

17

'OK,' I say, 'But only if it's cake.'

At the fête, I head straight for the squash and cake hatch once Dad has paid the entry fee and given me a quid to 'spend wisely' – which, in my dictionary, means to spend it all on home-baked triple chocolate fudge cake.

The last time I came to the village hall was two Christmases ago for the fundraiser to straighten the wonky church spire. I won a jar of pickled beetroot on the tombola, and also marked X in the exact spot on a map of a desert island where the treasure was buried and won first prize: my *Chambers* dictionary.

'Is there a treasure hunt?' I ask Mrs White, with hair to match her name. She's pouring weak orange squash into turquoise cups and saucers.

'Not today.'

I pay 20p for a slice of cake and a cup of juice and take them to an empty table covered in chequered cheesecloth. Dad's up the other end of the hall talking to the man who runs the Spread Eagle. Seems he's selling off his brass items – pokers, coal shovels and scuttles. Dad appears to be in the market for a horseshoe.

It's on account of watching Dad that I don't notice Richard until he's pulling up a chair next to mine. Perhaps he's no longer allergic to me.

'When's your birthday?' Richard asks.

'September twenty-eighth.'

'I'm thirteen next weekend. I'm having a disco in town...' Richard pulls apart a jammy dodger, and licks off the jam filling before eating the biscuit halves in one go.

Richard's sixth was the last village birthday party I was invited to. There was a clown, who made animals out of long, blue balloons. I chose two birds kissing in a heart. Richard chose a gun.

18

'...It's going to be radical,' he says.

'I'm at my mum's next weekend,' I say.

'Oh, you're not invited. Only my friends are coming,' Richard says as he gets up to leave.

My eyes are pincushions, but I will not let Richard see my tears fall. I turn my head, and make out the swimmy figure of my antique friend, Mrs Curtis, at her stall.

Mrs Curtis is selling jars of 1987 gooseberry jam, pot-pourri and rusted things like can openers, creaking whisks and empty tins of dried milk powder. Veins pump blue blood beneath her skin which is as thin as the airmail paper Mum uses to write to my grandma in New Zealand. Mrs Curtis's fingernails are long and cracked, and her hands are like claws, but come July they'll still be nimble enough to sort metal colanders of gooseberries into two bowls: tart and ripe. Thing is, Mrs Curtis's brain is dissolving slowly like sugar in one of her pans of bubbling jam. Plus she dribbles. But I don't mind. I love her: we're the village misfits.

I place 10p in a plastic pot for a sandwich bag of pot-pourri and go round behind her stall to stand right next to one of her face-long ears so she can hear me when I speak.

'How's school?' she shouts.

'I'm doing well in history!' I'm glad she's having one of her good days and that she can recognize me, though it probably won't be long before she gets confused. 'Last term we did the Romans and archaeology! This term we're studying energy and where food comes from! We're visiting a farm at the end of term for our school trip!'

She nods. 'How's your mother?' As well as being the only village person not to blank me, Mrs Curtis is the only one who ever mentions Mum.

'She's fine!'

'Any boyfriends?' she asks, her eyes searching my face like the beam of a lighthouse.

'No,' I say.

'What happened to the bank manager?'

'Didn't like him!' I say.

'The artist?'

'Flew home!' I remind her. The water of her broken memories is starting to pour through her colander brain.

'You deserve to be happy, Harper! You make sure she looks after you. She's a witch, your mum!' She looks at me with her cooked-fish eyes, and sighs. 'Care for a gooseberry, Gregory?'

'Thanks, Mum!' I shout.

When Mrs Curtis's colander brain overflows, she not only gets dead bitchy but she also calls anyone within gooseberry-spitting distance Gregory. I just ignore it and play along, especially since nobody else in the village tends to talk to Mrs Curtis, especially about her long-lost son; I guess we share the same Hardingstone jinx.

I have a fuzzy picture in my mind of Gregory as well. I remember his corrugated beige cricket pads that were strapped to his legs. I suppose he must have left for London when I was as tall as his kneecaps. He never visits Mrs Curtis, and village gossip goes that he got a divorce too when he moved to the capital. I suppose that's why he doesn't come back; nobody here approves of the D word.

Mrs Curtis presses a rusty cog into my palm as if it's an emerald. I wonder how long it'll be before she loses all her marbles and becomes a patient down the Hopkin Wynne Mental Hospital. Then I'll be able to go on the hospital treadmill without trespassing.

four

▼▼▼▼▼

I can invent dead clever tricks to exterminate those potential step-dads who don't pass my quality control; the latest one to head into the boyfriend bin was the bank manager, Mike Hyde. For Mum's third date he took the three of us out for tea down the Harvester; I nearly fell asleep in my salad with thousand-island dressing and bacon bits. He kept boomeranging what we were talking about back to asset strips, fat profits and bottom lines. When the waitress brought over the bill, he magicked a calculator out of his pin-stripe jacket pocket and worked out what his third of the bill came to. So, when he called one Friday evening to speak to Mum, I lied point blank and said she was on another date down the Shang High.

Mum thanked me afterwards.

Only thing I regret is that his car had electric windows.

Then, there was Alfonso. Alfonso Hope Follanger. I had a soft spot for Alfie because he could make thick pancakes in the shape of gerbils. But Alfie was Canadian. He was also a vegetarian and an animal rights activist. And he said that the only gerbils in the house would be made out of butter, eggs, buttermilk and flour. A few weeks after I asked him fifty times in a row to buy me a gerbil, he flew back to Manitoba. But I like the sound of Kit. I won't throw a poppadum on *his* lap when he comes round for tea.

I learn about Kit that Sunday evening after coming back from my Dad. Mum doesn't hear me come in on account of Dolly Parton crooning D-I-V-O-R-C-E in the lounge. I perch on the bottom step of the stairs with my duffle coat still on. The needle lifts from the LP, and I can make out what Mum's saying to Avon's-calling Oona.

'What's he do then?' Oona asks.

'Sells chocolate.'

A chocolate salesman? That has to be the best *potential stepdad job yet.*

'How old?'

'Forty-one next month.'

'Divorced?'

'Twice. No kids. How do I look?' Mum says.

'Fan-bloody-tastic.'

'Hope I can manage to do the same on Saturday,' Mum says. 'Kit's taking me out.'

'That can't be his real name.'

'It's short for KitKat. Cheque OK?'

'KitKat? Well, I'm sure Derek'll babysit. He needs the money. Spent his piggybank on a pair of winklepickers last weekend.'

I tiptoe to the front door, open it, then slam it closed so the letterbox rattles. 'Hi, Mum!' I yell.

'We're in the lounge! Stay for another glass?' Mum asks Oona as I go through.

22

'Best get back, check Derek's uniform's dry,' Oona says.

'Hell's teeth. Harper, did you put your uniform in the laundrette pile?'

I shake my head.

'You'll have to go in mufti again,' Mum says.

Two strips of gas fire are burning red and orange in the lounge, in the middle of which Mum is sitting on a dining chair. Her eyes are like two calm, blue lakes in a thunderstorm of colour. Her eyelids are painted purple fading into yellow then white; her eyelashes drip with electric-blue mascara and two red stripes storm up her cheeks to find the tops of her ears beneath her bobbed hair. Mum has the perfect face to practise colouring in, Oona says, because it's beautiful.

Oona loves layering make-up over her own face too. She calls it 'war paint'; I've never seen her without it on. Oona undoes her white cloak which she wears over beige culottes and a shocking-pink tubular top with a zip that goes up the middle at the front; it puts me in mind of my pencil case when I fill it full to bursting. Being careful not to break her ballerina-pink nails, she screws lids back on small pots of coloured powders, tiny bottles of varnish and the chemical-smelling bottle of nail-varnish remover which makes my eyes water. I take two chocolate bourbons from a plate on the coffee table and post them in my mouth like Mum does pegs when she's hanging out a hand wash.

'I'll let you know if Derek's free,' Oona says, as she waddles towards the front door, her heavy briefcase of Avon tricks at her side. 'Thanks for being my crash-test dummy!'

'We'll have spag bol once my nails are dry,' Mum says, wafting her hands through the air like she's trying to take off.

How nice Mum's food will be depends on what the hole-in-the-wall says. If she comes back from checking the bank balance in a good mood, it'll be spaghetti with bolognese sauce which she'll make a vat of, then store the rest of it in Tupperware in the deep freeze. But if she comes home in a sulk it'll be old baked beans on anything that she can squeeze into the toaster like crumpets, stale Scotch pancakes or frozen potato waffles.

I take one more chocolate bourbon before Mum clears the plate from the coffee table. She holds it by the rim so as not to smudge her nails.

'How was your weekend?' she asks.

'Fine,' I say.

'Just fine?' Mum asks, frowning. 'Was your dad OK?'

'He was fine,' I say. Bet what Mum *really* wants to ask is whether Dad mentioned anything about their row – or a rise in her allowance.

'I'm banning that word from now on,' Mum says, heading out to the kitchen. 'Everything's just *fine* these days...'

I zap the telly with the doofer and flick through the four channels. Nothing interesting's on, so I call Cassie to find out what she got up to at the weekend. Not only did she go down Our Price to see The Primitives gig, she's totally trumped my bag of pot-pourri by buying their new single *and* getting it signed by the band.

'Come round mine next weekend, H. I'm free on Sunday. We'll do something just as fun,' Cassie says.

'Thanks,' I say, but I feel like a charity case.

'Balls,' Cassie says. 'Mum's coming to check my teeth and homework. Better go.'

'Sounds like the sort of thing they'd do in a boarding school,' I say.

'Tell me about it,' Cassie says. 'See you tomorrow.'

I go through to the dining room to ink in my visit to Cassie's on the family calendar. The dining-room table doubles as an office desk and a place to eat. It's this table that we clear for takeaway meals with potential stepdads. I'm the firing squad. Anything can be used as a weapon and look like the innocent accident of a twelve-and-a-half-year-old. A poppadum, dripping in mango chutney; a well-aimed fork in the potential new stepdad's lap; questions about what they earn (which Mum blushes at and tries to stop me asking, but secretly wants to know); how many women they've proposed to before (ditto); and, of course, if they eat meat or object to gerbils as pets on 'grounds of animal violation'. For these greasy meals, Mum gets the special red tablemats from the top of the bookshelf, dusts them down then wraps them in plastic shopping bags.

The rest of the time, the dining-room table is where Mum works on her Open University English Literature degree after I've gone to bed. At one end of it, a tower of papers is stacked; it'll avalanche if one more essay is asked for. Half-drunk cups of coffee are balanced on second-hand books, and on the floor beneath there's a large hardback thesaurus which Mum uses as a footstool.

Above the table hangs the 1988 calendar. On it, Mum writes in different coloured ink each weekly event – Open University deadlines, benefits and allowance payments, piano lessons, repeat prescriptions, paydays – plus, the weekends are colour coded with orange highlighter for a Dad weekend, and blue for a Mum weekend with capital Ds and Ms depending on where I'm supposed to be.

D M D M D M D M
D M D M D M D

M D M D M
D M D
M D
M
D
M D
M D M
D M D M D
M D M D M D M
D M D M D M D M

Fifty-two capital letters that dictate my life.

I scrawl in the square of Sunday 27 March that Harper will be at Cassie's. Mum has already inked in her activity for that day. It says 'Mary is SLEEPING'.

five

▼▼▼▼▼

The town I live in now, Blackbrake, is famous for lager, lifts and loonies. Mum says they should print *that* on the 'Welcome to Blackbrake' sign. I've never seen a drunken mental hospital patient travelling in an elevator, but I do glimpse the patients sometimes when Cassie and I go trespassing on the grounds of the private Hopkin Wynne Mental Hospital; it's named after a famous poet who went potty there. The facilities are amazing compared to Blackbrake General Hospital. At the Hopkin Wynne, there's a gym with an electronic bike machine, rowing machine *and* a treadmill. Cassie and I use the rowing machine and pretend we're on the river Brake. There's no lock on the gym door, so even if we were caught by a mental nurse, we'd say it was fair game.

If Cassie's not with me, I don't have the guts to trespass down the private facilities alone, so I go down the public General Hospital instead. You go in the main entrance through two sliding doors that lead to a long sloping corridor. It smells of disinfectant, cancelling out all the smells you're certain to find lurking underneath, like boiled potatoes and dried blood. Brown and white signs announce each ward. Beds on wheels are parked by the flapping doors, waiting for an ill person to come out of Theatre, the Serious Injury Unit or Oncology. You pass patients snailing forward on wheelchairs or shuffling on flattened slippers. Some lean on thin metal drip stands from which bags of water dangle. The water is being injected into them, and you wonder if that's what is making them look so yellow.

The vending machine that gives you back more change than you are supposed to receive is next to Oncology. I have this week's 30p pocket money in my pink sparkly purse and I know exactly what it's going to be spent on: three packets of bacon-flavoured fries. While I press the pad and watch the metal hand corkscrew, the thought pops into my head that Mum's new boyfriend might be a vegetarian. And that would spell D-I-S-A-S-T-E-R. I pocket the 10p profit and hoover up the fries.

Mum spends every Saturday in town window-shopping. Once a month on paydays, she purchases as well: mostly clothes, shoes and Sainsbury's beef mince. Saturdays are also release days for mentalists down the Hopkin Wynne. They sway in their seats on the bottom deck of the Number 14 bus, talking to their reflections in the window. Mum and I sit on the top deck so that she can see into strangers' lounges, and comment on their choice of three-piece suites. That Saturday, I go in with her.

Blackbrake bus station isn't that different from the General Hospital: pale people sit in plastic bucket seats, waiting; it smells of disinfectant and the vending machine (which adds up properly) sells bacon-flavoured fries. The only difference is that I feel a sense of dread in the bus station: it means spending two hours of my life in the Black Knight shopping centre.

Mum announces as we walk along the glass gangplank between the bus station and the Black Knight that we're shopping for a new pair of shoes for her meal out with Kit later that same evening. First, though, it's Boots the Chemist for pink anti-wrinkle cream and hairspray. I stay upstairs to browse in the music department while Mum takes the down escalator towards Health and Beauty.

I spot the Pet Shop Boys' new release, 'Heart', in the seven-inch single section. On *Top of the Pops* on Thursday it was tipped for Number One. In the music video there's a bride dressed in a white, lacy balloon of a gown who ends up kissing a vampire and driving off with *him* instead of Neil Tennant which just goes to show what I already know: weddings aren't worth the bother.

At least I can tell Cassie that I've seen the sleeve for next week's Number One, even if I can't afford to buy it. Like me, Cassie's religious about the charts, and Five Star. The Top Forty is like a holy rosary. You need to tune into it every Sunday evening; it's the key to being cool, especially on a Monday morning when you're in assembly and you should be singing about Jesus being nailed to death on a wooden cross and coming back to life, but instead you whisper Bananarama lyrics.

Once Mum has got her Oil of Ulay and Elnett, we stroll across Blackbrake market towards the shoe shop. Plus-size Union Jack underpants dangle from hangers; grapefruit, apples and oranges are stacked on top of sheets of fake plastic grass. Underneath the stalls, crates of bruised fruit and reject goods gather.

The done thing at Blackbrake market is for stallholders to rock up in their white vans at dawn, unload their bulk-bought stock then write the day's hot bargains on neon-yellow stars. They shout them out at top-decibel level to anyone who happens to pass:

'GET YA MADONNA, KYLIE AND WACKO JACKO PIN BADGES 'ERE!'

'SHELL SUITS! ONLY FIVE NINETY-NINE!'

'NEON TROUSERS: TWO FOR A TENNER!'

Blackbrake is also where you should go if you need a new pair of shoes, as there is an ancient tradition in this town of shoemaking. Depending on the occasion, you can go to different types of shoe shops. If it's nearly a new term and I need black PE plimsolls, for example, it would be SpeedyShu – shopping there is a cross between buying a fast-food burger and going swimming down Blackbrake pool. You go through a metal turnstile, choose from two styles of plimsoll – black or white – which are stapled together at the heel. They all look the same and cost £1.49. Within five roly-polys in the school hall, they'll start to unstick at the seam.

Kit's date, however, calls for none less than Gordon Benét's. Mum is perched on the edge of a green velvet chair, twisting her ankle to inspect the pair she spotted in the window and is now trying for size: silver heels so shiny I can see my face in them, and so high I bet my ears would pop if I wore them.

'Don't they look lovely?' asks the sales assistant – Simon, according to his badge – who crouches at Mum's feet. He looks ready to kiss them.

'They're very silver,' I say.

'Do you have an outfit in mind?' Simon asks Mum's ten-denier legs.

Mum nods. 'They'll go perfectly with my C&A polka-dot number.'

'Do you like dressing up in Mum's high heels, m'duck?' Simon asks, dragging his eyes towards me now.

'I like trainers.'

'You'll succumb to them soon. Don't worry, pet,' Simon says. He uses the same tone of voice as my doctor when he identified a rash I had as measles. Simon places the heels in a nest of tissue paper in a shoebox as if they're made of glass.

At the till Mum says, 'I hope this works,' as she hands over a green and orange card. 'I just got it.'

'You've succumbed to the flexible friend?' he says.

'Hasn't everyone?'

Buying high heels is an illness. And, it seems, so is spending plastic money.

six

▼▼▼▼▼

Derek's quiff and the many flaps of his trench coat must arrive about a minute before the rest of him when he calls to babysit later that evening. When I open the door I think I've seen a ghost, and my face probably goes as white as his.

'It's just talcum powder,' he says, barging past.

He's wearing an LP-sized bag like a shield across his chest. His lips are deep purple – nearly black – as are his eyelids. He must have attacked them with some of his mum's Avon supplies.

Although Derek scares me, he might have some cash. And I am about to open a new shop, Harper's Bazaar, which stocks fag ends. Most sixteen-year-olds would be mental if they didn't want to buy them; I just need to know that Derek isn't going to bite me in the neck.

Rip-off Chanel Number Five and tobacco smoke mix together in the bathroom while Mum leans over the sink, powdering red slashes up her cheeks. From the lounge, I can make out the chorus to Adam Ant's 'Prince Charming'.

'Do whatever Derek says, OK?' Mum says.

'But he's wearing make-up. And black nail varnish!' I whisper.

'Let him try some out on you. Wouldn't hurt for you to be more *feminine*.' Mum whips the wand of her electric-blue mascara over her eyelashes.

'But he's a boy!'

'Relax,' Mum says. 'He's harmless. It's probably just a romantic Goth thing.' She flashes her dentures to make sure there's no fire-engine-red lipstick on them; if there were a stain, she could just slide her falsies out and give them a quick polish. Once she has finished painting her face, she air-kisses me and leaves in a silver flurry of wobbling polka dots, cursing that she'll be late because she can't run in heels.

Back in the lounge, Derek stands in front of the mirror over the mantelpiece where he squirts a meringue nest of hair mousse into his palm. I watch as he slaps it on to his quiff and adjusts the peak like it's a weathervane and the wind has changed direction.

'Centre partings are *so* last year,' he says to my reflection. Then he turns to face me. 'Fancy a re-style?'

I dodge behind the telephone table and touch the black velvet scrunchie that pins back my hair in a ponytail.

'Fancy a smoke?' I say; I'm not sure I'm ready to have Derek near my neck yet with a pair of scissors. 'I've got some fag ends for sale. Two pence each.'

'Cool,' Derek says.

I peg it downstairs to the cellar where I store my Harper's Bazaar stock to find the matchbox I've hidden the fag ends in. I have to think smart and think *quick*. I've been growing out my hair since I was eight when Mum thought it would be fun to copy Annie-Lennox-dressed-as-Elvis, and cut our hair short and dyed it black. I've been there, done that and had the re-growth and roots to prove it.

Back upstairs, I hand over the matchbox in exchange for some coppers. Derek has wedged Mum's small bottle of water for spraying houseplants on to his silver-studded belt where a pistol would dangle if he were in a Western. He lights a cigarette butt. It hangs from the corner of his mouth.

'What kind of look do you fancy, then? Something a little bit... edgy?' He slices at the air with his pair of slim silver scissors.

'I'm thinking Tanita Tikaram?' I know I'm safe with Tanita; she's dead natural with long, black hair.

'We've got to bear in mind what we're working with here, Harper,' Derek says, pulling out my ponytail so that my ginger curls fall on to my shoulders. 'I'm thinking more Molly Ringwald?'

'Who?'

'Or Belinda Carlisle?'

Seems Derek *is* harmless if he thinks Belinda Carlisle has edge, so I spread some newspaper on the floor and sit on a dining chair in front of the telly and let Derek spray and trim. While he's cutting, we watch the first half of *Blind Date*, where Cilla Black tries to find the perfect match for Our George, a painter-decorator from Lancaster. Three permed, blonde women sit on black swivel stools as if they're on death row, Derek reckons. Their shaggy fringes fall over their eyes when they lean forward to stress certain words. They say things like: 'Well, if *you* gave *me* the opportunity to make *you* a candlelit dinner for *two*, you'd *swoon* at my starter, *marvel* at my main course and positively *pounce* on me at pudding.'

'How d'you get a boyfriend?' I ask, over applause.

'My mum met Dad down the Working Men's Club,' Derek

says, resting his scissors for a moment at his waist. 'How did your parents meet?'

'Dad says they met at work over the photocopier. Mum doesn't like to talk about it.'

'Romantic,' Derek says. 'Course, some people use the Lonely Hearts.'

I crinkle my forehead.

'Look.' Derek reaches into our pine magazine rack, finds the most recent copy of the *Blackbrake Gazette*, and turns towards the back to the page opposite the obituaries.

He hands it to me; one entry reads: 'Forty-ish perfect lady with GSOH WLTM perfect gentleman with good taste in fast cars, dance music and exquisite food for friendship. And maybe more.' Grown-ups get all mysterious when they're looking for romance, like they need to complicate things with another layer of hair, or words.

Back on the telly, Our George chooses Our Sandra – a beauty technician from the Wirral – and Cilla hands them a golden envelope with tickets to a snorkelling holiday in Majorca inside.

'There!' Derek announces with a final snip.

I inch myself off the chair so I can look at my reflection in the mirror in stages.

If my hair cut is supposed to be channelling Belinda Carlisle, then it's Belinda after sticking her fingers in a live plug socket. I try not to show how I'm feeling, but there's not much hair left to hide behind.

'Let's use some product to calm it down a bit. Go for a wet look?' Derek suggests, squirting more mousse into his palm. He massages it through the tufts, some of which stand straight, like soldiers going into battle.

'Thank you,' I manage.

As Cilla finds her next match made in heaven for Our Pippa from Woking, I blot out my pain by drifting off to sleep to the sounds of Cilla's Liverpudlian lilt on the sofa. That night, I dream my hair is so long it could rival Rapunzel.

Next morning, I'm curled up like a poked hedgehog on the sofa underneath a woollen blanket. Pools of sweat have gathered where my skin touches the plastic cover. Derek has tucked his can of mousse into my hands while I was sleeping as if it's a weapon to foam at attackers. The telly's off. Coffee is brewing.

'All right, sleepy head?' A man with stubble as black and scratchy as a wheat field burnt after harvest peers around the lounge door. Then the rest of his body appears, dressed in Mum's fake silk dressing gown. He holds a smoking cigarette in his right hand.

'Are you Kit?' I ask, tightening my grip on the can of hair mousse.

'Enchanted to meet you.'

'You don't need to go outside to smoke that!' Mum shouts from the kitchen. 'There's an ashtray somewhere on the dining table!'

I watch as Kit, grinning at me, tugs the dressing gown around him and then shuffles to the table in the walk-through dining room.

The ashtray is nearly full.

Kit taps his cigarette on the edge of it and looks at me.

I narrow my eyes.

'You eat meat?' I ask.

'Certainly do.' He scratches behind his ear. 'Do you eat your mum's friends?'

I laugh – a little – and think over my tactics. If I want a gerbil, first of all I need to make sure that he's going to stick around.

'Did you have a nice time last night?' I ask.

'Lovely, ta.'

Mum nudges the door open, carrying a tray with a couple of bacon butties, a box of paracetamol, two mugs of hot coffee and a carton of orange juice on it. She's still got her war paint on.

'Not quizzing him already, are you?'

'Just *interested in your wellbeing*,' I rewind Mum's words and play them back at her. I know it gets to her, but sometimes I like to see her squirm. When I grow up, I'm going to talk straight, wear flat shoes and I am definitely not going to marry anyone, let alone go out with the wrong man.

'Where's the Elnett?' I ask, touching my hair, hoping yesterday was a nightmare. Turns out, it's not one I've woken up from yet.

'On top of the bathroom cabinet.' Mum's voice fades as she comes closer and realizes the lengths Derek went to in order to tap into my inner Belinda.

'Oh, Harper,' she says. 'Your lovely hair!'

'It's all right, Mum.'

'I'll get the hairspray for you, pet,' Kit says, ducking out of the lounge as if he's dodged a bullet.

Mum starts to cry; what Oona calls Mum's 'over-empathy' is kicking in.

'Please don't...' I say, and try to think of something to say to make her feel better. 'It'll grow back in a year or two.'

This sets her off even more.

I put my arm around her as she hunches next to me on the sofa. 'It's OK,' I try again. 'Remember that time we cut our hair to look like Annie-Lennox-dressed-as-Elvis?

Mum rubs the smudged blue mascara from under her eyes. She sighs, 'We looked great, didn't we?'

'Yes. And it grew back.'

Kit, who has reappeared from the bathroom, hands me the hairspray. 'Chin up,' he says to Mum. 'She's cut her hair, not her wrists.'

'Thanks,' I say.

'I'm going for a bath,' Kit says, taking his bacon butty with him.

Mum sighs and pops two paracetamol out of the packet, and downs her painkillers with her triple-strength coffee.

'Bad headache?' I ask.

'Bad wine,' she pauses to take a deep breath. 'Harper, I have some good news and some bad news. Which would you like first?' she asks.

'Bad headache. Bad wine. Bad news,' I say, and take a bite out of Mum's butty.

Mum pastes a smile across her face, but I can tell it's stuck on, like the lips from a game of Mr Potato Head.

'I'm afraid I don't have enough money to buy you a gerbil and a cage this summer,' she says. 'I'm sorry I promised. I shouldn't have. We need to save all the money we can for a deposit.'

Guess Dad couldn't afford that rise in allowance. 'Don't beat yourself up, Mum. I knew you wouldn't be able to. I've been saving up my 30p pocket money; I've already nearly £2. And I can take a paper round from Mr Power after my thirteenth birthday–'

Mum interrupts, 'But you should be able to enjoy your pocket money, Harper, and spend it on chips and chocolate like every other kid.'

'I'm not every other kid. What's the good news?' I ask.

'Kit's going to be our new lodger.'

'Will he sleep in your room?' I ask. There are only two bedrooms in thirteen Kendal Road, so he'll either be in my room, Mum's or on the sofa in the lounge. I'd really rather not share a bedroom again. Six months ago, Mum took in a Polish teenager called Magdalena as an au pair and she slept in my room. Magdalena was as pale as a parsnip and as bloated as a potato. Each night, she'd cry herself to sleep with homesickness and after three weeks she went back to Warsaw.

'He'll be on the Zedbed in my bedroom,' Mum says. 'We could do with the extra income, H. Kit's moving back to Blackbrake after several years away and he's struggling to get back on to the property ladder.'

'OK,' I say.

'Are you sure you're all right with that?' Mum asks.

'So long as he's not vegetarian and I can play my music loud and not have to tidy my room, I'm fine with it.'

'Great!' Mum says, and she stretches her arms out like a pylon. 'I'm going back to bed now, love. Wake me up at half one and I'll make lunch.'

seven

▼▼▼▼▼

I don't spot any change on Cassie's mum's face on account of my hair when she opens the door, but you never can tell with Mrs Pope – she's one of those people who say one thing, but mean another.

'Welcome,' she says, edging the door a tiny bit wider so I can just about squeeze in.

Looking through to the kitchen, I spot a stuffed chicken squatting by the side of the sink, its dead legs tied together with string. Simmering gravy has steamed up the window, through which I can just make out Cassie's dad mowing the lawn with a small, orange hovercraft.

'Lisa! Serve some cordial for Harper will you?' Mrs Pope has well posh ways of saying things: squash becomes cordial, tea is called supper and here, salad cream is known as *vinaigrette*.

Mum says this is *pretentious*.

I slide off my shoes – Cassie's is the only 'shoes off' house I know of in Blackbrake – and pad into the dining room.

The carpet beneath my toes gathers like cotton wool. A

cobweb-like tablecloth covers the mahogany dining table, which is already laid, with polished cutlery and tablemats ready for Sunday lunch, although it's only half past ten in the morning. Mrs Pope seems to think that there is a direct link between being successful and being clean. Mum reckons Mrs Pope's bathroom is as antiseptic as an operating theatre; she says it's that disinfected that you could eat a meal off the floor. This is something Cassie and I intend to try one day.

Cassie's sister, Lisa, is at one end of the dining room in a peach and turquoise shell suit zipped right up to her neck. She's polishing wine glasses with an ironed tea towel – 'iron' and 'tea towel' are not three words that are ever heard in the same sentence at my house. Underneath Lisa's shell suit, her boobs balloon; they get a cup size bigger each week, I swear.

Cassie's doing origami with starched napkins so they stand up in the shape of swans. 'All right?' she says. 'I can come out once I've finished my chores.'

'Has someone mistaken hairdressing for topiary?' Lisa says, pouring me some squash into a glinting wine glass with a dangerously thin-looking stem.

'Just fancied a new hair-do,' I reply, taking the glass from her.

Cassie whispers, 'Ignore her. You look great.' I love friends who lie to make you feel better. I take a large gulp of the bitter lemon squash.

'Are you doing anything special for Easter?' Lisa asks, placing the wine glasses by the tablemats with the same amount of care as if she ran an art gallery and was deciding where to show sculptures.

'Not this one, but I am going to Brighton with my dad in the May half term.'

'We're skiing next week,' Lisa replies, looking up.

'Are you?' I ask, turning to Cassie.

'It's only for five days,' Cassie says.

'Six if you count the flight,' Lisa says.

'You're going on an aeroplane?' I ask.

'We leave tomorrow. It'll take eight hours from door to door,' Lisa says, her eyes as wide as a DD-cup.

The furthest away I've ever been is Pontins on the Isle of Wight when I was four and a half.

'Want to go down the playground?' Cassie says, as she does the final fold.

Outside, a jumbo jet crosses the clear blue sky in silence, joining up mushrooming clouds with its white trail as if it's a pen in some heavenly dot-to-dot. I can't believe Cassie hasn't told me about her skiing holiday – I may like it when she lies to make me feel better about myself but I don't like it when she keeps secrets. She's done this before, like when she was the first in class to have a car with electric windows and heated seats. I only found out that she had a new car because I spied her sitting in it when her dad stopped to let me cross the Greytown Road pelican crossing; she was on her way back from Argos, where her dad had bought her a ghetto blaster. We get the same pocket money, though Cassie has always got the latest trainers. But I'm not complaining any, because I get her hand-me-downs.

I suppose you can't hand down a holiday.

We head towards what's left of the playground on Cassie's estate, the Old Marshes. Just a few months ago the playground was torched by the borstal boys from my side of the Greytown Road. This made Mrs Pope doubly nervous about letting Cassie out after five o'clock; her curfew has only just returned to six each evening. The council haven't got round to replacing the roundabout which is now just a deadly skeleton of charred metal bars. The only sign that there was ever a wooden shed is a pile of blackened planks, the few which didn't go up in flames. The borstal boys didn't set light to the swings, perhaps because they were afraid they might be gassed by the burning rubber seats.

Cassie and I take a seat each and start to swing.

Until a couple of months ago, there used to be a wing of the Hopkin Wynne Mental Hospital neighbouring the playground. After they bulldozed it, Cassie and I spent several afternoons picking over the rubble to look for scraps of straitjacket that the patients were rumoured to wear; legend goes, this was the electroconvulsive wing where the patients were allowed to go truly fruitcake. The windows were barred, and I swear there were padded walls. Daffodils are now poking their closed yellow heads up in between the crumbled walls, waiting to bloom in warmer weather. A new sign has been put up since we were last there saying that Vanguard Housing is about to 'commence construction of an exclusive estate of executive five-bedroom homes with detached carports for the modern family' in the wasteland.

'Lisa went to me the other day: "You're not allowed to wear denim coats at private school,"' Cassie says, putting on a posh accent.

'Why not?' I ask.

''Cos apparently the headmistress reckons only troublemakers wear them. You have to wear a regulation wool one from John Lewis!'

'That's *mental*,' I say, jumping off the swing and turning to look at Cassie. 'My acid-washed denim jacket is my coolest! There's no way I'd be seen alive in a wool coat anywhere, let alone in a private school.'

'I know,' Cassie slows to a gentle swing, then tugs hers tighter over her chest as if someone's about to take it off her there and then.

'Let's make a pact, that we'll both wear denim till we die...' I say.

'And that we'll never change schools,' Cassie adds.

I cross my fingers behind my back. Who knows where I'll be living come September. '*And* that we'll be buried in our denim jackets to boot,' I add.

'Denim till we die!' Cassie shouts, her voice echoing across the demolished wing. A pair of crows takes flight from the hospital rubble, croaking as they go.

eight

▼▼▼▼▼

Holidays are awkward for single parents, Mum says. How are you supposed to work *and* look after kids? Mum's answer, having tried Polish au pairs, is to take me to the advertising agency where she works. I'm given simple jobs such as putting files in alphabetical order, Tipp-Exing names off Rolodex cards when business contacts have been sacked or quit, making strong coffees or buying iced buns from the bakery next door for Mum, Spike the designer and me. It's only when cake products are on offer that Spike pushes back the curtains of his long hair and looks up from his CMYK book. Otherwise, he wears his wet-look hair like a visor. We never offer cake to Mum's boss, Joanna: she avoids saturated fats, as well as daylight. Joanna has a private office that she arrives at before sunrise and leaves after sunset. Mum's desk is just outside it, next to the grey metal coat stand from which Joanna's jet-black raincoat and closed umbrella hang to attention.

While a caller is on hold, Mum explains that Joanna won a contract with Inspirations Ltd, a direct mail company, to copywrite their seasonal catalogue of festive junk for all ages. Joanna won it off the rival agency in Blackbrake. It's the biggest contract of the year, and the year hasn't been a good one so far; a 'year on year' graph is pinned to the wall above the water cooler on which the 1988 profit line plummets like a lemming.

Mum's in and out of Joanna's office like a battery-powered rabbit, taking dictation, typing up letters and memos on the Amstrad, faxing them off, calling for couriers. At two minutes past eleven, I remind her about our mid-morning snack. I'd finished my filing by half nine and had spent the next hour and a half flicking through the books on the coffee table – *Fat Profit? Fair Game* and *How to Sell India Rice* – and 'mocking up', as they say in the trade, a newsletter for Harper's Bazaar. I used a typewriter I found in the stationery cupboard beneath boxes of fax ink. The 'N' key doesn't work, so I've had to write that letter in by hand.

'CRISIS MEETING!' growls Joanna's lion-like voice.

'Christ,' Mum says as she hands me a fiver from the petty cash tin. 'Go and get those bloody buns, then,' she says, kissing me on the head, 'And whatever you fancy.'

Spike peels himself off his chair like he's a sticking plaster and his chair is a scraped knee. The two of them file into Joanna's office armed with pens, notebooks and black coffee. Joanna fuels her office on caffeine and fear.

When I come back with a large box of chocolate éclairs, cream horns, iced buns, jam doughnuts and pink fondant fancies, Mum's not yet back at her desk but Spike is sitting at his, an unlit cigarette poking out from under his hair-head around the point where an ear should be. He nods towards the crinkled glass door of the CEO office.

I set down the cake boxes on Mum's desk, take a glass tumbler from the kitchen draining board and crouch at Joanna's office door, my ear pressed against the bottom of the glass. The fax machine churning makes it difficult to hear, but I can just make out jigsaw pieces of the conversation.

Joanna: '...Step up to the plate...clients inside out...woman to woman...staff copywriter...'

Mum: '...pay rise?'

Joanna: 'Sleep on it...by lunchtime tomorrow...'

I hear a sucking-then-sighing noise as Mum gets up from a chair. I go snooker-cue-straight and beetle back to the kitchen. There, I grab the small watering can for giving the desk plants a drink and I go round topping the saucers up. Mum's plant is a ticklish one with tiny leaves that curl up as you brush your hands along it as if it's shy of being touched.

Throughout the afternoon Mum doesn't chatter away to me, not even during her fag breaks on the sofa next to the water cooler; instead she concentrates hard, keeping her fingers glued to her keyboard, jumping up the moment she's buzzed through to Joanna's lair.

At five o'clock sharp, Spike, Mum and I creep out of the office as if we've just burgled the place rather than spent seven and a half hours fattening Joanna's profit margin.

Outside, Mum sparks up and sucks hard on her Silk Cut.

'Is something up?' I ask as we cross the High Street to the council estate.

'You could say that.'

Mum may have gone all mysterious on me, but twelve and a half years of being on this planet has taught me one important life lesson: flattery gets you everywhere.

'You worked really hard today,' I say.

Mum massages her forehead. 'I could do with a quick sit down, actually, Harper. These heels will be the death of me.'

There are tree stumps lining the council estate: the remains of elm trees which were attacked by a Dutch disease in the 1970s. Mum sits on one and nudges off her high heels. I sit on my denim jacket on the pavement opposite. I munch on an iced bun left over from elevenses, and watch Mum as she rubs her ankles and toes.

'I've been offered a promotion,' Mum says. 'Staff copywriter. Full time.'

I fake surprise: 'That's brilliant, Mum! Congratulations.'

'I'm not going to take it, Harper. I don't think I'm clever enough. Then there's fitting in my OU course which I'm already behind on. And then there's you. It would be longer hours, H, and I struggle to keep up with all the laundry, cooking, gardening and cleaning...'

I'm not about to offer to do all four of these things, but I can make my own raspberry jam sandwiches for my packed lunch, I tell her. I don't need looking after any. Plus Mum's always telling *me* not to be 'crippled by self-doubt', and that I should 'feel free to be my own person'.

Mum's not convinced.

'What's more important?' I ask. 'Keeping your job or keeping on top of the housework?'

'It's not even our house, Harper.'

Thinking on my feet now I say, 'Ah, but that's why you should take it. You'd get a pay rise?'

'That's negotiable.'

'Well, then,' I say, '*neg-o-tiate.*'

Mum laughs, but I'm deadly serious.

nine

▼▼▼▼▼

The last time we used the red tablemats and cleared the dining-room table for a posh meal was when Mum was still trying to impress the bank manager, Mike. The same evening that Mum's offered a promotion, Kit rocks up with the ingredients for a special tea: frozen shell-off prawns; Co-op cola; ketchup; mayonnaise; red wine and pizza from the deli counter. Luckily, Kit arrives while Mum's having a soak with a novel from her OU reading list in the bath, so I can get his opinion on Mum's new job offer.

Kit stashes the prawns in the Snow Queen 'freeze chest', a compartment as narrow as one of Mum's many shoeboxes on account of the impacted ice: Mum takes a hairdryer and roasting tin to it to when she needs to make room for another gin bottle or pot of bolognese sauce.

'I need your advice,' I say.

'Sure.' Kit sits opposite me at the kitchen table where he pours himself a large glass of red wine and takes a generous gulp.

'Mum's been offered a new job as a staff copywriter, but she doesn't think she can do it.'

'Course she can,' Kit says. He reaches into his pin-striped jacket, produces a medicine packet, and swallows two tablets.

'Tell her, then, will you? She won't listen to me.'

'She just needs to think positive.'

I'm not sure Mum's capable of this. I must be frowning because Kit sighs and says, 'Look, if you can manage to make us tea, then your mum can take the job.'

I frown at him. 'I can't cook tea! Not unless you fancy pin-wheel jam sandwiches with crisps for starters.'

'You're just as bad! You've got to think *endemically* positive.'

'Right,' I say, still unsure.

'I'll go and tell your mum what her twelve-year-old is doing downstairs, and it'll show her what you're capable of. Inspiration, innit?'

'OK,' I say. I do actually know what seafood sauce should look like; I tasted it once round Cassie's house when she ate prawns for starters served in half an avocado.

Kit leaves the ingredients – except the wine – next to the cooker, which I set to gas mark nine. I play side one of my *Now That's What I Call Music! 11* cassette on the stereo above the sink, put on my 'I'm a little rascal' apron and start to cook. We have covered cooking pizza in school, but we haven't yet covered Marie Rose sauce, so I shall use my common sense.

Marie Rose sauce should be light pink. Mixing five tablespoons of tomato ketchup and five of mayonnaise together makes sure it is. You should always add a pinch of salt to everything you cook, and throw a handful over your shoulder. Frozen shell-off prawns take a long time to defrost, even the littlest ones. I try sitting them in a bowl of hot water from the tap, but Mum has emptied the tank so they just float in lukewarm water staying pink, hard and frozen. It's when I put one in my mouth to try one that I have a brainwave – throughout the whole of 'Gimme Hope Jo'anna' I defrost the bag of prawns by sucking them in my mouth, and spitting them out again.

In the fridge salad drawer I uncover an iceberg lettuce, a little brown and icy on one side, but green on the other. I shred it with a bread knife and decorate three glass bowls with it. Sadly, what was once a cucumber is now mostly green liquid in the bottom of the drawer but the tomatoes are ripe, so I slice these into quarters, and shower lemon juice from a yellow bottle over everything and dollop the Marie Rose sauce on top after adding the prawns.

The oven is hot now, so I unwrap the cling film from the pizza – which I am pleased to see is pepperoni – and slide it into the oven.

I think this is a good time to admit that people do some things on purpose, and some by accident. Often, when people do things on purpose, it is because they *want* things to be noticed. For ex- ample, sometimes Mum says her boss leaves her car keys on tables when she meets clients so that they have to run out after a meet- ing, and it's then that they notice Joanna drives a soft-top BMW. This, Mum says Joanna says, makes men take her more seriously as a woman.

That evening it happens that Kit leaves his large, black briefcase *open* in the lounge. Inside, I can glimpse – without rummaging – what you'd normally expect to find in a briefcase: keys, clipboard, pens. But underneath the Cocoa Creations Inc. catalogue, I can see, peeping out, a selection of chocolate bars. On their plain red wrappers is printed: 'Secret Mixes: for Market Research Purposes Only'. Now, I have learnt from watching how Shaun Lewis gets a right bollocking at school that you should 'take a moment to reflect' before acting. So I weigh up the pros and cons of taking the packets out of the briefcase. This is roughly how it goes.

Pros of taking the chocolate bars now:

- Kit might not hang around much longer, in which case I'd never get to taste them.
- It's March and the days are getting warmer now. They might melt.
- They're probably intended for me anyway and I'd save Kit the bother of having to give them to me if I take them now.
- I can be his market research.

Cons of taking the chocolate bars now:

- I cannot think of a single con.

I grab Mum's ring-bound reporter's notebook and leg it out into the garden, then tear the red wrapper off chocolate bar number one. I've seen chefs on TV enough times to know how to perform a professional tasting: you sniff the product, taste a bit, suck your cheeks in, swill the product around your mouth and then spit it out and describe it in flowery words like 'overtones of blackcurrant' and 'rose-like aroma'. I do all of those steps, except I swallow the prototype chocolate after tasting.

An alarm clock beeping loudly interrupts my tasting notes – the nurse next door at number fifteen must be oversleeping from her nightshift, I guess. Only, now that I lean into the sound I realize that it appears to be coming from our house. Smoke – which isn't from a cigarette – is wafting out of the open kitchen window.

The pizza.

I run to the back door. In the kitchen, Kit is waving the *Blackbrake Gazette* at the smoke alarm.

'I've managed to defrost the prawns, Kit! And made the seafood sauce!' I shout, over the alarm.

'Two out of three ain't bad!' Kit shouts in reply, then he presses the red button on the screeching smoke alarm. 'Shame we couldn't get your mum's three-piece suite to go up in flames too,' he adds, in the sudden silence. 'Don't worry. We'll have the chocolate I've brought home with me for pudding.'

My cheeks glow gas mark nine. 'About the chocolate...'

Kit frowns.

'I found the secret mixes in your briefcase. I thought I could be your market research, so I ate them all and took tasting notes.'

I offer Mum's notebook to Kit, who takes it and sits down at the kitchen table to read through them: 'Like eating an airy yellow car sponge, laced in butter and sugar...Flavours of gravy made with prunes plus peppery notes...Overtones of Blackbrake Balti's tarka dhal...*Aftertaste of blackberries and Mum's day-old coffee?*'

I scrunch up my shoulders, ready to take the full weight of Kit's bollocking.

'This is *GENIUS*!'

'It is?'

'You've saved me a day's work of running a focus group. If you could just type this up, I'll give you a commission: ten per cent of my day rate.'

'Twenty per cent,' I pitch in.

'Fifteen. And you can have a monthly supply of chocolate off-cuts.'

'Deal,' I say, and we shake on it.

Mum joins us in a pale pink jumpsuit, her blow-dried hair like spun sugar, her fingertips as shrivelled as nuked pepperoni. Kit doesn't mention the cremated pizza, which is now a black disc on the oven shelf.

'Here she is,' Kit says, as Mum comes into the kitchen. 'Ready to jump off a plane. Ready for anything!'

Mum snorts, and tops Kit's glass up with some more red wine. 'I'm going to take the job,' Mum says to me. 'But I can't let it get in the way of my studies. Or you.'

'Which is why I've suggested she should borrow an Amstrad from work,' Kit says. 'That way, she can write her OU essays as well as her catalogue from home if she needs to do overtime—'

'If you're getting an *Amstrad*, can I have your electrical type-writer?' I interrupt. 'I'll need it for typing up my notes, anyway,' I add.

'What notes?'

'Harper and I have come to a little financial arrangement – she's going to be my focus group,' Kit explains. 'Her palate is very refined.'

'It's refined when it comes to tasting sugar, Kit, and that's the extent of it. Well, Harper,' Mum says, turning to me now, 'Looks like we've both got new jobs.'

'Your catalogue will be a work of great literature to rival Dickens,' Kit says, patting Mum's confectionery hair.

'Shall we have tea in front of the telly to celebrate?' I suggest.

We leave the dusty tablemats where they are on top of the bookshelf next to Mum's Wedgwood vase and eat the prawn cocktails on the sofa while watching telly. Both Mum and Kit ask for seconds.

It's my idea to play Monopoly after tea, but it's Kit's brainwave that he should help us to buy thirteen Kendal Road.

Mum has remortgaged King's Cross, the water utility and all her properties, and she's down to her last hundred quid. Kit has built red hotels on all of his complete green, yellow and orange property sets. I've bought the other three train stations, and I'm managing quite well by catching both of them out with a hotel on Old Kent Road and Whitechapel Road. I still have a £500 note in my kitty.

'Imagine if the post office took this,' I say, waving the prawn-pink note in the air. That's what sets them off.

'We could buy anything we wanted,' Mum says as I roll the dice and move my old boot seven squares to safety in 'Free Parking'.

'You could buy this place,' Kit says.

Mum snorts. 'The mortgage would still be astronomical, even with another five hundred quid towards the deposit.'

'You read the spring Budget headlines, though?' Kit asks. Mum never reads the news – unless you count *Woman's Own* – and the only 'headlines' she's familiar with is the hairdressing salon on the Greytown Road. Mum shakes her head, and the dice – a six and a two – and sails into jail via the Community Chest for the third time without a 'Get Out of Jail Free' card.

'I'll stay here, I think,' she says. 'Keep out of trouble.'

'From the first of August, Lawson's abolishing tax relief for unmarried people. Everyone who's been thinking of getting a house is buying now before the tax break disappears. The market's going bonkers. If you want to get on the ladder, now's the time.'

It's my go: five and a one, which lands me on 'Chance'. I'm ordered to pay school fees of £150.

'Landlord's going to sell this place,' Mum says. 'There was even a valuer round the other day. What do you reckon it's worth?' Mum asks.

'Around twelve thou for a two-bed terrace like this,' he says, shaking the dice. 'But you could reckon on eighteen by the end of the year if things turn out like they reckon they will.'

The grand total in my pink sparkly purse at the moment is £2.35: not even enough to buy a doorknob, let alone the deeds to this place.

'My mortgage applications have always been rejected. Nothing screams potential default as loud as a single mother with a part-time job,' Mum says.

'Two hundred and fifty pounds, please, Kit. Hotel on Old Kent Road,' I say, as Kit parks his silver top hat on my property.

He hands me the notes. 'Course, if you were married, you'd probably get a mortgage.'

'Is that your idea of a proposal?' Mum asks.

'Might be,' Kit says, reaching into his trouser pocket. He brings out a small, navy box with a gold edge.

I can't believe my eyeballs.

'Now, it's not the real deal. It's just something temporary until we can get down Elizabeth Duke...'

Mum opens the box as if it's glued together, her forehead knitted. She tries the plastic ring on each of her fingers, but the only digit it'll stay on is one of her thumbs. It's clearly out of a Christmas cracker – plastic, yellow and without a precious gemstone.

'We'd better get down a proper jeweller's pronto, hadn't we?' Kit says, elbowing me.

I don't like to evaporate romance like Mike Hyde but, as I watch Mum put the ring on, I can't be sure if we'll end up on the credit side of the balance sheet or the debit. The credits are obvious: we get our own house and I get a stepdad who sells chocolate. The debits? I looked up the meaning of the word 'mortgage' the other day. It means 'dead pledge' which sounds more like the diagnosis of a terminal illness than a money product to me. Although we'd own number thirteen, we'd be heavily in the red. Plus, it could all go DD-cup up and Mum would be disappointed again and get into another one of her downward spirals. And all this would be just when, she said to me the other night, she feels like she's finally getting her shit together.

And if Kit and Mum were to divorce, then who'd keep the house this time? And what *would* Dad think if I changed my surname? Surely that would be rubbing out-of-date baked beans into his wounds?

While Cassie collects beautiful pebbles from beaches that she's visited in a large glass jar, I collect unanswered questions and useless pop lyrics in my head. If you hold one of Cassie's pebbles, they're light and smooth – but she has that many now in her jar that she can't lift it any more. It's the same with my questions. The more questions I store up, the heavier my head becomes. One day, I swear I'll collapse with the weight of carrying them around.

As Monopoly bank manager, I declare the game a draw by bankrupting everyone. Mum's already distracted by thinking about which pair of shoes she could afford from Gordon Benét's for the occasion. Kit slinks into the kitchen and comes back with a bottle of fizzy pink wine and two glasses. He pops the cork, and a tiny volcano of drink spills on to the rug before Mum manages to get her wine glass beneath the bottleneck. I'm not allowed a taste, but just sniffing the bubbles makes my head spin like a top-loader down the Full Cycle laundrette.

Whatever side of the balance sheet you choose to look at, I'm going to be a stepdaughter. And maybe there'll be a honeymoon via aeroplane, and I could smuggle myself into one of Mum's suitcases. Let there be cake, champagne and canapés: I intend to taste all three.

ten

▼▼▼▼▼

When I knock on Cassie's front door a week later, her mum answers, dressed in her fluffy white dressing gown and slippers with little heels and a bobble of white feathers that tickle her purple toenails. It's the first time I've seen Mrs Pope without a pinafore.

'Harper,' she mumbles. 'You'll have to excuse me. Our flight was delayed. We only got in five hours ago.'

I look at their wall clock and do the maths; they must have got home at around six in the morning. That's often when my mum goes to bed when she's got an OU deadline.

'It's all right,' I say.

'Cassie's still asleep. You're welcome to come in,' she says. 'I suppose.'

I'm already through the door and spying in the dining room to see what Mrs Pope has laid out to eat. It's not quite prawns in avocado, but I'm not disappointed: there's a tower of flaky cakes in the shape of the letter C, a jar of strawberry jam and a block of butter.

'Help yourself, Harper,' Mrs Pope calls from the kitchen. 'I need to keep an eye on the pan of milk.'

While I'm going into the dining room, Lisa calls from the hallway, 'It's called a *continental* breakfast.' When she comes in I'm in for a surprise: one of Lisa's legs is in plaster up to her thigh. She leans on two crutches. 'They're croissants.'

'Cool,' I say. 'You broke your leg.'

Mrs Pope calls from the kitchen, 'I'm afraid Lisa's lost her place on the school team as goal attack.'

'Didn't know you played basketball,' I say.

'*Netball*,' Lisa says.

I used to play basketball down the compound before some health and safety officer from the council took the basket away. Netball's new to me.

'Is that anything like basketball?' I ask, then regret it immediately.

'Once you have the ball in your possession,' Lisa says, as she tears one of the flaky croissants in half like Mum does bounced cheques, 'you can take one step, but then you can't move. It's like playing stuck in the mud. You can only bounce the ball once. There are seven players on each team at any one time...'

I hope Cassie comes down soon because Lisa's off on one of her I'm-cleverer-than-you-that's-why-I-go-to-a-school-where-you-pay lectures. At least Cassie's pretty thick like me; otherwise I reckon she'd be sitting the entrance exam at Blackbrake School for Girls. BSG is for the kind of girls who don't turn off the tap while brushing their teeth, who think it's worth learning dead languages that nobody speaks any more and who parade their hockey sticks down the Black Knight as if they're sub-machine guns. One time, double-hard Shaun Lewis called one of those rich girls a poofter. She said it took one to know one.

'...and then there's Goal Defence...'

I peer down at Lisa's plaster cast which is sticking out beside her seat, and notice Cassie's already had a go at graffitiing it. '*Get stoned! Drink wet cement!*' she's written on the back of Lisa's calf where she can't read it. I'd write, '*I swear! They're not silicone!*'

As Lisa drones on like an aeroplane on autopilot, she's also eating her croissants in a strange way, dipping pieces smeared with butter and strawberry jam into her bowl of hot chocolate, which she sips in between boring me. Doesn't look like they teach good table manners down BSG. Finally, when Lisa has worked through the entire rulebook of netball, and I've torn three croissants to shreds, Cassie comes downstairs. She's far browner than before her holiday, except around her eyes where she's a lighter shade of brown in the shape of large goggles. Because her skin is dark, Cassie once told me, it doesn't burn easily like mine. I hadn't noticed that her skin was a different colour until she said that.

Luckily, Lisa's been told that she should rest on the sofa every hour so she hops back to the lounge and over my fourth croissant Cassie tells me about how you have to be X-rayed at passport control before you can even get on the plane, and how, once you're on it, oxygen masks will fall from the ceiling when it looks like there'll be a crash. She says you have to leave your high heels behind if you land in the sea, going down an orange slide to get out, and you breathe recycled air on board.

I'm glad I've never been on a plane after all.

'What've you been up to?' Cassie asks, after an ice age.

'Not much,' I begin, 'though Mum's getting married and so we're going to buy our house...'

Mrs Pope is being an earwig over the washing-up. She comes

in with her rubber gloves still on. 'Your mum's getting married?' she says.

I nod.

'Who to?'

'A salesman.'

'I'll have to invite your mum round to the next Tupperware party,' Mrs Pope says, more to herself than to us, as she wanders back into the kitchen. 'Mine her for details.'

It took about six months for me to pass Mrs Pope's quality control when I moved to Kendal Road and first made friends with Cassie. Because we live on the wrong side of the Greytown Road, Mrs Pope was nervous about me, like I might have nits, be really thick, or – even worse – cleverer than Lisa. I wonder what Mrs Pope will uncover about Kit with her X-ray questions next time Mum goes round to buy plastic pots for bulk-cooked bolognese sauce.

eleven

▼▼▼▼▼

After the Easter holidays are behind us, the strata in our house start to shift like the coloured sands on the coast of the Isle of Wight. First, it's the hallway which gets cluttered with Kit's shoes, all worn down at the heels. Then, it's the bottom step of the stairs which becomes the dumping ground at 'gin and tonic o'clock' for his paisley ties, trench coat and calling lists; then, it's his Aladdin's briefcase filled with chocolates which I trip over each time I reach the top of the stairs. Kit also brings with him a hatbox of wigs from the local joke shop which finds a new home beneath the television stand. I let him use half of my share of the bathroom cabinet so he can house his shaving brush, foam and razor along with various other grooming tools. Kit keeps his lucky dip of drugs in a small, wicker basket in the kitchen. The medicines have long names that remind me of the zodiac. Their packets state that they should be kept both out of children's reach and direct sunlight, but Kit is one for breaking the rules and he leaves them in plain view in a sunny spot by the kettle as if they're meant to sweeten a cup of coffee.

This is the spring that my head reaches high enough to see – without standing on the top of *Chambers* – the turned-in pink spines of novels on the top tier of the bookshelf. They have titles like *Hot Flash for Frances* and *Uniforms, Underwear and Ulrika*, and drawings of half-dressed grown-ups on the covers.

Mornings, we settle into a rhythm: Mum is the first in the bathroom where she showers and gets into her staff copywriter costume, then Kit washes and dresses in his pin stripes ready for his travelling chocolate-selling. I'm last. The water's always lukewarm.

Over Easter I finished making my final version of the Harper's Bazaar newsletter. Mum suggests that I should carbon copy them rather than photocopy so as to get better at typing. This means sandwiching very thin, bluebottle-coloured paper in between sheets and typing it out key by key. At least the typewriter I'm using now is electrical and types the letter N. But given that I want to make at least twenty copies to meet demand, it takes me a whole day to finish.

Kit explained to me that it's good to think in terms of 'soft launches' and 'hard launches' for business ventures. 'Like flying to the moon in a spaceship made of marshmallow before getting into the real metal thing?' I asked. Kit said, 'Don't take things so literal.' So I took his advice and splashed out down the Co-op on some Reduced for Quick Sale salt and shake crisps to offer to customers for my hard launch.

My range of products and bottom lines have increased, thanks to customer feedback from Derek at my soft launch. He suggested that I undertake some market research down It's a Gift so I spent an afternoon with a clipboard examining products, and noted that, like the gadgets that Mum's writing about, they were mainly imported from China.

The next best thing to importing goods is making them yourself out of raw English materials. It being spring, I found inspiration outdoors.

Although the garden in thirteen Kendal Road isn't ginormous, there is enough soil to fill several washed-out yoghurt pots, which is what I spent one morning doing after breakfast while Mum was in the shower. You take one trowel, your empty yoghurt pots and some soil. Once the pot is nearly full to the brim, you poke a little hole in the soil with your finger and plant a sunflower seed; these can be bought at any reputable pet shop, as I know from going down Mr Goodman's to cuddle gerbils. Priced at 20p each a pot, I'm on to a fat Mike Hyde profit margin.

I discover another unusual source of products down the Old Marshes estate. Cassie's next-door neighbours have been building an extension – a new garage for their second sports car. The yellow skip outside their house is a treasure chest of old toys buried beneath broken bricks, chipboard squares and empty sand sacks. The small keyboard I found in there worked fine, apart from the 'Jazz Demo' which just made the speakers crackle. I've marked it up at £1.99.

There is one other product line which should make my bottom line bulge: blue bubblegum. Earlier in the week I was opposite Mr Power's corner shop eating a paper bag full of penny cherry lips and chocolate cigarettes when I spotted something shiny in the gutter. Someone had dropped a whole 10p coin! Dad says it's good to save but I decided to spend my winnings there and then on the bubblegum machine rusting on the red-brick wall. It sells three for 10p a go. But the machine didn't stop at three bubble-gums; it spat out at least a hundred, I swear. I had to take off my neon-yellow fake mohair jumper and use it as a bag to harvest the bubblegum in. When I heard the corner shop bell tinkle, I hit and ran.

Inspired by Gordon Benét's, I'm displaying the bubblegums on a bed of cotton wool in reject Tupperware boxes with missing lids. Kit says non-violent music can make people spend more because they relax, so I've brought the stereo downstairs into the cellar and have fast-forwarded side two of *Now That's What I Call Music! 11* to find Vanessa Paradis singing about Joe *le taxi* driver, which I keep rewinding. Fag ends are stashed in empty match-boxes so that Mum doesn't realize what's in them. The sunflower yoghurt pots are grouped together on a paper doily at the front of the low table. The idea for my top-end range comes from Kit's proposal: it's the twelve deluxe toys stolen out of some Reduced for Quick Sale crackers that Mum bought in January. I found the box in Mum's shoe-polish cupboard at the top of the cellar stairs, which she calls Cupboard Love. There are small plastic whistles, bracelets, mini catapults, tiny spinning tops and pencil sharpeners, all at 10p a pop. As manageress, I'll be nice, but I'll keep my eyes peeled; often shops pay policemen to dress in plain clothes, pretend to be shoppers and look out for robbers stealing expensive products.

I'm ready for my hard launch.

'My loyalest customer!' I say, from behind the shop counter: it's Mum. She ducks as she enters the cellar. 'I've got money to burn,' she says.

I show her my newsletter. The fine lines around her blue eyes crease as she smiles, and I watch her fire-engine-red mouth move as she reads it: '*We now have more stock in jewellery. We hope this will please the lady customers who shop here. H. M. Richardson: Manageress, Editor, Illustrator. Harper's Bazaar Enterprises, 27th Floor, 13 Kendal Road.* Impressive. Enterprising, even,' she says. 'I'll take a bracelet, then.'

'Might not be your size,' I say. 'They're really for the *little* lady customers, but the sunflower plants are British. Quality goods.' This is what the market seller said to me down Blackbrake market when I bought my two pairs of flammable lime-green and pastel-pink trousers. 'Two for thirty pence!' I add, to clinch the deal.

'Sold! And I'll have a bubblegum too, please.' Mum pops one in her mouth and hands me 35p. This makes my grand total over £2.50 now.

'Isn't it Kit's birthday soon?' I ask.

'It's next Sunday, as it happens. Why?' she asks. I notice her dentures are staining blue; her mouth is a chewing Union Jack.

'Just wondering about getting him a present. What do you think he'd like?'

'You could make him something.'

'I want to buy him something special.'

'Well, he's almost out of Filofax paper...' Mum says. '...And Grecian 2000.'

'What's that?'

'Special shampoo.'

'Like Vosene?'

'Similar. They sell it down the Co-op.' Mum grins widely.

'Your teeth are blue,' I tell her, and she clasps a hand across her mouth.

'It's OK, I don't mind. I'm used to seeing all sorts on your dentures.'

Mum's brow ridges and furrows like a medieval field down

67

Hardingstone plains but I'm saved by the doorbell's metallic version of 'When the Saints Come Marching In' before I have to explain. I leg it upstairs to answer the door – it's Dad come to collect me an hour early.

'Come in, Dad,' I say, opening the door. 'I'm not packed yet.'

'I'll wait in the car,' he says, turning on his heel as Mum comes down the hall.

'Wait, Pete,' she says.

The air is as thick as an unsliced white.

Packing your bag twice a month gets dead boring, so I try to liven things up a bit by making it into a game. Upstairs, I sort through what few clothes aren't in the laundrette pile. My most recent challenge is to see how small a bag I can pack – the trick being to roll rather than fold clothes. Packing like this, I manage to use a small, American Indian rucksack with tassels – Alfonso Hope Follanger's parting gift: fake leather, course.

Once I'm packed, I go back downstairs to say goodbye to Mum, who's now at the sink peeling potatoes in a basin of muddy water. Her eyes are red.

'Have you been chopping onions?'

Mum dries her hands on a tea towel and gives me a hug.

'Have a lovely weekend, my love,' she says, as if this is an answer.

Dad's just as bad. When I get into his car and ask him how he is, in reply he asks if I'm going to be a bridesmaid.

To be honest, the thought hadn't even crossed my mind. 'Not if I have to wear anything from Laura Ashley,' I reply.

Dad lets out a small laugh, leans over and gives me a kiss on the cheek. He says: 'Let's beat it,' and we cruise to the Blackbrake Co-op.

twelve

▼▼▼▼▼

They're threatening to turn the Co-op into a bingo hall. Dad signs the petition after we've gone through the turnstiles. Then he walks as if a magnet is drawing him towards the Reduced for Quick Sale shelves where there's a collection of products all marked at under 20p each: broccoli which is turning yellowy-brown; dented cans of alphabet spaghetti; half-open packets of freeze-dried soup, and unwanted bottles of chocolate-flavoured conditioner.

'It takes a long time for butter to go rancid,' Dad says, placing four cheap blocks into his metal basket.

'I'll be in the Health and Beauty aisle,' I say.

'Out of hairspray?'

'I'm after some Grecian 2000.'

Dad looks up from fingering some Twiglets multipacks marked down to 15p each. 'Why?'

I decide not to tell him the truth. I know he gets jealous of Mum's new squeezes.

I cross my fingers behind my back. 'Mum says Vosene makes

my hair brittle.'

'You know it's made for men, and–'

'I know, I know,' I say, walking off to find the right aisle. 'I'll meet you at the checkout,' I call, over my shoulder.

At the hair care aisle, I find Derek comparing two boxes of dye.

'This one has more ammonia...'

'All right, Derek,' I say.

'All right, Harper.' He turns back to the boxes. '...But this one's cheaper.'

'Can you reach the Grecian 2000?' I ask him.

'Um, yes,' he says. 'But do you know which tint you're looking for?'

'Mum didn't say anything about tints.'

'I don't think your mum needs anything else adding to her hair, H. She'll combust. Spontaneously. Either that, or it'll all fall out.'

'It's not for her. It's for me.'

'Oh, I'd go for middle of the road, then. Nothing too dramatic,' he says, handing me a box. 'Remember to wear the gloves!' he calls after me as I head to the checkout. The man on the front of the shampoo box looks like one of the patients I see down Oncology. Except that he has hair.

I find Dad at the checkout loading the black belt with four blocks of out-of-date butter, a large bottle of Co-op ketchup, a dimpled tin of cocoa, eight Twiglets multipacks, four chicken tikkas on sticks and a family-sized bottle of antiseptic. I hope that this isn't our tea.

I put on a dividing sign that says 'NEXT CUSTOMER PLEASE' and add Kit's birthday present to the queue. The lady at the cash register wears a sprout of bright red hair. She peers over the green rim of her car-wing-mirror-sized glasses as she checks the price label and rings it up.

'One pound sixty-nine please, m'duck,' she says to me. 'I'm a wash-in wash-out gal myself,' she adds, winking at Dad.

'Oh. Oh, no, no, *no*! *She's* buying it. It's not for *me*.' Dad sounds as scratched as his over-played Genesis LP.

I turn to him. 'Can we go down the pet shop and look at gerbils through the window?' I ask. '*Please*?'

'Not today,' Dad says. 'I want to get back in time for a documentary on World War Two on the radio.'

'Great.' My mouth is a closed zip.

When we arrive at Ivy Cottage, I'm fish-and-chip-tired. Since my last visit, Dad's nailed the brass horseshoe he bought from the village fête above his front door. Ivy Cottage is that old that the doorway is only just high enough for me to get through without banging my head. In the olden days, people must have been at least two feet smaller. If you ever time-travelled back to the middle of this millennium, you'd look as gigantic as Dorothy does among the midget-sized Munchkins.

Dad announces what we're doing at the weekend while he's unpacking the shopping: 'Bric-a-brac fair tomorrow morning in the village hall.'

I sigh, and make a mental note to lie in. I wish I was in Blackbrake; in the town centre tomorrow Cassie says there's going to be a human flytrap. She gets to wear a suit made entirely of Velcro and fling herself at an upright bouncy castle. She says there are two blokes to catch you in case you don't stick.

'In a couple of weekends it'll be a bit more exciting, perhaps,' he says, poking his head round the kitchen door. 'There's a Lone Rangers disco in Coventry.'

I join Dad in the kitchen and yawn. 'I think I might go to bed.'

'You'll miss the documentary,' he says, pouring milk into a battered pan.

Dad's obsessed with the Second World War because he lost his own father in the Normandy landings in 1944. My grandma was pregnant at the time, so Dad never knew his father and as Grandma died of a heart attack when I was seven, Dad's now officially an orphan.

He opens the tin of cocoa and spoons it into two mugs, thickens it with a tablespoon of cold milk. He auctioned off most of Grandma's belongings from her house in Brighton after she died, bringing back to Ivy Cottage just a few things to remember her by: a mantelpiece windmill model; a set of scales with brass weights; bone-handled cutlery in a wooden box; and the battered red pan in which the milk is now starting to simmer.

Dad also inherited Grandma's habit of drinking cocoa each night before bed, but not her need to spring-clean once a week. Mondays, Grandma would borax the bedding, whack the door-mats and sofa cushions with a broomstick, wash everything she could put her hands on, including the pink fluffy mats that cosied up to the sink, toilet and bath. Her day didn't begin until she had swept and mopped the pavement outside her house, pushing the cigarette butts, leaves and rubbish into the gutter. Nor was I allowed to go to bed until I'd had a bath, sanded off any flaky skin with a pumice stone and scrubbed the rest of my body with a nailbrush and the foam from a bar of see-through orange soap.

Being her only child must have been lonely.

Dad pours the hot milk on to the chocolate paste and whisks the cocoa until it froths.

'I'll stay up with you till I've drunk that,' I say.

We sit by the fire and listen to the closing headlines from the news bulletin. Guerrillas are still holding passengers hostage on a jumbo jet in Kuwait.

'Imagine being trapped in an aeroplane by terrorists...' Dad says, poking the fire.

Something tells me he doesn't want to be alone this evening, so I sit on the sofa next to Dad and listen to the hour-long documentary about the Normandy invasion, hear how soldiers secured their helmets, guns and magazines of bullets across their chests, saying quiet prayers to God before their landing crafts hit French sand.

Imagine growing up without a father. It's not like I need my dad most of the time, but I reckon it would feel like going into battle without a bullet-proof vest. As the programme ends, I turn to look at Dad. Tears are streaming down his cheeks.

I have never seen him cry.

For a couple of seconds I am frozen to the sofa, but then I jump up to grab the tissue box from the mantelpiece.

'Are you OK?' I ask, handing him several tissues.

He dabs his face and turns to me.

'I miss you, Harper.'

I'm not expecting him to say this. Not at all. Thing is, I don't miss Dad much.

But what else can I say?

'I miss you too, Dad.'

*

73

The next day is more April storms than April showers. When I wake up at ten o'clock, I think it's still night, the sky is that dark. Horizontal rain hammers against the windows and the metal frames rattle from the bass line of thunder rumbling overhead. Hailstones the size of golf balls drop like bombs on to the street outside. They don't melt for at least half an hour. All electricity is cut off and praise be to Zeus, the bric-a-brac fair is cancelled.

Thrown back into the Dark Ages, Dad and I do what every caveman surely did in bygone times: we toast bread on forks by the fire and raid the puzzle cupboard. With Dad's emergency torch, I light upon the present Dad bought me for Christmas that we haven't opened yet – it's a 550-piece jigsaw of a vat of baked beans.

We start by finding all the edge pieces and the four corners. By twelve o'clock we have made the frame. I decide now is the time to fill in some gaps I have of my own.

'Dad?'

'Yes, love?'

'How did you meet Mum?'

'It's complicated.'

'I can do complicated,' I say. 'I'm thirteen in September.'

Dad half-smiles. He clicks a bean into place.

'Did you meet her over a photocopier?' I try again.

'That's right.'

'Was it at work?'

'Yes.'

'Why won't you tell me about it?' I say. I'm getting frustrated now, and it's not on account of the jigsaw.

'It's just – I think it best if it comes from your mum. It's her story.'

'It's my story, too,' I say.

'You weren't even born.'

I leave Dad to his puzzling and stomp upstairs to my bedroom, banging the door behind me. Dad must think I'm a complete dimwit. I'm sure I could handle whatever it is he thinks he's trying to protect me from. I crumple on to my bed, and pick up my favourite book, *The Almanac of Spooky Happenings: A Compendium of Weird Tales, Strange Sightings and Odd Occasions*.

Life, the *Almanac* promises, is weirder than meets the eye. I return to the stories I know by heart between the covers: rose-coloured frogs dusted in Saharan sand falling from the sky in Cirencester. Showers of red rain and flakes of beef. Icicles that form in the shape of hands. Hoofprints in fresh snow – on roofs. Children who vanish. Boats that disappear in the Bermuda Triangle. Alien big cats on deserted moors. Dead people who turn up in photographs of their own funeral. Seems I'm not the only one who's haunted, only my ghosts are alive and kicking.

It's time I did some of my own ghostbusting.

My old nursery is now used as a storeroom for wood-wormy furniture and broken junk. I creep into the dark room, and flick the light switch then remember there's no power. A faded paper chain dangles along one wall. On another hangs a poster of the *Mary Rose* tall ship before it sank, its white and green sails and St George's flag flapping in the wind. Thirty cannons are set to shoot, the sailors keeping watch from the crazily high crows' nests.

Next to a box file of papers labelled *Decree Nisi* is a collection of damp cardboard boxes of toys – shape sorters with blocks missing, stuffed bears spilling their woolly tummies, broken rattles – nothing worth selling at Harper's Bazaar. As I'm investigating

I find a large brown envelope, its seal having long since lost its stickiness; it's marked 'Super 8 – Developed'. Inside, there's a large reel of film. I shake the envelope upside down in case there's anything else inside and a photo flutters to the floor like a helicopter seed in search of soil. I sit cross-legged and lean against what's left of my cot after it was used for emergency firewood last winter.

It's a close-up photo of Mum and Dad rewound fifteen years or so; Mum's wearing a school uniform with a striped tie. Dad's in a brown corduroy suit with a large-collared orange shirt. They're both looking into the sun, squinting, and far from smiling. On the back of the photo is written, in handwriting I don't recognize: *Mary's Last A-Level Exam, 5 June 1972* – that's just over three years before I was born. I return the photo and film reel to the envelope and take it back to my bedroom where I hide it under the mattress. Looks like Mum and Dad didn't meet over a photocopier, after all.

thirteen

▼▼▼▼▼

Insomnia. If I went to Blackbrake School for Girls, I wouldn't have to look it up.

> **Insomnia** *in-som'ni-a, n.* sleeplessness [from the Latin
> *insomnis,* meaning sleepless]

Since finding the photo of Mum and Dad last week, I've become an insomniac. Some nights it's impossible to sleep at all. The second week of the summer term, I struggle to stay awake at school. When I'm supposed to be working out fractions in maths, I fall asleep and dribble on my graph paper.

The first time I greet the milkman at three o'clock in the morning he's that shocked he nearly drops our pint of full cream on the pebbledash doorstep. I pour myself a glass full and sip it at the kitchen table, the milk so fresh I can almost taste the grass.

I take to reading the dictionary at random, memorizing song lyrics from back copies of *Smash Hits,* doing sums to figure out how long it'll take me to save a down payment on a gerbil cage now that I've only got just over £1 since buying Kit's birthday present. In the silent kitchen, I notice for the first time that the Snow Queen fridge freezer grumbles just like Mum. I go that ga-ga with lack of sleep that these noises start to mean things. I christen the fridge Freddie Mercury and we become best of friends.

Freddie and I have some deep and meaningfuls well into the small hours. At half three one Saturday morning, I'm sipping milk with a pirate station playing on the radio and 'Under Pressure' by David Bowie and Queen airs. Freddie joins in. Seems he knows all about being under pressure on account of his compressed gas: 'Um bo bo be lap,' he burbles.

I would join in the duet; however, at that exact moment, I hear footsteps on the staircase. I sit tight. Freddie gurgles gas. Before too long, I hear human humming coming from the front room.

I nudge the lounge door open. The only light in the room comes from the glowing picture of a little girl playing noughts and crosses with a clown on the telly. Mum's lying on the rag rug, playing dead fishes, a blanket covering her so the only body parts I can see are her head and her hands. Her thumb and fingertips touch to make an O-shape. The hum is coming from the telly and Mum is being a tuning fork, humming with it.

Printouts of the *Inspirations* catalogue are snow-drifted to one side.

'Are you OK?' I whisper, kneeling beside her.

Mum doesn't answer.

'Would a cup of tea help?'

Through her closed mouth she says, 'I'm medicating.'

I know that medication means she has a headache and that means she has been drinking wine. I've never seen her like this before on medication – usually she just sleeps in till gone midday.

I'll wake Kit up; he'll know just what to do.

As I'm leaving the room, Mum stands up, her eyes still closed. The blanket falls to the floor to reveal she's wearing her pink jumpsuit. Mum bends over slowly, puts her hands on the floor in front of her and waggles her bum from side to side. She takes a loud, slow breath out and stands up again, stretching both hands up in the air in a V-shape and takes one foot off the floor and places it against her inner thigh.

Up in their bedroom, Kit's fast asleep on the Zedbed.

'Kit,' I whisper. He grunts and turns over to face me. 'Kit!' I whisper, this time more loudly.

'The only London Underground station not to have the letters from the word "Mackerel" in it,' he says. 'For ten points.'

Sleep talking: I suppose he's on a quiz show. I wonder what the prize is?

I try once more, 'Kit!'

'Time's up!' he shouts, sitting upright as if I've electrocuted him.

'Mum's medicating downstairs,' I say.

'What?'

'Mum! She's medicating! Downstairs!' Kit rubs his eyes. I perch on the edge of the Zedbed. 'She's humming in her jumpsuit, posing like a flamingo.'

'It's called procrastinating,' Kit says, yawning.

I shake my head. 'She definitely said she was medicating.'

'She's supposed to have started work on the catalogue proofs this week, isn't she?' Kit asks, awake now.

I nod.

'She's taken up yoga and meditation as a way to avoid it.'

'Oh. Is that what it is? Has it got something to do with drinking wine?'

'It's got everything to do with drinking wine.'

'I think I'll stick to milk.'

'I would,' Kit says. 'What were you doing up at this hour anyway?'

'I can't sleep,' I say. 'I realized how long it would take me to save up for a cage and I can't get a gerbil without a cage, can I? Or a water bottle. Or a wheel.' I start to cry, and I'm really not putting it on.

'Why don't we see about all this in the morning?' Kit asks. 'Perhaps we could go down the pet shop and work out exactly what it's going to cost.'

'That's the other thing,' I sniff. 'I thought I should stop having pocket money so that we can afford the house.'

'Save your pennies,' Kit says, ruffling my hair. 'And go to sleep, OK?'

Seems my insomnia was linked to gerbils as I sleep deeply for the rest of that night after halving my troubles with Kit. It's the rare sound of vacuum cleaning that wakes me up at half nine. Mum gave up trying to figure out how to empty the vacuum cleaner bag last year; Kit must be disturbing twelve months of dust, crumbs, our toenails and tufts of hair. Then I remember: today is the day that Kit's taking me to see about getting gerbils. I spring out of bed and put on the first clothes that tumble out of the broken bottom of the top drawer: dungarees and a Five Star fan club T-shirt which is too small for me, then I slide down the banister to the hall.

Kit is passing the vacuum cleaner ov
a bath-towel wrapped round his head.
player, the music so loud it makes my brain
hear me as I come in and sit on the plastic-cov

Mum's papers on her desk in the walk-throug
have been tidied away. The glass ashtrays are all emp
have felt like the Flag Fen archaeologists who dug up
of ancient wood when he found Mum's keyboard. There
have been a few crispy pancake relics beneath the paperwo
well, I bet. I'm sorry to spot that the mould experiments I'd bee
enjoying in Mum's coffee mugs have also disappeared. They'd
started to give off a fine, green talcum-like powder when you
wobbled them.

The stylus lifts from the record.

'You gave me a shock!' Kit says.

'I'm nearly ready. I just need to find my trainers.'

Kit unwraps the towel from his head and hangs it over the
radiator. 'Do you know, your mum didn't come to bed till after
four. She's an effective procrastinator,' he says.

'So are you,' I say. 'The pet shop might run out of gerbils! Come
on!' Mr Goodman did run out of budgerigars in January; there
may well be a gerbil shortage.

Kit finishes vacuuming as if in slow motion then goes to get
dressed. To make time dissolve, I prepare a space for the gerbil
cage on the bookshelf. De-rolling twelve rolls of toilet paper into
two plastic bags so that the cardboard can be used for gerbil gnawing takes up another ten minutes. When Kit still hasn't appeared,
I look through my View-Master at pictures of Paris. After about
twelve hours, Kit slings on his leather jacket and we go down the
High Street.

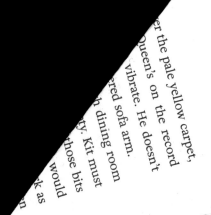

...Mr Goodman's pet shop is
...gerbils, hamsters, chin-
...e off a smell of sawdust
...; the 'Avian and Aquar-
...their bowls having to
...e seconds, toxic-green
...nselves, and one old
...obody wants to buy
...s, the parrot sits on
...mands pieces of eight. You can
...or accessory here to do with keeping pets –
...sawdust to seeds, squeaking balls to water bowls.

'Here to look at the gerbils again, Harper?' asks Mr Goodman's long white beard.

'I might be buying one this time. Are there any left?' I say, clutching my sparkly pink purse. I don't think Mr Goodman gets plain-clothed policemen in his shop.

'Plenty. And we just got an albino in yesterday.'

'Albino?'

'One with white fur...'

...I wonder if it is nesting in his beard...

'...and red eyes.'

I peer into a large cage of male gerbils, and spot the albino. Eyes the colour of blood pop out of a tiny white head; he shrinks back into a corner of the cage with a sunflower seed between his minute claws. It's as if his black and brown brothers don't want to talk to him.

'He's gorgeous.'

'They're best off in pairs,' Mr Goodman says, scratching his beard where it's yellowing. 'They're happier with someone else to play with.'

There's a black gerbil whirring around the wheel in the cage, his front and back legs never seeming to touch the floor as he runs. 'Look at him go!' I say.

'How much for two gerbils, a cage and all the trimmings?' Kit asks.

'Fifteen quid.'

Kit looks in his wallet. I turn albino-white. Fifteen quid! It would take me at least three years to save up that much.

'And I'll throw in an extra packet of sawdust,' Mr Goodman adds.

'Deal,' Kit says, handing over the cash.

'Isn't your dad kind?' Mr Goodman says, as he opens the cage. I don't correct him, and neither does Kit. 'You'll have to look after them very carefully.' He bundles the two gerbils into a red-bottomed cage on a bed of sawdust.

'I'll be the perfect mum,' I say. 'I won't flush them down the loo or anything.'

On the way home through the council estate, I carry the cage by its handle on top. The gerbils hide in the plastic house Kit bought as part of the deal; it's as if they have never seen daylight before.

'What do you think your mum would like for a present?' Kit asks.

'But it's *your* birthday tomorrow. Not hers,' I say.

'I know, but I can buy presents whenever I want, can't I?' Kit says, smiling.

I know Mum would *really* like a new set of falsies – the set she's got clatter around her mouth, especially when she laughs.

Apart from teeth, she has been talking about going back to Gordon Benét's for a pair of heels like the silver ones, but in pink for the wedding. Then it pings into my mind: *bona fide* perfume. When we were down Boots the Chemist the other Saturday, she got a piddle stick with a 'refreshing fragrance for the woman who's streets ahead' on it. I can't remember what it's called or how much it costs, but Kit says perfume's always cheaper 'duty free'. I know without asking that this means going on a plane or a ferry, because Cassie has told me all about duty-free shops and the chocolate bars in purple wrappers the size of bricks that they sell.

To buy Mum perfume must be cemented in Kit's mind when we get home. On opening the door, a wall of smell hits us: boiled cabbage. Oona must be in. Every so often she comes round to share a large pot of cabbage soup that she's made too much of, followed by a course of chocolate bourbons.

Kit disappears up the stairs taking three at a time. I set the cage down on the bookshelf and the gerbils nose their way out from under the twitching sawdust. Bubble and Squeak, Ebony and Ivory: they're vegetarian names. I want something with more bite. I decide on Bangers and Mash, and take down my library copy of *Keeping Gerbils* from the bookshelf. 'Dehydration is the primary cause of death in the young', it says, on page one.

I brave the cabbagey kitchen to fill their water bottle. Oona and Mum are already on to the chocolate bourbons. I unscrew the bottle and fill it up at the tap.

'Don't know why I bother,' Oona says, wiping crumbs off her breast-shelf. 'It's like I was *born* a size sixteen.'

'Why don't you take up yoga?' Mum asks.

'It's calories I need to burn, Mary. Not incense.'

'You lost two pounds last month,' Mum says.

'That's what I mean! It's as hopeless as trying to redecorate your house with a bottle of Tipp-Ex!'

'You just need some more willpower,' Mum says.

'My willpower has the restraining strength of a KitKat,' Oona says, taking a chocolate bourbon from the plate which balances on top of a pile of Mum's catalogue printouts. Mum offers me a biscuit; I take four. Then I peg it back to the lounge with the water bottle. Bangers and Mash are busy gnawing the loo-roll tubes just like Derek's rats, Adam and Twenty-Twenty. I've stashed the spare loo paper in two plastic bags and hidden it in Cupboard Love. I'm sure it will come in handy one day.

fourteen

▼▼▼▼▼

Carrying a tray of two boiled eggs with soldiers and black coffees along with Kit's birthday present, I climb the stairs to Mum and Kit's bedroom the next morning. As usual, Mum's fast asleep with wax earplugs jammed into her ears. She keeps her earplugs in a net bag on her bedside table next to her new silver engagement ring that she has to take off at night so it doesn't give her a rash. Each Friday she puts the earplug bag in with the week's laundrette load. *Gross*, I say, but Mum says it's no different from pegging out teabags for a second dip.

'Breakfast in bed?' I whisper to Kit, who's half-awake on the Zedbed. I set the tray down beside him on the floor.

'You're a star,' Kit says, inching up his pillow. He reaches for a brown bottle of pills by his bedside, unscrews the lid and swallows a couple of capsules with his morning coffee.

'Happy birthday!' I say, handing him the shampoo which I have wrapped that morning in an article from *Woman's Own* about losing weight by eating more.

'You shouldn't've,' he says.

As Kit's unwrapping the small box I notice that Mum's teeth are in and she's twitching as if she's having a bad dream.

'How did you know?' Kit says, when he sees what I've bought him. 'It's perfect!' I'm pleased Derek made the right choice of tint.

Mum pings awake. 'Happy birthday!' she says, laughing.

'I don't get it!' I say. I take a closer look at the box. Reading the small print, it seems that Mum has tricked me into treating Kit to a hair dye product for 'greying gentlemen'.

'Mum! It'll be Oil of Ulay for your birthday for the next ten years,' I say.

'Come here, pet,' Mum says, trying to cuddle me. 'It was quite a funny joke, don't you think?'

I shrug her off. 'If I wanted to buy Kit a practical joke, I would've bought him a whoopee cushion.'

I hope she's got a better idea for a present up her armpit when it's my birthday.

I leave them to their breakfast and go to cheer myself up by putting on my set-aside Blackbrake Carnival outfit: Mum's yellow and black striped T-shirt worn as a dress with one of her black patent leather belts tied twice round my waist.

If you stand on the blue water-butt cover in the back garden, you can see down the back lanes which lead to the High Street where carnival floats are being towed. I can make out the God Squad one: there's a large white cross and a bloke dressed in a torn white pillowcase. The Second Coming, I guess. According to Derek, the borstal boys have a float this year; they're going as Daleks who'll shoot chocolate coins instead of exterminating death-rays.

Later that morning I head through the council estate to the

High Street. I've some coppers in my denim jacket pocket from my Harper's Bazaar profit to throw at the people holding buckets on the passing floats; in return they throw penny sweets towards the pavements. Kids gather along the length of the High Street like racehorses straining on their reins at Aintree: at Blackbrake Carnival, it's each to their own. Forget frogs, blood or UFOs falling from the sky, here we're talking hailstorms of Black Jacks, Mojos, cola cubes and flying saucers; fistfuls of Flumps, fizzy cola bottles, jelly beans and, if you're lucky, you might even score an Atomic Fireball.

Police cars will be waiting at each end of the roadblock with their blue lights flashing, the bobbies telling adults to turn off their car engines as there are some serious amounts of sweets to be distributed.

The first float which inches along the High Street is one organized by the Brownies. They've come as Snow White and about twenty-five dwarves. I hide behind a lamppost as they pass so that Brown Owl, who's dressed as the Evil Stepmother, doesn't spot me: I've bunked off the last six weeks of Brownies, and spent the subs Mum gave me on stock for Harper's Bazaar instead. When I edge back towards the front of the pavement again, I scoop up a handful of Polos. I stuff the miniature life-saving rings into my cheeks like a squirrel sensing winter. My cheeks start to burn from the sugar, so I decide to pull back from the front line and get a drink; there are dozens of floats still to go.

Next to It's a Gift there's a fried-food van. I do a double-take when I realize that the boy behind the counter with a skin-coloured face free from make-up and with white-blond hair beneath a net is Derek. I wonder which centre-fold *Smash Hits* poster he's got pinned next to his bed now?

He leans over a steaming vat. 'Can you keep a secret, Harper?' he whispers.

'Course,' I say.

'I'm saving up for the bus fare to London. I'm going to run away and work for Vidal Sassoon.'

'Cor!'

'Don't tell no one, mind.'

Running away. I've done that once before; I got as far as Blackbrake bus station before I realized that the only places I could afford a coach ticket to were Luton or Walsall. When I got home, Mum hadn't even noticed I'd gone. It was just as well; when I unpacked I discovered I'd forgotten to take any knickers.

'I don't know exactly when yet,' Derek says. 'But I wouldn't tell you if I knew. It's *classified*.'

'Don't forget your boxer shorts!' I whisper, as Derek's manager heaves himself back up the steps into the trailer carrying a cardboard box labelled *Dehydrated Fried Onion Slices*. I hand Derek 10p for a Panda Pop, cross my heart and press my finger against my lips.

I'm very good at keeping secrets.

This is just as well.

I sit on the wall outside It's a Gift where they've a seasonal line in battery-operated Easter bunnies marked down to £1.99 in the window. I sip my lemonade and wonder how long it'll be before I'll find battery-flat bunnies in the skips around Blackbrake that I can rescue.

I spot Lisa on the Blackbrake School for Girls float as she sails past, waving one of her crutches in the air to her imaginary fans. The rest of the girls have decorated their hockey sticks with yellow ribbons and they're holding them up to make X-shapes.

A teacher in a black cape and a yellow bonnet with a red slash for a mouth is standing as straight as an upright coffin on the float, occasionally throwing a handful of mint humbugs into the gutter. It's while I'm watching the float sail past that I spot Kit on the other side of the High Street.

It's illegal to cross the road, so I'm about to get up and head to the police car check point to cross when I see Kit kiss a woman who's standing next to him. Bang on the mouth kissing between the sexes is something people do when they're going out or married. Either that, or when they're trying to bring someone back to life. This woman is clearly not in need of resuscitating because she's smiling as Kit licks his lips. She laughs, tipping her head right back so he must be able to see her tonsils.

Cassie wouldn't understand what's legal when you're dating because her parents have been married for so long, they're practically the same person. I won't mention it to Mum, because she's getting as fragile as the Wedgwood vase that stands out of bounds on top of the bookcase. So I bury another pebble question in my head-jar. I'll keep it there safe until I can find someone who will understand, and then I'll root it out and try to grasp what the hell is happening.

fifteen

▼▼▼▼▼

Many bombs exploded in the nearby city of Coventry, Dad tells me over the chips we're eating in the car on the way to the Lone Rangers disco.

'Some people kept the bunkers they'd built in their gardens after the Second World War just in case there was a Third,' Dad says.

I wind down the car window to peer out at the flats next to us. They're built out of huge blocks of grey concrete. I can't see any gardens, let alone bunkers. Occasional colour does drip down the balconies, but that's on account of wet washing, not flowers. With the car window open, the smell of fat from the chip shop opposite mixes with car exhaust fumes and another smell I can't quite place.

'Dad, have you got rip-off perfume on?' I ask.

'Aftershave.'

'It smells of peanuts.'

Dad sniffs his collar.

'I have some Exclamation! in my jelly bag if you'd like to borrow some?'

Instead, Dad changes into his emergency shirt which he keeps in the cardboard box in the boot along with a shovel, blanket, a luminous orange triangle and five litres of diesel. We polish off the chips, and then drive to a large church hall where white balloons are tied to the iron gates. A banner has been strung on the railings. It reads:

LONE RANGERS DISCO

For Single-Parent Families

You're Not Alone: Let's Party Together!

Sounds to me as if the Lone Rangers are trying to convince parents to split up rather than stay together. Ditch your marriage and disco? *Please.* I've been to enough Lone Rangers firework parties, picnics and mingle mornings to know the score: the kids are chucked together to 'have fun' while the adults get bitter about their exes. Once they've exhausted each other with tales of being back on the shelf, with raw deals and colossal mortgages, the kids are given the job of taking black bin liners around to collect the stale crisps and plastic cups which have been crushed in frustration by grown-ups and children alike. Lone Rangers discos may be billed as for the kids, but odds on it'll be the lone parents throwing shapes by the last dance.

Dad and I are the first to arrive, if you don't count the DJ, a man who's wearing a Radio One T-shirt and setting up on a wallpaper table at the front of the hall. Chairs are pushed back against the wall to make a dance floor in the middle. The DJ billows smoke from a machine into it, then flickers lights like a traffic signal on fast forward.

'Can we come back in half an hour?' I whisper to Dad. Not even wearing leg warmers can make me feel cool about being five minutes early for a Lone Rangers disco.

'But we've got the best seats,' Dad says.

We are sitting near the emergency fire exit and a green sign that says Children are the Responsibility of their Responsible Adults AT ALL TIMES.

It turns out that the DJ is a dad, too. His son, who looks about fourteen, must have been sent down It's a Gift to bulk-buy party poppers because he's carrying a dozen boxes of them in a tower tucked under his chin. My dad bulk-buys too, things like tinned sweetcorn, UHT orange juice, mayonnaise, firelighters and teabags. He says it's because of the war as well.

The DJ's son has a crew cut and wears a black T-shirt with 'CND' in white letters on the front. I'm sure I memorized some CND lyrics about ten Smash Hits issues ago, but I can't remember what the song was called. The disco lights catch his braces as he laughs at something his DJ dad shouts to him over the top of Shakin' Stevens's 'This Ole House', and his mouth glints. If the DJ had been listening to the lyrics, he mightn't have chosen that track to kick off a disco for single parents and their kids, seeing as it's about a man whose wife and children have left him alone in his leaky house with shingles, floors and hinges that need fixing.

I hitch up my leg warmers and wait for a cooler track to be played. Meanwhile, two girls in matching tight white jeans and black leather jackets arrive and go up to the DJ table, I hope to request something that's less break-up and more breakdance.

Bananarama's 'Nathan Jones' comes on next. This song seems

to attract more kids into the disco, their Responsible Adults flocking to the drinks hatch to sniff out the bad alcohol. Now, I've taped Bananarama lip-synching 'Nathan Jones' off *Top of the Pops* on the Betamax, and I've not only memorized the lyrics with help from Freddie, but also the moves. I hit the dance floor; at first I feel like Halley's Comet would if it fell to earth – totally out of place – but after the first chorus, I forget that anyone is watching. When the song ends, the DJ's son with the CND T-shirt comes over to chat up one of the cool girls in tight white jeans. But, no.

No, wait.

Hang on.

He's making a line like a bee towards me.

He's making a line like a bee towards me and he's handing me a drink.

'Do you want to go and sit outside?' he asks.

Breathe, Harper, I tell myself. *It's not like he's asking you out on a first date down the Shang High Noodle Emporium or anything. He's just asking you if you'd like to have some weak orange squash outside a church hall in Coventry.*

I nod, finally finding my words: 'Better just tell my dad.'

Dad's still sitting next to the fire exit, but he has been joined by a Lone Rangers mum of three, Louise.

'OK, love?' he asks.

'Did you see me dance?' I say.

'No. I bet you were great,' Dad says, more to Louise than to me.

'Are you having a nice time?' she asks and her make-up, which is as thick as icing, cracks as she raises her thick eyebrows. Even I could have done a better job of choosing colours for her face. Her eyelids are caked in bright blue powder, her cheeks are nearly purple and her lips are somewhere in between.

'No,' I reply, grabbing my duffle coat.

'Oh. Well. There'll be lots of games to play later,' she says.

I raise the corner of my mouth into a half-snarl.

'Louise is hosting the Lone Rangers committee meeting later tonight,' Dad says. 'I'm joining to help with fundraising!'

'I'm going for some fresh air,' I announce.

'OK but not too far. I'm your Responsible Adult, remember!' Dad says.

I screw my face up at Louise like a piece of scrap paper heading straight for the bin. I know what these Lone Rangers women are like: territorial and two-faced. Dad dabbled with one once: Michelle. He ate only traybakes for at least two weeks after they split up.

Outside, gloomy clouds have ballooned, their edges tinted with orange. The air feels heavy with soon-to-bolt thunder. We sit outside the gates and sip squash. CND Boy introduces himself as Craig.

'That's your dad?' he asks.

'Afraid so. Yours is the DJ?'

'He's not very good at socializing,' Craig says. 'That's why he DJs. He's only had one girlfriend since the divorce.'

'Mine, too. Michelle, her name was. Her five boys were mentalists.'

Craig laughs. 'Why?'

'All they did was beat each other up, I swear. It ended after we visited one time and I threw up over a defrosting chicken in the sink.'

Craig passes me a stick of chewing gum. I tear it in two and give him the other half. We sit and chew the white, minty gum in silence for a while, watch the traffic rumble past.

'How old were you when your parents split up?' I ask.

'Five,' he says.

'Me too.'

'Mum says she won't marry again,' Craig says. 'Just as well because her boyfriend's an arsehole.'

'I don't believe in marriage,' I say, to colour in the silence which follows. 'But when my mum marries her boyfriend, then we can afford to buy our house.'

'Sounds like a good reason.'

'I wish I could make my parents less embarrassing,' I say.

'Don't think you can make people change, especially not your parents,' Craig says. He seems clever, though not in an Intellectual Quotient kind of way. Craig is the first boy I've met who seems to understand what it feels like to be a Lone Rangers freak like me. And I bet he knows if you're allowed to kiss another woman even if you're engaged to be married to somebody else.

'I wish they'd tell the truth,' he continues. 'I mean, why do they always say they've split up because "Mum and Dad don't love each other any more"? We're not babies. We can handle the truth.'

'They think they're protecting us,' I say.

'That's impossible,' Craig says, standing up, knocking the last of his orange squash over.

I change the compass of our chat by asking what pop song CND charted with. It does the trick; Craig laughs.

'CND stands for the Campaign for Nuclear Disarmament,' he says. 'You know anything about nuclear war?'

I blush at getting my pop music knickers in a twist.

'Splitting the atom is like divorce: there's always fall-out and it makes you sick...' His sentence fizzles out, like a spent sparkler. Raindrops begin to make dark black circles on the grey pavement.

I decide that now isn't a good moment to ask him what he thinks about Kit's mystery kiss.

'My dad seems to be getting on with Louise,' I say. 'Something about her makes me suspicious, though. Maybe it's her make-up.'

'She's a two-timer.'

'How d'you know?'

Craig scuffs his shoe against the kerb. 'My Dad used to go out with her.'

'When did they split up?' I ask.

'Ended last month I think. But that was the fourth time she called it off. I'd be glad if she moved on, but not if it's with your dad.'

Just then, Craig's dad comes out to tell him that it'll be time to go soon. We must have been outside for an age. His dad ignores me, maybe because he thinks it's my fault that my dad is taking his ex-girlfriend away from him. After all, if I didn't exist, then Dad wouldn't be here, entertaining me at a lame Lone Rangers disco in Coventry on a soggy April afternoon.

Craig's dad slams the door shut behind him, leaving the two of us on the kerb.

'Your dad seems as sensitive as mine,' I sigh.

'Sensitive?' Craig says, as he leans his face towards mine. 'Well, he's got nerve endings.'

His kiss is as sweet and cold as an orange lolly.

'Craig?' I ask.

'Mm?'

'Why me?' I can't help myself; I have to know.

'Cos I can tell you're different, Harper.'

I look down at what I'm wearing: yellow leg warmers, thick black tights, a red and white polka-dot ra-ra skirt, an orange T-shirt and matching fingerless gloves.

'I don't mean what you're wearing,' Craig says.

Before Craig can explain his dad comes out again and shoots us evils. The chorus from Phil Collins' 'Easy Lover' spills on to the street. Back inside, three Lone Rangers mums are dancing around their black handbags which are grouped together like cats with arched backs, ready to pounce.

Inside the loos, one of the girls in tight white jeans leans over the sink and peers into the stained mirror as she applies a coat of peachy lipstick.

'All right?' she says.

'All right,' I say and rub my mouth with the back of my hand, wondering if it shows that I've been synchronizing lips.

'Who d'ya snog, then?' she asks.

'Craig,' I say, then disappear into the cubicle and sit on the closed lid of the cold black toilet seat.

'Where'd you learn to dance like that?' she says, after a pause.

'Off of the telly!' I shout, over the door.

Then there's silence.

'Like your moonwalking,' I say, but my voice echoes around the walls of peeling white plaster. I sit tight and watch the chain dangle overhead until I'm sure she has left before coming out again. On the mirror is a message, written in lipstick: *Craig Arrowsmith. 1, Vicarage Crescent. Cov. CV1 7AL. Your love birds ain't you?*

I have a pen in my coat pocket, and before wiping off the lipstick with bog roll, I scribble the address down on a scrap of paper in my pocket. I never thought to ask for his address.

sixteen

▼▼▼▼▼

Dad's emergency shirt is all sweaty from dancing. After the disco we have a couple of hours to kill before the Lone Rangers committee meeting starts at six o'clock, so Dad says we'll go down Coventry shopping centre to get him a new shirt. In British Home Stores, Dad buys one identical to the one he was wearing – white with thin, blue stripes as well as a new packet of Y-fronts. He's in a spending-money mood, and asks me if I'd like something.

If you're going to find anything to like about Coventry shopping centre then I suppose it would be that it does have a Woolworths. There, I choose a single called 'Doctorin' the Tardis' and nick a couple of prawn-shaped pick 'n' mix from underneath the plastic flaps of the containers when I'm sure no plain-clothed policemen are looking. There's still a good hour before the committee meeting starts. Dad suggests we turn up early, but I say this would be worse than turning up in a peanutty shirt, or death itself. We're rescued by a last-minute visit to Patrick, who works Saturdays at his Photographic Palace.

As I push the door open, a doorbell with a nearly-flat battery drowsily ding-dongs. Skew-whiff on the wall is a display of wedding photographs on brown cardboard with a golden trim – the photos of brides and grooms fade out at the edges as if a fog suddenly appeared as they were taken. Reels of black film spill out of crumpled cardboard boxes. I step over a set of small wooden drawers complete with slides of ancient ruins from the turn of the century, for sale at thirty quid the lot. Glass cabinets display dusty single-lens reflex cameras. At Patrick's you can also buy or have repaired – if you can reach the counter without serious injury – binoculars, new film, padded camera bags, slide viewers and projectors.

A customer has risked her neck and stands at the counter just ahead of us. In one hand, she holds a set of negatives which she's asking to have reprinted; in the other, she grasps a white handkerchief.

'Thirty-six or twenty-four?' Patrick asks without looking up from his counter.

'It's not polite to ask a stranger's age!' I whisper to Dad.

'It's the number of exposures, silly,' Dad replies.

'Thirty-six,' the lady says.

'These are all over-exposed,' Patrick says as he places the brown negatives on his light box.

I frown at Dad. 'They've seen too much sunlight,' he explains.

This is not a problem that could be laid at Patrick's pebble-dash doorstep; his skin is so pale he's practically a poltergeist. It appears to me that Patrick spends far too much time under-developing in a dark room. In fact, he would blend right in down Oncology with the Grecian 2000 crew.

'It would be a waste of chemical to reprint these,' he says.

The customer sniffs; seems she's on the verge of tears. 'They're all I have left of my mother's wedding day,' she says. 'I found them in the attic when I was clearing out her house. *Please* will you try?'

Her words ring clear as church bells between my ears: *They're all I have left of my mother's wedding day.*

Bingo! Patrick's my phantom photographer. I thought I was Harper May Richardson in a Photographic Palace. But no, I'm Marty McFly in a DeLorean, and Patrick is my Doc Brown. If I can just get Patrick on his own, I'll get him to time travel back to 1972 and ask him to explain how my parents met and the story behind the photo of my mum's last A-level. He's also bound to have a projector somewhere that I can hijack so I can see what's on that film. Just like Doc does for Marty in *Back to the Future*, I'll get Patrick to explain to me why on earth my parents ever thought it was a good idea to get it on.

I have to think over my tactics here.

I have to flux my capacitors.

Best thing to do is for me to bore for England about the pink and purple Le Clic pocket camera I can see in the cabinet that's for sale and that I quite fancy, actually. Dad'll switch off if I ask enough questions – then I can take Patrick to one side and ask to borrow the projector.

The customer's waterworks display has convinced Patrick to have a last stab at salvaging what little is left on the lady's negatives. She leaves the door trumpeting into her handkerchief.

'How are tricks?' Patrick asks Dad once we reach the counter.

'OK,' Dad sighs, in a voice that suggests the opposite is true.

Patrick raises one bushy eyebrow.

'British Steel's looking dodgy,' Dad says.

'You need a back-up plan, mate. Not that I'm the best business adviser in this backwater,' Patrick says, looking around his shop.

'What can be so dodgy about steel?' I ask.

'Margaret bloody Thatcher's selling off utilities and public companies. She'll be privatizing the damn water we drink before you know it,' Dad says.

I wish Dad would swear more when he talks to me; it makes me feel like I'm a grown-up. Like I'm old enough for underwired bras and Judy Blume.

'Won't happen,' Patrick says. 'Bet you a lager top.'

'Dad,' I begin, while the going's good. 'You know Louise?'

'Yes,' Dad turns to me.

'I think she might already have a boyfriend.'

Patrick hinges over his counter and peers at me through his thick spectacles.

Dad says, 'Where did you hear this, Harper?'

'I...just heard it through the grapevine,' I say, scrabbling around for the right words, and pouncing on some I've heard on the radio that say it without getting Craig into trouble.

'How old are you again, Harper?' Patrick says, his eyes narrowing as if he has photographic chemicals in them.

'Twelve and a half,' I say.

'Bloody hell! You've got your mum's tact already.'

Dad turns to look at Patrick, opens his mouth, then closes it again like a letterbox. We leave just as soon as Dad and I can clamber back over the boxes of stock.

seventeen

▼▼▼▼▼

Dad leaves me to wait in the car round the corner from Patrick's saying he'll be gone two minutes and then he marches down the High Street out of sight. I tune into Radio One on the car stereo where Madonna is singing about being a virgin. Pulling down the sun visor, I look at my reflection in the rectangular mirror. I snaffled one of Mum's black eyeliners from her make-up bag the other day, which I use now to colour in the mole just to the right of my lips. To pass the time, I also colour in my eyebrows and draw along the watery red bits at the bottom of my eyes; I reckon I look instantly at least thirteen.

I really thought I was doing the best thing by telling Dad about Louise. I don't want to see him get hurt. While Mum may be fragile, she's always the one who does the dumping and I know it hit Dad hard when Michelle of the defrosting chicken ended it – as well as just eating traybakes, he also grew his beard back, and that only happens when he's depressed.

The clock on the dashboard tells me that Dad has been gone

for at least five minutes. Madonna's song comes to an end and the DJ plays something by ABBA that I turn down until it's over. At first, I think it's silly to worry. *I'll be gone two minutes* is something people say to mean they'll be gone for ten, after all. But once he has been gone for over quarter of an hour, I can't stop the old panic rising in me: Dad's gone. And he's never coming back.

By the time he does return, my eyeliner is reduced to black streaks which have poured down my face.

'What's wrong?' Dad asks.

'I thought you were never coming back,' I say, gasping for air.

'You silly thing. I wouldn't leave you.'

'But you said you'd be gone two minutes, Dad!'

'I was, wasn't I?'

'They played *six* singles while you were gone,' I say, jabbing my finger towards the radio.

'I'm sorry, love,' Dad says, and he does sound apologetic. He also smells of lager.

'It's just, I don't like it when you make promises and then break them.'

'I would never break a promise,' Dad says coolly, and he crunches the gears into first quicker than he needs to then streaks down the street.

Louise's is a brick terraced house like those on Kendal Road – hers is the one that backs on to a scrapyard where old cars come to die in the crushing teeth of huge, hungry machines.

'Would you like to play Trivial Pursuit with the other kids upstairs?' Louise asks as we go into the hall.

I ignore her. Dad fills in the silence. 'We've brought Twiglets!' he says, offering Louise five multipacks.

'How generous!' she says.

'They're beyond their best-before date,' I say, as I head into the kitchen to check out the snacks. There's bound to be a cheese and pineapple hedgehog; there's always one of those at crap parties.

From the kitchen, I can make out what the kids are saying upstairs: 'Ask us a green question, Troy! This one's for a cheese!'

In the front room, the Lone Rangers committee meeting is declared open by someone freeing the cork from a bottle of sparkling alcohol.

I destroy Louise's display of chocolate finger biscuits and take several cheese and pineapple cocktail sticks. I can't help but tune into the ideas being discussed at the committee meeting in the front room. Some dimwit with an Intellectual Quotient of a flea suggests they should consider introducing badges, ones that you'd sew on to the arms of your shirt, like you get at Brownies.

I doodle on the back of an envelope, write up some genius badge ideas of my own.

You get:

- A bronze star if you have a step-parent
- A silver star if you're screwed up enough to have an ex-step-parent
- A gold star if your parents are able to have a conversation lasting longer than two minutes without crying or cutlery being thrown
- A bronze coin if you get pocket money from one parent
- A silver coin if you get pocket money from both parents

- A gold coin if your mum and dad have opened, out of parental guilt, a trust fund and you'll be rolling in it come your eighteenth birthday

A knock at the front door interrupts my thinking.

'Hi, Phil,' Louise says. 'Let's get you a drink.'

I dive into the downstairs toilet with a handful of cheese puffs.

Phil and Louise walk past the toilet door through to the kitchen. 'I've brought a six-pack,' Phil says and I recognize his voice instantly: it's Craig's dad.

'Two six-packs, you mean?' Louise says, and then I hear silence, probably being filled in by an orange lolly kiss.

I have to get a message to Dad that Louise is going out with Phil again. Chinese Whispers would do the trick. I could say something in mirror writing like, 'Esiuol tuoba tegrof,' but then I don't want to spoil his chances like I did the time I threw up on a defrosting chicken.

I wish Craig was here so I could ask him what to do. And so I could kiss him again.

'Harper? Are you in there?' Dad shouts through the door.

'Yes, Dad,' I say, flushing the cheese puffs down the loo.

'We're going,' Dad says. 'Get your coat.'

We don't say goodbye to anyone.

As we drive home, 'Red Red Wine' comes on to the radio. Dad turns it up loud so that there's no white space left to talk in. Once we've pulled up outside Ivy Cottage, Dad gets his British Home Stores bag with his spare Y-fronts out of the boot of the car and throws it in the metal bin. The lid crashes and echoes down the empty street.

In bed I don't want to think about anything complicated, so I turn to my favourite chapter in *The Almanac of Spooky Happenings*, the one about a feral child who was raised by wolves in the jungles of Sri Lanka. He walks like a monkey, eats with his hands and bites anyone who tries to hug him.

eighteen

▼▼▼▼▼

Harper May Richardson
*Shop Manageress * Daydreamer * Lone Ranger*
Floor 27, 13 Kendal Road
Blackbrake, BKI 3JF
England, The Universe
The Solar System

Craig Arrowsmith
1 Vicarage Crescent
Coventry
CVI 7AL

Sunday 1 May 1988

Dear Craig,
You were right about Louise; she is going out with your
dad again. The committee meeting was D-R-E-A-D-F-U-L.

Can you help me? I think my mum's new boyfriend is *also* two-timing. I saw him kiss another woman down the Blackbrake Carnival.

I copied this quiz out of *Just Seventeen*, but changed the words. Can you fill it in and send it back? Pretty please.

My best things are the Top Forty, gerbils and Five Star. What are yours?

Harper x

Reasons why my mum's boyfriend kissed another woman:
__ She's his girlfriend (two-timer)
__ She's his wife (two-timer)
__ He likes the feeling (two-timer)
__ She's his sister (illegal – double gross!)
__ She's his cousin, second cousin etc. (Legal. But still double gross!)
__ She/he needed mouth to mouth (doubtful)
__ Her gerbil/grandma/grandpa/best friend just died (no excuse)
__ Other reason (state)_____

Put these in order of probability by writing 1–8 next to them, with 1 meaning the 'most likely' and 8 being the 'least likely' then cut out and return in the enclosed self-addressed envelope. Thanks a trillion.

nineteen

▼▼▼▼▼

It's not long before I get to ID the mystery kisser. The next Wednes-day afternoon I'm practising scales on the piano after school while Mum's at the dining-room table making plastic gadgets sound like they're worth a hundred times more than they are with her copywriting. Two earplugs are jammed down her listening chim-neys, so she doesn't hear the doorbell when it rings in the tune of 'She'll be Coming Round the Mountain When She Comes'. I go to answer it.

'Good afternoon,' the woman at the door begins. Then she takes a deep breath: 'I'm-Melanie-I'm-here-today-representing-Blackbrake-Windows-Conservatories-and-Doors-to-drop-off-a-catalogue-with-the-man-of-the-house-is-he-in?'

I'm positive it's her; she has the same bubble-perm and wide mouth. I have two options: warn her off or slam the door in her face.

'Sorry, I'm the only one here right now,' I say, thinking over my tactics as I lie through my teeth, which are set in a sneer. 'But my mum's fiancé will be back later. He's a salesman too,' I say.

'Oh yes?' The woman says while feeling in her bum bag for a leaflet.

'He sells chocolate.'

'Is-that-right-here-you-go,' Melanie says, handing over her leaflet, but her smile is frozen. *Gotcha!*

'His name's Kit-short-for-Kit-Kat,' I say, adding splintered double-glazing glass to her punctured face.

'Right-then-thank-you-for-your-time-please-call-the-office-if-you'd-like-a-quotation...' She's already power-walking up the dead end, her bum bag bouncing behind her. I turn the leaflet over in my hand. On the back is a box where she's written her name in order to get her commission: Melanie. What a dumb name. Back in the lounge, Mum notices that someone's called. She looks up as I go in but doesn't take out her earplugs.

'Bloody double glazing!' she shouts, and tosses the leaflet I hand her into the wastepaper bin to join hundreds of *Inspirations* catalogue printouts which are slashed through with red ink.

That evening, Kit calls a summit to discuss the wedding over crispy pancakes. When the telephone rings, Mum lets the answering machine take the message from Joanna. Her voice growls into the tape recorder: '*I hope you'll be feeling better by tomorrow, Mary...*'

Kit writes up an agenda on the back of an unopened brown envelope which he fishes out of the wastepaper bin. I think he notices the double-glazing leaflet, but I can't be sure. If he does know it was that moron Melanie who dropped it off, he doesn't let on.

The agenda reads:

1. Booze
2. Date
3. Mortgage
4. Party
5. Invitations
6. Music
7. Religion??
8. AOB

Kit explains what AOB stands for and I add:

8.   AOB:
8.i   Laura Ashley ban
8.ii Harper's name
8.iii What happens in case of divorce

'Well, that'll be a fine note to end on,' Kit says, opening a can of Blackbrake lager.

Mum takes minutes in her reporter's notebook on account of her memory-sieve. The most important points are that:

- I can wear whatever I like;
- Religion isn't coming into it, thank Five Star, because they're getting married in a register office where you don't need to mime prayers;
- We can bulk-buy Panda Pops;
- I can invite one friend (Cassie);
- My name will be double-barrelled like a sawn-off shotgun (with Dad's approval), and,
- I have the job of baking the wedding cake.

I've always wanted to know how to bake a cake, but what I really want to know is what'll happen if Mum and Kit split up, especially if he fancies double-glazed Melanie. When I ask about potential separation (without mentioning that I've seen Kit kiss another woman), Kit drains the dregs out of his can. 'I'll look into a pre-nuptial agreement in case of death, divorce or derangement. OK? But first things first. About these supplies...'

'The cash and carry's always a good bet,' Mum says. 'I bought twelve bottles of Vosene down there last month for less than a fiver.'

'I was thinking of somewhere a little bit more exotic, Mary...' Kit says, a smile unzipping across his face.

Mum doesn't get it.

'Where better than the land of grapes and wrath?' Kit says.

'Is that land duty free?' I ask.

Mum leaps out of her chair. 'France! I'll go and find my passport, make sure it's still valid.' She's already halfway up the stairs, her voice fading as she goes. 'God, that photo was taken *years* before my permanent...'

Where I imagine paranoid people stash guns, knives or victim alarms, Mum hides her passport: under the mattress at the top of the bed where she lays her head in case, she says, anyone tries to steal it in the middle of the night. Not that she has ever used it for foreign travel as, like me, she's never been abroad. She just uses it to certify who she is when applying for credit.

'I don't think I've got a passport,' I say to Kit.

'It's all right, H, you're just a minor.' Which makes me sound like a scale my crinkly piano teacher makes me learn, not a twelve-year-old with a mind of my own. 'You can just be inked on to your mum's.'

twenty

▼▼▼▼▼

For *le weekend*, Kit borrows a car to drive us all to France – a bright red 2CV Dolly with a striped red and white roof which peels off like the lid on a tin of sardines. It's an upturned deckchair on wheels, and feels about as safe. I've found an outfit to match the car: red and white stripy leggings and a blue T-shirt with a picture of the Eiffel tower on the front; I found it in the 10p bargain bin down A Dog's Not Just for Christmas charity shop. Derek has lent me his navy beret. I haven't accounted for it being so cold at half four in the morning, which is when my talking alarm clock detonates its strangled cockerel alarm. I have to spoil the look with my yellow fake mohair jumper.

While Mum gets ready, I sit at the bottom of the stairs and check the contents of my green jelly bag. Inside, I've packed a pair of prototype sunglasses with windscreen wipers that Mum's writing about for the gadget catalogue and my pink sparkly purse with this week's pocket money – 30p – inside. As I haven't been to Mr Power's, my snack supply is just what's left over from Blackbrake

Carnival: a half-sucked Atomic Fireball and a packet of space dust. Plus, I have smuggled two of Mum's cigarettes in between this week's *Smash Hits*. This is France we're going to after all, and I have seen more than just View-Master pictures of what French kids get up to, *n'est-ce pas*?

Mum's chucking things in her handbag in between outfit changes while she thinks of them: two packets of Silk Cut, lighter, emergency lighter, electric-blue mascara, pocket mirror, Chris Rea cassette, cough medicine, earplugs, sunglasses, French phrase book for utter beginners, a Mills and Boon, mints, her passport... While she's upstairs on her fourth change of clothes, I fish out her passport and look at her small photo. It wasn't just taken before her permanent, it was also taken before she had her teeth pulled out: they look like yellowing toenails.

I spit my atomic fireball out, and wrap it up in a centre-fold poster of Glenn Medeiros from *Smash Hits* which I can live without.

Mum nudges past me, bare-legged, having decided on a white blouse paired with a skirt with swirling patterns of purples, greys and reds and a blue jacket with cardboard in the shoulders. The silver heels finish it off, of course.

'*On y va!*' she says, going out to the car. I'm heading for the front door when Kit stops me in the hall and hands me a ten-franc note.

'Pounds sterling are academic in France, you know,' he says.

'Thank you,' I say, stunned. I wonder what you can get for ten francs?

'*De rien,*' Kit replies, as he closes the front door behind us.

I buckle the seat belt across my lap in the back of the 2CV where Kit says French peasants store sheep. Kit peels back the roof and secures the material with the same kind of poppers you might find on a pair of cheap shoes.

'You're good at that,' Mum says.

'Just like rolling up!' Kit replies, far too chirpy for five-thirty in the morning. He gets into the driver's seat in front of me and pulls the throttle out as he fires up the engine. We crawl out of the cul-de-sac, the sky over our heads shepherd-warning red. As he indicates and turns left on to the Greytown Road, the indicator stick falls off in his hand.

'It's OK!' he shouts over his shoulder to me. 'It's still attached by the cable.'

I peer out of the back window; the only other traffic on the Greytown Road is our milkman, his float droning like a bee drunk on tinkling bottles of milk. I wave as he overtakes: Kit has stalled. He blames the gearstick. 'It's like changing gears with an umbrella!' he says.

The last thing I see before falling asleep is Blackbrake's totem pole – the tower where the Dynamo Elevator Inc. tests lifts. Inside, I imagine crash-test dummies whizzing up and down the concrete pillar in prototype elevators.

An urgent feeling in my tummy wakes me up about two hours later. It's light outside now and we're hurtling down the slow lane of the M1 motorway, coaches and towed caravans overtaking us. My body buzzes as if I'm sitting on a washing machine set to spin cycle down the laundrette.

'Can we stop soon? I need the loo!' I holler above Chris Rea, whose 'Steel River' is struggling to be heard over the screaming engine.

Kit turns the music down.

'You should've gone before we left,' Mum murmurs from the passenger seat. 'We'll miss the ferry.'

'We can spare ten minutes,' Kit says. 'I'll get us both a coffee.'

He indicates left for the next Little Chef services. It's while I'm hopping towards the café that my tummy starts to fizz like a bottle of shaken pop.

'I feel like I've been here before,' I say to Kit.

'*Déjà vu*,' Kit says, opening the door for me. 'That's French,' he says, puffing up his chest like a penguin.

A waitress greets us by asking us if we'd like breakfast or just coffee.

'Just coffee, please. And we were hoping she might be able to use your conveniences,' Kit says. I pogo by his side.

'Conveniences?'

'The bogs!' I say, desperate now.

'Oh, course,' the waitress says, pointing out the door near the kitchen.

Customers are tucking into oval plates overflowing with fried eggs, sausages, hash browns, bacon, buttered toast and baked beans. The body of one man in oily blue overalls takes up the whole side of one table; he's drinking an extra-large mug of coffee and smoking at the same time. On the table next to him, a baby in a high chair spits out globs of soggy toast into its plastic bib, which its mum then re-posts through its frothing mouth. As I run past the half-wall at the kitchen, a chef wearing a tall white hat winks at me then flips a fried egg. I peg it into the ladies' and wait for the one available toilet to become vacant. An elderly lady with violet hair nudges the lock open then sprays perfume from a lavender-coloured bottle behind her.

Although I feel relieved to be on the toilet at last, the churning in my stomach doesn't go away, and the scent makes me feel even more sick on top of the *déjà vu*.

Kit is reading a newspaper by the entrance while the waitress peers over his shoulder, giggling.

'All right?' he says, rustling the paper shut.

'I want to get out of here,' I say. 'I feel weird.'

'Car sick,' Kit says. '*Mal voiture.*'

'Would a Little Chef lollipop help?' the waitress asks, bending behind her station.

I nod.

'I wouldn't say no neither,' Kit says, picking up the two take-away coffees.

The waitress unwraps an orange lollipop for us both; she hands mine to me, and pops Kit's into his mouth.

'*On y va,*' Kit says, speaking out of the side of his face.

As I suck on my lollipop, the *déjà vu* becomes too much. I throw it on to the tiled floor in the entrance, and it shatters like glass. Flinging the doors open, I run to the nearest bush, where I throw up.

Mum rushes over to me, scrapes back the little hair that I still have and puts her jacket over my shoulders.

'Was it something you ate?' she asks. 'Or Kit's driving? I can tell him to slow down. I'm sure we won't really miss the ferry...'

'Neither,' I say. 'I just know that I've been here before and I don't like the feeling...'

'You've never been here with me. Perhaps you've been here with Dad?' She soothes my back as she speaks.

'I've definitely had one of those orange lollipops,' I say. Then, like water through a colander, the memory floods into my head: 'This was halfway.'

Mum looks at me blankly.

'It was halfway between Ivy Cottage and Grandma's in Brighton. I came here lots one summer when I was younger. I'd always get a lollipop.'

Mum stiffens.

I ask: 'But where were you?'

twenty-one

▼▼▼▼▼

Kit says the *déjà vu* will wear off if I look dead ahead, so I examine the number plates on overtaking cars, searching for Mum's, Dad's and my first initials all on the same plate. Mum is a mollusc when I ask her about my Little Chef memory: she curls up in her seat, hides behind her sunglasses and takes a sudden interest in the map, despite it being upside down.

When we arrive at the ferry terminal, we are somewhere even flatter than Blackbrake, but here the sky meets sea – not buildings – on the horizon. We are in Dover, Kit announces as we join a snake of cars queuing up to drive off the edge of the tarmac into the ferry, the inside of which looks as dark and hollow as a bin truck. Mum passes me two triangles of jam sandwiches, then lights a cigarette.

In the car opposite a girl's face is pancaked against the window, her head surrounded by a purple flowery duvet and black plastic bags. Tied down with straps on the car's roof rack is a tower of three suitcases stacked in size order like tiers of a wedding cake.

In the front seats her parents, I guess, share a flask of a hot drink, and their plastic cups kiss before they take a sip.

The metal tongue that we drive across into the ferry seems too thin to carry the lorries that go on first, but it doesn't snap. When we've parked, I nudge my car door open so as not to scrape the Skoda next to us.

I climb up the narrow steps to the main deck following Mum, who click-clacks in her silver high heels ahead of me. Then, once we're on carpet, like Gretel following a trail of sweets I track the smoke that wafts behind her towards the bar. Mum sits on a stool next to Kit, who orders two vodka tonics and a cola for me. I take my drink over to the rectangular windows which are so cloudy I can barely see through them. I peer at the chalky shore of England. Ripples plough the surface of my flat cola as the ferry chugs out of the port.

Once we're at sea, I follow signs to the observation deck where the heavy door swings open in a gust of wind. I step over a metal doorframe designed to trip you up, and head towards a row of faded red seats that are nailed down just like in Blackbrake cinema. At the end of one row, a bunch of French teenage boys are huddled together, sharing cigarettes. I sit at the other end of the row, glancing over when I feel they're not looking at me, and remember my two fags that I nicked last night. I place one between my lips.

One of the boys, dressed in a baggy T-shirt and loose jeans, rises from the pack and pads his way over to me.

'*Bonjour,*' he purrs, sitting on the lip of the seat next to mine. '*Tu veux du feu?*' he says, miming flicking a lighter with his thumb.

I nod and do a quick check to see if there are any Responsible Adults within sight. The boy cups his hands around my cigarette

121

and lights it. I blow the smoke out of my nostrils, because I know that is what sexy movie stars do.

'*Tu es un dragon?*' he says, a bulge in his neck bobbing up and down like a busy cistern in the Little Chef toilets.

I nod, puffs of smoke making my eyes water, but luckily I have my sunglasses on.

'*C'était un plaisir,*' the boy says, and with that he and his bobbly throat get up to leave.

I don't like the taste of cigarettes one bit; it's like eating an ashtray. And it can give you a cancer. Once I have let the fag burn to the stub, I drop it on to the floor and pound it with my white plimsoll heel.

Back below deck, Mum and Kit are swotting up on French with their phrasebook, which is now beer-stained. The French barman is helping Mum to perfect her pronunciation.

'*Jay voodoo cat temper, silver plates,*' Mum says.

'What does that mean?' I ask.

'I'd like four stamps, please. Can't you tell?' Mum laughs.

I *knew* my Rolodex of lyrics would come in handy one day! To the barman who's polishing his brassware, I channel Vanessa Paradis and sing about Joe the taxi driver's *embouteillage* and love of mambo music. It seems to go down well.

'*Merde!*' the barman says, snapping his tea towel over his shoulder. '*Tu as l'esprit français, quoi?*'

The *hypermarché* opposite the ferry terminal in Calais is so gigantic you could park six aeroplanes in it, easy. French tannoy messages bounce off the metal walls like bullets. This is no Blackbrake Co-op. There's an aisle just for squared-paper notebooks called *cahiers*! There's even an aisle for clothes. Kit whisks Mum off to choose a bottle of birthday perfume while I browse the toy aisle. I opt for a walkie-talkie set with batteries included, then track down Mum and Kit in the spirits aisle, their trolley veering left, so heavy are the bottles of red wine, cheap bubbles, and bulk packets of cigarettes.

The only restaurant that's still serving at two thirty in the afternoon in Calais is called *Le Petit Prince* and it's at the end of a narrow, cobbled lane. I'm about to suggest we hunt down *le big mac* when Kit spots it. There's no way of telling it's a restaurant other than a faded menu hidden behind steamed-up glass in a wooden box which is nailed to the wall – at first I think it's advertising church service times. But sure enough, when Kit pushes open the door, on the other side of which hang thick velvet curtains, there are six small, round tables set for diners. Two French women inspect us over their burgundy menus. A waiter with wax for skin leans against the bar, sipping from a doll-sized coffee cup.

Bet he has to avoid naked flames.

'*Bonjour, vous voulez manger?*' When the waiter speaks, his lips barely move, but stay pouted like a trout on a fish counter.

'*Wee,*' Mum says. '*Silver plates.*'

'Hell's teeth!' Kit says, into his hands, stopping a giggle fit.

'*Très bien.*'

We're shown to the table nearest the front door where the breeze from an open window whips around my legs.

'I don't think we've got off to the best start with our new French friend here,' Kit whispers to me.

'Let's try snails. You're only young once!' Mum says, from behind the large menu.

Kit downs a carafe of red wine as if it's water before we've even ordered. I sip cola in between slices of stale baguette which thins the skin on the roof of my mouth. Mum tries to translate: '*Salade*. Well, that's obvious, isn't it? Though I haven't got a clue what *pamplemousse* or *niçoise* is. How about an *omelette*? Or there's *le rumsteak...*'

And so it goes on until I'm fairly sure that if I order a *salade*, I won't be eating insects or amphibians. Kit goes for *le rumsteak*. When asked if he wants it '*saignant, bleu, à point ou bien cuit,*' he just polishes his steak knife with his heavy, white napkin and says, '*Wee!*'

'A robot could deliver cutlery with more grace,' Mum says, as the waiter tosses tools that would be at home in a dentist's surgery on to the tablecloth.

'The French have a lot to learn in personal relations,' I say to Kit.

'What matters most is the *clientele* – another French word – coming back. Good work,' Kit replies.

After five minutes or so, the waiter wheels a squeaking trolley towards us. Breadcrumbs are swept from the ironed tablecloth with a quick flick of his wrist. Something must have short-circuited, Mum says, as the waiter smiles and, with the air of a magician pulling a rabbit out of a hat, lifts a silver oval lid off a plate of twelve snails drowning in garlic butter. '*Voilà!*'

'*Triple gross,*' I say, under my breath.

'Try one,' Mum says, scooping a snail out of its shell with a tooth tool, and plopping it on to my plate. 'Garlic's good for you.'

I can see no difference between eating one of these and eating one of the slugs Mum declares war against by shaking blue crystals on to the crazy paving. But I bet for all her foreign travel Lisa has never eaten one and it would be something for me to brag to her about for once, so I bite into it, close my eyes and hold my nose at the same time.

Now, Cassie once dared me 10p to touch her tonsils that she

kept in a jam jar after her tonsil removal operation, but no amount of money would have made me *eat* them! I spit the snail out into the napkin, and look up to see Mum biting into a frog's leg.

'It tastes *just* like chicken,' she says, wiping frog juice from her lips.

'Are you all right?' Kit says. 'You've turned, well, *green*.'

'I'm going to wash my mouth out in the bathroom,' I say.

'Green like a frog. Boom-boom!'

I push back my chair and follow the *toilettes* signs through the back of the restaurant, out into a smoky lean-to conservatory and then into an empty car park. There's no queue. Perhaps that's because the toilet's outside, in a shed and, I discover, it's a hole in the ground. I stare down into it, and wonder how you're supposed to use *that* when the smell hits me and I run back.

'France is weird,' I say, sitting down again at the table.

Kit looks up from a slab of bloody steak that he's now tearing at with a large, wooden-handled knife. The meat's that raw it looks as if the cow could have taken its last breath while I was in the 'toilets'.

My *salade niçoise* has arrived. I peel off some moustache-sized purple fish and scoop out the sliced egg.

'Where's the protein in that now?' Mum says.

I nod towards the two French women with bodies as straight and as slim as ladders. They've only had a plate of lettuce each in front of them the whole time we've been there. They eat as if they might discover diamonds in their dish, raking a lettuce leaf at a time on to their forks.

'It's how the French eat, Mum,' I whisper. 'Sophisticated, like.' I peer more closely at my excavated *salade niçoise* but nothing twinkles.

'I must let Oona know the latest fad,' Mum says. 'They must be burning more calories than they're eating.'

By the time we've demolished the meal, Kit has also disappeared a second carafe of wine. There's now just the four of us in the restaurant: me, Mum, Kit and the waiter. Three, if you count people with a pulse. The other two French diners were scared off as soon as Kit began his Meatloaf impression.

'...I'll be gone, gone, gone!' Kit sings, wobbling like a ninepin ready to topple from the wooden chair on which he is trying to stand upright.

Mum is sitting with her head in her hands as if it's the heaviest bowling ball in the alley. 'You certainly are,' she says.

'*Vous voulez l'addition, Madame?*' the waiter asks Mum.

'*Excuse mon ami, il est un complete nincompoop,*' I say, looking up the sentence in the phrasebook.

'Come on, Harper, let's get the hell out of here,' Mum says, taking Kit's wallet and fishing out enough francs to pay the bill.

Kit zigzags back to the 2CV, its boot far lower now because of the many boxes of booze. He collapses across the back seats, and I shotgun the front. In the ten minutes it takes to join the queue at the ferry terminal, Kit's sleeping like the dead.

twenty-two

▼▼▼▼▼

Kit's hangover lasts a whole week after we return from France and turns into what Mum calls Man Flu. He says he feels as if he left his batteries behind in France, so the wedding planning goes on ice – along with the cheap champagne – just until Kit gets better.

Halfway through the week, Kit starts sleeping on the sofa in the lounge because he keeps waking Mum up with his coughing. His stuff starts to mushroom on the coffee table – first it's a bedside lamp, then it's joined by an alarm clock, a jug of water, purple-bottled cough mixtures, his wicker basket of medicine and boxes of tissues. Meanwhile, Mum's in the middle of a copywriting crisis: the deadline for the first draft of the *Inspirations* Christmas catalogue is the same Sunday of the May half term that I'll be getting back from Brighton. Mum takes to wearing earplugs all day and I give up speaking to her, and instead send a semaphore message with a red napkin if there's an emergency, such as us nearly running out of electric or chocolate bourbons. I also threaten to call up the Hopkin Wynne to see if they have any straitjackets going spare, since Mum has started talking to herself.

Kit calls in sick to work all week, and instead he lies on the sofa, drifting in between being asleep and half-awake. He groggily watches cartoons with me in the morning before I check the post for a reply from Craig and head off for school. When I come home, Kit is in the same position: lying on the sofa in Mum's fake silk dressing gown.

One afternoon, in a bid to cheer Kit up, I make him hot buttered toast, stamping the slice of bread with one of Mum's prototype catalogue toys before putting it in the toaster. I press the yellow stamp on to the bread, and it comes out of the toaster with 'DON'T WORRY BE HAPPY' magically printed on it.

He doesn't even take a bite.

The Friday that I'm due to leave for Brighton for my holiday with Dad, I give Kit a present.

'This is for you,' I say. It's the sunflower seed that I had planted in a pot and was selling at Harper's Bazaar. I place the plastic pot among the screwed-up used tissues and empty medicine packets.

'If it germinates, which I doubt it will,' he says, 'we'll plant it out the back.' It is the longest sentence he's said all week.

To prevent thirteen Kendal Road going nuclear, I wait at the end of the cul-de-sac for Dad to pick me up. I don't know how far the fall-out of rows can carry, but I don't want to blow our chances if Kit hears Mum speak to my dad when she's having one of her eppies.

On the drive down the motorway, Dad asks how my daytrip to France went, and I tell him about the snails and the hole-in-the-ground toilet. I don't mention the Little Chef.

'That's nice,' he says.

It's my job to follow the plotted directions Dad has typed out, having looked up the most efficient route. After two and a half hours in a car like a greenhouse, we're drawing up outside the Seaspray B & B.

The blades of grass on the front lawn are that uniform they look as if they have been brushed with a hair comb and clipped with nail scissors. When I get out of the car, a long-haired tortoiseshell cat wraps itself around one of my legs like candyfloss. Dad hauls his suitcase up the steps to the front door and presses the doorbell.

'Welcome to the Seaspray,' says the woman who opens the door. 'You're Pete and Harper?'

'Correct. We're right on time,' Dad says.

'I'm Miranda. And that's Marmalade,' she says. Do you like cats?' Miranda asks me.

'I love them,' I say.

'Come in,' she says, tightening the apron around her waist, which she doesn't need to do. Miranda reminds me of the kind of witch that I wouldn't want to squash under a clapboard house in a hurricane; she even carries a wooden broom. I follow her wobbling bottom to our bedroom.

'Are you planning anything nice this afternoon?' she asks us as she unlocks the door.

I look at Dad.

'We're visiting the War Memorial,' Dad says.

'Oh,' Miranda replies. 'That will be fun, won't it?' she says, quizzing me with her eyes.

I go inside our room and check out the en suite bathroom. There's a sign over the hot tap which reads 'Caution! Hot Water!', another sign over the door saying 'Watch Your Head!' and one above the loo shouting 'FLUSH WITH PRUDENCE'. Woollen hats keep spare loo rolls warm and a doll's head is stuck on top of the toilet brush; its googly eyes roll back into its head as if it has overdosed when you pick it up.

Not only Dutch diseases kill trees. Last October there were terrible storms in which several ancient oaks in Old Steine Gardens toppled over. Most of them have been removed, but a man who wears an orange hardhat and ear defenders is still chainsawing thick branches off the last couple left. It feels somehow rude to look at the trees' nude and helpless roots which point at least twenty feet skywards, large craters left where the oaks once grew. While Dad heads over to the War Memorial, I investigate an upright stump of one of the casualties that have already been cleared.

I trace the felled oak's age by counting the dark rings; the stump I'm sitting on is over one hundred and fifty years old.

In the distance, Dad's walking around the memorial: several white Roman columns, metal plaques gone green with age and an algaed pool with a little fountain in the middle to represent eternity, I guess. Dad stops beneath one of the columns and takes out a notebook. Above me, the sun is a burnt apricot slung low in the sky.

When Dad comes over, he joins me in silence on the stump. I sneak a peek at the inscription he has copied down in his notebook:

> *A GOOD LIFE HATH*
> *ITS NUMBER OF DAYS*
> *BUT A GOOD NAME SHALL*
> *CONTINUE FOR EVER*

I wonder how it feels never to have known your dad but to carry his surname. A bit like carrying the Olympic torch perhaps? You don't want to go dropping it and ballsing it up for everyone. How do you live your life in the shadow of a dead man who sacrificed his life for our freedom? Even though my dad's totally taking in oxygen, I feel I know him about as well as my dead grandpa sometimes. God knows what's going on up there. Dad clearly has no idea what's going on in my nearly-teen head area.

He looks over at me, stares for a minute and then says, 'Harper, are you wearing a bra?'

'*DAD!*' I say, squirming. 'You can't ask *that!*'

'It's just,' he says. 'You're growing up so quickly. I can hardly keep up–'

'It's called a *crop top*?'

'Oh, I see.'

'Can we talk about something else, please? Like the war or what's for dinner?'

We choose Chinese.

My fortune cookie reads: 'Build the great arch of unimagined bridges.'

The next morning we breakfast in the front room, listening to panpipe versions of Elton John songs. A wrinkly couple has the best table in the bay window where they eat their porridge and stewed prunes staring across the perfect lawn to the Royal Mail depot opposite. I'm glad to read on the menu that Miranda also does a full monty fry-up. Like the Tiger Who Came to Tea, Dad and I eat everything that Miranda puts in front of us: white toast; diced fruit salad; Rice Krispies; fried sausages, bacon, egg, mushrooms and watery tomatoes, all washed down by a miniature glass of sour grapefruit juice. Miranda comes over to top up our metal teapot.

She asks Dad what we're up to.

'Today is a "Harper Chooses" day,' Dad announces. 'So we do whatever she wants.'

'Lucky you,' Miranda says, winking at me. 'More toast?'

After breakfast, we go down Brighton fairground and arcades. Dad gives me two quid that I change into 10p pieces with which to gamble. I try my luck at the Hi-Lo card game machine where you guess if the next card dealt will be higher or lower than the last one. I am good at it, Dad says, because I have 'a logical mind with an intuitive grasp of the law of averages'. It isn't a MENSA test, but I do make a 50p profit.

This, I spend on my entry fare for the pirate ship – a fairground ride which swings you backwards and forwards, building up gently until you are practically upside down. Dad and I sit at the prow of the ship where you feel the most swing. We grip on to the cold metal bar for dear life, eyes shut tight. Once the ride has finished and the white-faced passengers are clambering off, Dad quickly scours the floor of each row for fallen loose change and pockets a £2.46 profit.

Next I choose the only PG film that's showing at the cinema, *Willow*, about a dwarf protecting a precious baby from an evil queen. There's a long queue, but we manage to get seats right in the middle. This is a shame, because as soon as the trailers are over, I realize I need the loo. They stink, but not half as badly as French toilets. I breathe through my mouth like when Mum's having a chemical treatment, but when I try to get out of the cubicle, I realize that I'm locked in.

I don't get upset straight away. First of all, I think through my logical options. The walls are made of brick and the gap between the floor and the bottom of the door is too narrow for me to squeeze through. Nobody else hears me when I scream for help because the film has started. When I'm about to cry, I realize I've had my jelly handbag with me all along in which I have a felt tip pen and one half of my walkie-talkie set; the other half is with Mum.

'Echo Bravo,' I say, pressing the red 'TALK' button. 'Do you read me? Over.'

The walkie-talkie fuzzes and crackles. Mum must be working with her earplugs in.

'Echo Bravo,' I repeat. *'Mum, do you read me?* Over and out.'

A whole day must pass before Dad comes in to rescue me and by then, I am writing a long note on the loo roll – which is more like baking paper than tissue – to explain to whoever might find my fossilized body how my death happened. Concentrating on the story has stopped me from crying.

'Harper?'

'Dad! I'm locked in!' I say, jumping up.

He opens the door. It wasn't locked, just a bit stuck and I'd been trying to push it open instead of pull. The loo doors open the opposite way down the Optimum Cinema in Blackbrake, I explain to Dad as he dabs my face with a cotton handkerchief; the odd tear does seem to have fallen without my noticing.

'Not to worry,' Dad says. 'The film isn't very good, anyway. Let's go and get ice-cream instead, hey?'

We leave the cinema and head into the sunshine for the pier where we both get 99s with extra chocolate sauce and chopped nuts.

'Are you having a good time?' Dad asks.

'Yes.'

'Better than in France?'

'It's about the same.'

'What do you want to do next?'

'Write postcards?'

'Fantastic. I'll get the paper and read it while you write them. I'll be back in exactly three hundred seconds,' Dad says, setting an alarm on his digital watch and then scuttling off to the newsagent's. I sit down on the boardwalk to write on some of the complimentary Seaspray postcards I took on the way out of the B & B this morning.

Mum:
Went to the cinema. Got stuck in loos!!! Miss you tonnes. PS Can I have a long-haired tortoiseshell cat for my 13th birthday?

Cassie:
Brighton is wicked. Say hi to everyone from me (except your sister).

Derek:
How's Vidal? Don't forget to top up Bangers and Mash's water bottle once a day.

Dad:
Thank you for a lovely holiday.

Craig:
Hi Craig. How are you? I'm fine. Did you get my quiz yet? Brighton's cool. See you at the next disco? x

Kit:

*I'm having a lovely holiday. It is about the same as France. I hope
you are feeling better now? Weather is here. Wish you were lovely.
Ha ha.*

twenty-three

▼▼▼▼▼

After breakfast the next morning I don't worry about meters as I run a bath right up to the brim and soak in some White Musk bubble bath that I bought from the Body Shop with the rest of my gambling profits. Dad's still in bed with one of his Second World War books. The bubbles don't fluff up as much as those down under in Kylie Minogue's unlucky bathtub, but I soak for a good half hour with my *Facts of Life* book for company.

A few weeks ago, when Mum still communicated in speech not semaphore, she took me to one side after school and presented me with my copy of what Cassie and I call the *Puberty Bible*. Seems most parents in Blackbrake think that the best way to make sure your kid doesn't end up *in the family way* is to hand over the *Bible*, with a knowing nod and let the book do the talking. On the cover are cross-sections of DNA, breasts, bones and ovaries as well as one close-up picture of a man shaving and one of some uncooked trout, two oranges, a bunch of cherries, a cabbage and a carton of cherry juice.

Seeing as Mum's more extra-curricular than most, she also took it upon herself to discuss *menarche* with me, which according to *Chambers*, is Greek for 'moon-beginning'. And for those of us who live in the twentieth century, this means when girls start to bleed monthly from the other kind of down under. Although I'm practically as flat as a gerbil under rubber, Mum said the 'red enemy' could come any time, regardless of cup size, and that I should be prepared.

I said this sounded like the USSR were going to invade my uterus.

Mum also took the initiative to find two make-up mirrors in her handbag and she positioned one each in between our feet in the bathroom. We took off our knickers and she pointed out which hole to shove a tampon up. Compared to what women had to do in the olden days (according to the *Bible*, this involved damp rags, boiling water and mangles), putting a rolled-up bit of cotton wool wrapped in cardboard up your vagina four times a day doesn't look so bad.

It's while I'm drying myself that I notice a pinkish stain on the white towel. First of all, I wonder if I've cut myself. And then I realize: I'm under attack from the red enemy.

As luck would have it, I packed my 'starter kit for light bleeds' which a lady who visited our biology lessons gave out to each girl in year seven, compliments of her sanitary pad company, in the same biology lesson as when our teacher got us to put a condom on a courgette.

A clever piece of marketing, I think to myself as I peel the sticky strip off one of the large pads included and secure it to my knickers: get the pre-teen girls hooked on your range of pads with 'new absorbency technology'. Seems to me this particular technology makes the pad every bit as uncomfortable as having three slices of Mighty White shoved down your pants.

I wrap myself in a towel, sit on the toilet lid and turn to Chapter *Period*, Verse *Day One*.

And so, on the First Day, it shall be thus:

The period starts. At the same time, the hormone FSH from the pituitary is making an ovum mature in a tiny sac or 'follicle' in one of the ovaries.

I didn't even know I owned a tiny sac other than the fake leather one from Alfonso I pack for Dad weekends.

'Are you OK in there, Harper?' Dad shouts from the bedroom.

'Yes, Dad!' I call back.

'I'm reading a fascinating chapter about V Day celebrations,' he says, 'Take as long as you want.'

In my head I make up an imaginary paragraph to describe my own:

V Day. Saturday 28 May, 1988. The day monthly bleeding commenced via Harper May Richardson's vagina. The red enemy first attacked in a hotel bathroom in Brighton. Resistance was futile. Girlhood surrendered. The occasion will henceforth be marked each anniversary in the back garden of thirteen Kendal Road, Blackbrake, with a ceremony which shall include attaching a looped sanitary napkin to a belt, then hoisting it up a beanpole.

I cry off the Fishing Museum visit that day, and opt instead to stay in bed in my pyjamas with a hot-water bottle and a cup of tea with a shovelful of sugar – Mum does this every month for at least three days in a row. Dad says he'll bring back lunch by two o'clock.

After one hour and barely a teaspoon of blood on my sanitary device, I get dressed and wander down the corridor. Miranda's in the lounge clearing away the breakfast items. She finds a cat brush and lets me detangle Marmalade's furry coat as I sit in one of the large easy chairs. The cat sits on my lap, purring as loudly as an idling motorbike.

It's once I've finished that I jolt to my senses, remembering I've left Bangers and Mash round Derek's and I haven't called yet to make sure that he hasn't done a runner to Mr Sassoon's salon without handing over the Bangers and Mash manual. I shove Marmalade on to the floor, and waddle to the telephone booth in the hall. I dial Derek's number, putting in 10p when he picks up.

'All right?' Derek says.

'All right,' I say, relieved he hasn't run away yet. 'All right?'

'No,' Derek says. 'Mash has gone missing, I'm afraid.'

'...'

'I last saw it...' Derek begins.

'Him,' I correct.

'I last saw *him* under the sofa.'

'Has Kinnock eaten him?' I ask, my voice cracking. Kinnock is Derek's incontinent ginger cat.

'Cross my heart and hope to die he hasn't,' Derek says. 'Bangers is fine,' he adds.

Before I can say anything else, the money runs out, and the line goes dead.

I search in my jelly bag for my walkie-talkie and radio Mum to tell her to look for Mash on the cul-de-sac.

She doesn't reply.

Back in the lounge, I ask Miranda if Marmalade can keep me company in our room until Dad returns with lunch.

'Course she can, pet,' Miranda says. 'Are you OK?'

'Yes,' I whisper.

I scoop up Marmalade, hide my face behind her furry coat. Back in our room, I lean back against the pillow with Marmalade on my lap and I sob quietly. I stroke her until she falls asleep.

Dad gets back about an hour later. 'OK, love?' he says, bundling in with two portions of scampi and chips. Marmalade wakes up, and leaps over to swaddle his ankles. 'Get off with you!' Dad says, booting the cat out of the bedroom door.

I burst into the complete works.

Dad dumps lunch on top of the chest of drawers.

'Whatever's the matter?' he asks, coming over to me.

'Mash is missing, presumed dead,' I wail. I don't want to confess to my dad that I've also just started my first period and am suffering from stress of the menstrual kind.

'Oh dear. That's terrible,' Dad says.

'I don't know what I'll do without him if he never comes back...'

'Oh dear,' Dad repeats, and then he asks me to remind him who exactly Mash is.

'My albino gerbil, Dad! Don't you know anything?' I start to cry again.

'Oh dear, love,' Dad says, putting his arm around me.

Dad sits with me as I cry, getting snot on my sleeves. After a while, he asks if I'd like my scampi and chips.

'No! I want Mash back!'

'Sometimes there's no rhyme or reason to what happens,' Dad says.

'I *know*,' I say, turning away from him.

'You still have the other gerbil, though, don't you?' Dad says.

He's right, I still have Bangers. And perhaps, if Mash *is* dead I could get a cat instead. I ask Dad how much he thinks long-haired tortoiseshells are. While I start on the chips, Dad goes out to check with Miranda, who says you can get them for a small donation down the Cat Protection League if there's a spate of people who were bagging them up to chuck them in the river, but had a last-minute change of heart and left them instead on the doorstep of the CPL.

twenty-four

▼▼▼▼▼

We leave Brighton after an early tea that Sunday and arrive in Blackbrake in twilight, just as the street lamps are starting to buzz and glow orange. Dad doesn't want to get out of the car when we pull up outside thirteen Kendal Road, but instead stays sitting in the driver's seat, leaving the engine running as I get my rucksack out of the boot. When I go to lean in through his open window and give him a kiss, Dad reaches behind his seat to grab a plastic bag which is full of empty loo rolls.

'For the gerbils,' he says, as he hands it to me.

'Where did you get all these from?'

'Miranda. I remembered you saying that gerbils like to gnaw cardboard.'

'Daddy, thank you,' I say and give him a kiss on the cheek.

Dad puts the car into gear and does a three-point turn, waving as he leaves. It's a funny thing; when Dad has just left, I want to be with him. But when I'm with him, I just want to be at home; I want to be at home with my mum, my things, my own proper bedroom with a window I can see out of, and a radiator. And, now that I'm officially *on* and everything, I want to be at home with access to an unlimited supply of sanitary gadgets and clean knickers.

As I enter the house, I can hear Mum in the dining room punching her keyboard as bluntly as she hits nails with hammers when attempting self-assembly furniture. I dump my bag at the bottom of the stairs and head straight up to my bedroom, where I rifle through my wardrobe to find my luminous yellow jumper.

'Hello!' Mum shouts as I come back downstairs and into the lounge. 'Good holiday?'

From the bookshelf, I grab a packet of sunflower seeds for bait and a mirror for doing under-car chassis checks. 'Search party. Mash is MIA,' I say. 'Didn't you get my walkie-talkie message?'

'I've had these in all weekend. I'm sorry,' Mum says, taking her earplugs out. 'I'll come and help look when I've—' I peg it out of the lounge mid-Mum's sentence.

Outside, I crawl on all fours along the pavement on each side of Kendal Road, sprinkling sunflower seeds alongside the gutters, poking the mirror behind the tyres of parked cars as if looking for a yet-to-detonate device. I find a dead hedgehog, plenty of white dog poo, a hubcap, a box of driven-over tissues and eleven cigarette stubs. With the fag ends in my pocket, I ring on Derek's door.

'All right?' he says.

'Not really,' I reply. 'I've come for my gerbil. *Gerbils*,' I correct myself.

Derek follows me in silence as I walk into the lounge, where I find the cage next to the telly which is muted and showing some crap black and white movie. Bangers is hiding in the beige plastic shed, his little brown eyes peering out of the dark.

'Not run away yet, then?' I ask Derek as I head back towards the front door, the cage banging into the wall.

'*Ssshhh!*' Derek whispers, nodding upstairs. 'Dad's in. He's having a migraine lie-down.'

'Well, don't expect me to cover for you,' I say, and turn on my plimsoll heel with the cage.

Back at home, Mum's still at her desk, earplugs jammed back in as deep as the corks she stuffs down her half-drunk bottles of red wine. I'm rearranging items on the bookshelf to make space again for the gerbil cage when the telephone rings.

I go to answer it.

'Wait!' Mum shouts, then she suctions out her earplugs. 'If it's Joanna, tell her I'm not available. I'm behind on my deadline.'

I nod and pick up the receiver.

It's Kit. He must have finally got off the sofa while I was away; his stuff is still on the coffee table, but in neat piles. The used tissues have all been thrown away.

'All right?' he says.

'Not really,' I say, then I turn to Mum. 'It's OK. It's only Kit.'

I tell Kit all about Mash's escape. 'Do you think he'll come back?' I ask.

'I'm sure he will,' Kit says.

'I hope not, because I want a long-haired tortoiseshell cat next.'

Kit laughs. A little. 'Can I speak to your mum?'

I pass Mum the telephone.

'Hi, Only Kit. Where are you?' she says.

'...'

'Why? What's wrong?'

'...'

144

'Shit!' Mum says, and she sips her coffee as if it's just that.

I tug at her arm. 'You told me to tell you when you say "Shit!"' I whisper. 'You wanted to make swearing out of bounds.'

'...'

'Of course.'

'...'

'Don't be. It will be OK.'

'...'

'I know.'

'...'

'I'll just finish my coffee, then I'll come and get you.'

She places the telephone receiver back in its cradle as gently as if it's a sleeping baby.

'What's wrong?' I ask.

'Kit's got cancer,' Mum says.

'Cancer?'

'What a way to go.'

PART TWO

twenty-five

▼▼▼▼▼

Cassie has bagsied her mum's first-aid trunk and uses it to stash old issues of *Just Seventeen* that she steals from Lisa. We're sifting through the problem pages, reading them out loud to one another to dissolve the time it's taking for my mum to buy pyramids of coloured plastic pots which, within a week, she'll either have lost the lids for or have melted on the hob.

'"My boyfriend says he wants to finger me, but I don't know what that actually means. Help! L from Clapham,"' Cassie says, then sniggers.

I don't have a clue what it means either. 'God, she's so naive!' I say.

'Yeah,' Cassie agrees, then after a moment she says, 'Read one of yours, then.'

'"I can't make my tampons stay in. Am I doing something wrong? They keep falling out in PE. Katrina from Gloucester." That's so embarrassing!' I squeal.

'At least she won't get toxic shock syndrome,' Cassie says.

Cassie's in the club, too. She first came on just a few weeks before me, so we're Blood Sisters now. It's just as well Cassie is adopted and therefore not related in the blood to Lisa, because otherwise she'd need a bra made out of steel to keep whatever's going to grow up there above her knees. Rather than mix their spermatozoa and eggs together and wait for nine months to see what pops out of Mrs Pope's down under, as adopting parents, the Popes got to choose which kids to love enough to buy wool coats for.

'Let's go and scrounge some more chocolate from downstairs, shall we?' I suggest. 'It's high in iron, you know. You're supposed to keep your iron levels up when you're on.'

'Chapter thirteen, verse four?' Cassie laughs.

We stash the *Just Seventeens* back in the first-aid box and return the most recent copies to Lisa's bedroom. We don't have to avoid her as she's doing an IQ test down the Blackbrake Young MENSA club.

We creep downstairs into the dining room where what's left of the snacks are fanned out on doilyed silver platters on the mahogany table. In the lounge, Mrs Pope announces that they're going to play a game where the women have to write a pitch to sell their husband. Avon Oona says she's game, but she can't think of a selling point aside from the fact that her husband doesn't produce much dirty laundry on account of sitting around in the same clothes for days on end.

All that's left of the chocolate fingers and bourbon biscuits is a few crumbs, but there's still Oona's crispbreads that taste and look like sandpaper, untouched tubs of cottage cheese and some wrinkled cucumber sticks. Cassie suggests we raid the kitchen cupboards where we find, hiding behind a packet of red lentils, a purple box of chocolates with one layer scoffed. As we're checking the guide to make sure neither of us chooses the pink ones which look and taste like wax earplugs, we overhear both our mums say they're feeling peckish so we bolt back through the dining room into the hallway and perch on the bottom of the stairs with the box of chocolates between us.

'So, Mary. Might you be interested in becoming a Demonstrator?' Mrs Pope asks. No doubt Mrs Pope would get a slice of Mum's income if she did decide to turn to Tupperware selling. But Mum replies that she's full time at the agency since her promotion and doesn't have any spare time.

'I understand,' Mrs Pope says. 'But if you wanted some extra income—'

'I don't think you do understand. They're evening parties,' Mum interrupts. 'I can't drag Harper along with me everywhere.' I make out Mum worrying her dentures with a slice of crispbread.

Cassie nudges me with her elbow. I roll my eyes skywards.

'Well, you've a man at home—' Cassie's mum says.

'I haven't, actually.'

'Oh?'

Mum can't stand it when Mrs Pope holds make-up mirrors up to her private life, trying to sneak a peek at what it's like to be a single parent. Mum reckons Mrs Pope's so nosy on account of having nothing better to do than sell plastic and memorize parables from *Good Housekeeping*. The only reason Mum doesn't tell her which short glass gangplank to take a long walk off is because Cassie's my best friend.

'He's been in hospital all of June,' Mum says, 'undergoing tests and sorting out his pain relief and palliative care programme for Stage Four lung cancer.'

'I'm sorry to hear that,' Mrs Pope says, after a pause.

I don't hear what Mum says next because Cassie tugs on my arm and whispers that we should go back to her room. I grab the box of chocolates, and leave the loony ladies to their airtight wonder bowls, winking seals and gossip.

Mum sometimes uses being a single mother or her repetitive strain injury as an excuse to get herself out of tight spots like missed deadlines or bad first dates. One time, before she'd even gone out the front door with a date she whisked me into the bathroom and whispered instructions for me to telephone the Shang High in half an hour saying I was having an epileptic fit; her date's breath smelt of cheesy feet. Mum also finds it useful sometimes to use me as an excuse when she's had enough of Mrs Pope's X-ray questioning. Not long after Cassie and I have finished the last of the chocolates, Mum comes upstairs to find me.

She's fibbed to Mrs Pope that we have to get back home in time for me to do my extra reading homework. That sets Mrs Pope off in a tailspin because Cassie hasn't been sent home with any, and she worries that Cassie will fall behind. I don't mind being used as an excuse or even faking eppies just so long as I get something out of it like a bag of prawn crackers or staying up for an extra hour. So, that evening, we leave the Tupperware party early with a bowl to keep lettuce crisp and a tower of orange-lidded plastic pots. As we head down Cassie's drive, Mum promises me I can watch half of *Annie* when we get home.

Overhead, the sky's as grey as my school uniform. Front rooms with curtains still ajar spill television on to the crazy paving. Back on Kendal Road, I catch a glimpse of *EastEnders* through the window of A-Rottweiler-Is-For-Life-Not-Just-for-Christmas-Edna's house next door. It's Mum who spots that all the lights are on in our house, despite having absolutely definitely turned them off before we left. Mum's super strict about it: the clicking meter eats electricity.

'Perhaps Kit's back from hospital?' I say.

Mum's searching for her keys in her handbag with one hand, the other clutching the stack of orange plastic pots. As she's about to put the key in the lock, the door opens and Mum drops the pots in shock so they fall, then roll across the pavement and mostly dive under the baked-bean Mini as if heading for shelter. It's our landlord; I recognize him from the time he came round to brick up the chimney and install the gas fire.

'Mary, this is Dave,' he says of the man next to him who wears a tape measure around his neck where a doctor would a stethoscope.

'Hello,' Mum says. Her lips are Tupperware-tight.

'Pleased to meet you.' Dave offers his hand for Mum to shake. She crosses her arms.

'Well, we've just finished,' Dave says, drawing back his hand and using it to smooth down his oily hair which puts me in mind of sealskin.

Mum frowns. 'Finished what?'

'You got my message?' Dave says.

Dave. Now it floods back into my colander brain. He rang last week when Mum was down the General with Kit buying me five packets of bacon-flavoured fries. Something about measuring rooms and taking photos?

'You won't need to show people round. The estate agency will take care of that,' the landlord says and with that, the two men bundle into a red car with suspension so low to the road as to

153

be practically scraping tarmac off it. They drive over and pop a Tupperware pot; it echoes around the cul-de-sac like a gunshot.

Mum pours herself on to the bottom step: she's flat cola, no fizz. 'They didn't even bother to turn off the bloody lights,' she says, into her cupped hands.

I leave her on the step and run into the house, where I find that it's true – those two idiots have left every single light blazing. The numbers on the meter at the top of the cellar stairs are going mental, like Bangers round his gerbil wheel. I peg it into each room, turning off all the lights. In the bathroom, I find they've turned on a light on the bathroom cabinet above the sink where I didn't even know there was one.

Back on the pebbledash doorstep, Mum takes a long suck on her Silk Cut.

'Shall we go and check the bank balance?' I ask: that usually seems to cheer her up. I can watch orphan Annie go and live with a billionaire any time.

'That's a great idea,' she says.

I scoop up what's left of the pots from the gutter and bung them in the boot of the Mini. Mum starts the engine and turns up her Chris Rea cassette. I don't ask if we can switch over to Radio One.

twenty-six

▼▼▼▼▼

Imagine winning a lifetime's free laundry. That's the competition Oona's running down the Full Cycle laundrette where she works nine till five; a poster in the window shouts *WIN FREE WASH FOR LIFE!* Mum takes our dirty clothes there every Friday after school and I tag along unless I'm on a Dad weekend. I suppose if Kit entered the competition it wouldn't cost Full Cycle too much because he'll likely die in two to four months. But if I won, it would mean giving me free washing for approximately sixty more years, which would cost much more. I'm not sure if Oona will try to make it so that someone terminal wins the competition but if I were her, I'd fix it like that. Apart from Oona, Mum and me are the only people there – if you don't count Madonna, who's singing 'Material Girl' on the ghetto blaster. A good choice of song for a laundrette, I guess.

While Mum's sorting our basket of clothes into colours, whites and net bags of dirty earplugs I pop along the High Street with this week's pocket money. The greengrocer is selling punnets of strawberries at 30p a pound. Next door to the grocer's is a bank with a sign outside saying 'Trust Is Everything. Trust Carlisle Bank.' Mum said that was horse manure when we walked past it; she said they wouldn't even give her an appointment to see the bank manager about a mortgage because she's divorced. Trust isn't everything, she said: banks don't just want to see your passport, they also want to see a wedding ring and several years of steady income before approving an application.

I'm half a punnet of strawberries heavier when I get back to the Full Cycle.

'...I reckon Mike's the only bank manager that'd touch me with a snooker cue,' Mum's saying to Oona as I come back in.

'Snobs.'

'Probably helps that I've slept with him,' Mum says.

I close the door behind me.

'Harper!' Mum says. 'I didn't notice you come back.'

'Take her with you,' Oona says. 'Might make 'em feel more charitable.'

Mum watches my uniform spinning around in the grey water. I perch next to her on the hard, wooden bench. If I were manageress, I'd make it a nicer place for people to wash two hours of their complicated lives down the sudsy plughole. Maybe buy a few cushions, think about link-selling some disposable goods. I've noticed, for example, that people connect laundry with smoking or reading Mills and Boons or figuring out anagrams.

The buttons of my second-hand cardigan click against the glass. Now and again the waxy bag of earplugs screeches across the porthole.

'Mrs Pope has to fork out for a pure wool navy coat from John

Lewis for Lisa to wear to private school,' I say, to see if I can pop Mum's thought bubble.

'Three quid a time to dry-clean,' Oona says, without looking up. Her nose is stuck in her copy of *Heal Your Body*, which she's started carrying around like the God Squad do bibles. Affirmations from it blossom daily all over her house – and ours – on yellow post-it notes. There's one stuck next to the dials on the machine my uniform is spinning in. 'I now go beyond other people's fears and limitations. I create my own life,' it says.

When we get up to leave, Mum turns to the poster advertising the free wash competition and asks Oona if there is a cash alternative. Oona's laugh blows us out of the door as if she's breathed fire. I've looked at the small print already, I tell Mum, as we bowl back home down the High Street; the prize doesn't even include dry cleaning. And if Full Cycle closes for business it's tough titty.

There are three surprises waiting for us when we get back, all sitting in a row on the doorstep: Derek, Kit and back-from-the-dead-Mash.

'You changed the lock!' Kit says to Mum, stacking his body back together as he stands up, like an ancient Jacob's ladder. There's a large white pad taped on to the back of one of Kit's hands covering up the hole where I suppose the doctors inject pain relief.

Mum dumps the basket of laundry by her feet and opens the door with her newly minted key.

'You'll have to change his name to Bobby Ewing,' Kit says, pointing to the Gordon Benét shoebox. Inside, Mash is curled up in a nest of sawdust.

The gerbil's red eyes blink at me as Derek explains, 'I found him in Mum's wardrobe. He'd made a nest out of bubble wrap.' Then he adds quickly, 'Don't tell Mum, mind.'

157

'What did he eat?' I ask.

'Blusher and eye-shadow.'

His fur does look pinker and his eyes are redder than I remember; I guess that's what happens if you're a gerbil and you eat make-up. I should be happy, but I've already done a ceremony for Mash in our back garden, burying a plastic mouse by way of a crash-test dummy; Mum said it would help with the 'grieving process'. I got a day off school out of it. Plus, I've already got my eye on a cat from Mr Goodman's that I quite fancy.

I close the lid.

'Not run away then, yet?' I ask Derek.

He lowers his voice to a whisper. 'I decided to call up Vidal before I spent my savings on a coach ticket. He said they don't have any openings right now, but that I should call him back when I'm seventeen.'

'Just as well, then.'

'I've got a Saturday job sweeping hair down Headlines for now. They need models, H, if you fancy getting a re-shape.'

For tea that evening Mum pushes the Mini out: she cooks faggots. Mum tells me while she pours boiling water over beef stock that Kit won't move out again until he absolutely has to, which I reckon could mean – without being too dramatic about it – until he leaves feet first in a coffin. I guess things with Melanie haven't worked out, then. Maybe she said she'd rather not have to share a man with a short shelf life.

Once dinner's ready, Mum strikes a match so it bursts an orange and blue flame and lights a candle on the dining-room table. It must be a special occasion because even the Amstrad has been moved off the table and on to the floor.

Kit doesn't seem himself at the table; it's as if his spirit has been sucked out and flushed away in the hospital. He's as awkward as a mannequin in a shop window with stiff, pale limbs looking like they're about to fall off. He checkmates his lumpy mash with a faggot.

Mum strokes his thin arm. 'It'll give you some oomph if you eat,' she says.

'Not much point, is there?' he says.

'Come *on*, Chris. You've got to stop feeling sorry for yourself if you're going to enjoy what time you have left,' Mum says.

'Who's Chris?' I say.

'*You're* not the one with a half-life,' Kit says.

'Who's Chris?' I say again.

'You were always banging on at me about being more bloody optimistic,' Mum says, ignoring me, pouring more gravy on to her potato. Her sympathy seems in short supply.

'You're already referring to me in the past tense,' Kit says.

'Is that your real name?' I ask.

Mum gets up. 'I'm going to check the bank balance,' she says and bums past me.

'Depends who's asking,' Kit replies, turning to me as if he's only just remembered I'm there. 'It's not if the bank manager's asking.' He puts his knife and fork at twelve o'clock.

'Can I have your faggot?' I ask.

'Course,' he says. 'The food was so bad in hospital, I turned vegetarian.'

He gives a little laugh, but I don't see the funny side.

twenty-seven

▼▼▼▼▼

Turns out, treating cancer and nuclear war aren't that different.

I recently signed a petition for the Campaign for Nuclear Disarmament – a man with a clipboard was getting people to sign it opposite Gordon Benét's. Since then, he's written me a letter asking for my pocket money, and sent me a leaflet all about the radioactive things that are happening the other side of the Iron Curtain. Even a curtain made of iron can't stop you getting sick if you're on the wrong side of it when a nuclear reactor explodes. On the leaflet, there are pictures of the roofless Chernobyl energy plant after the explosion a couple of years ago. The people, cats, dogs and trees who lived and grew nearby the plant got toxic shock syndrome and many died on account of being exposed to too much radiation. One cat born not long after the explosion had seven legs. Kit says that down the General they make sure that treatable cancer patients get just enough radiation to try to make the tumours shrink, but not enough to give you seven legs or worse still, kill you. He explained, by doodling a figure of eight called a DNA double helix on the back of an empty fag packet, that it was the genes inside him that mutated and gave him cancer.

Over dinner of instant mash and burnt tofu, Mum announces she's going to have an operation in hospital too, on a Dad-weekend Friday.

'Partial hysterectomy,' she says.

'You stealing my thunder?' Kit asks. 'Or trying to make me feel better about my loss of lung capacity?'

'I've been on the waiting list two years, actually.'

I peel myself off the sofa and sneak into the dining room. Underneath the dining-room table I cross my legs and look up 'hysterectomy' in *Chambers*: it means 'to remove a woman's uterus'.

Kit leaves his tea half-eaten again and announces that he's going for a lie-down on the Zedbed, his second of the day. Mum sighs and comes to sit next to me under the dining-room table, squeezing her head underneath and crossing her legs.

'I need to tell you about Kit's illness, Harper. It will affect his moods and might make him more volatile. When they did the scan last month, they found—'

'Mum,' I interrupt.

'Yes?'

'He's going to die very soon, isn't he?'

'Yes,' Mum says.

'I don't want to hear any more,' I say. 'I'd rather just not know.'

'I understand, sweetheart,' Mum says. 'You know how much he loves you, don't you? As much as if you were his own.'

'You should write copy for Love Hearts sweets, not Christmas catalogues,' I say, shuffling away from her.

'You're getting so teenagery,' Mum says, squidging my arm.

'*Mum!*' I say. I'm not a teenager yet: I'm still only twelve and I'm not wishing my life away any. In fact, I wish I could pause time like a video and be this age for ever. Kit would get to live as long as he wanted. My ova wouldn't multiply and nor would Kit's cancer. I want the deathly egg timer to magic its pink sand upwards.

'It's not fair,' I say, wiping a tear away.

'What isn't, poppet?' Mum asks.

'Life,' I sniff.

'I know.' Mum shuffles closer to me, craning her neck even lower. She's not even crying.

'Why do you always have to be so brave, Mum? It's like you don't care!'

'I do care, Harper,' Mum says. 'I care very much, but I have to stay strong for Kit. It's no good if he spends the little that's left of his life wallowing in misery.'

'You're not strong. You're weak,' I say. I hate it when Mum pumps herself up like this, like she's a Roman city that no Trojan horse can enter; I know she has weak spots.

'Can we have a pretend fight?' I ask, after a long silence.

'We've not had one of those for years,' Mum says. 'Of course we can.'

Mum crawls out from under the dining-room table and offers me her hand to pull me up. In the lounge, she pushes the coffee table to one side and then lies down on the carpet like I would do at a birthday party when playing dead fishes. I straddle my legs across her hips, sitting on top of her, and hit her gently on her shoulder.

'Harder!' Mum says, so I punch her harder, this time on her arm. 'I think you can do much better than that.'

'I hate you!' I say, as I punch her on her tummy, right where the surgeon will be scooping out any chance of me ever having siblings.

'I can't hear you,' Mum says.

'I said I *HATE* you,' I say and punch her even harder.

'I'm sorry?' she says.

'*I HATE YOU*,' I shout at the top of my voice and then I crumple into her arms and weep. Mum doesn't say anything else. She just strokes my back and lets me sob until my tank of tears runs dry.

When Mum had her teeth extracted, she was still giggling an hour after the operation. Oona gave Mum a lift home because the dentist said Mum shouldn't operate heavy machinery, drive, sign anything legally binding or make any big life decisions for twenty-four hours after the extraction. Her lap was covered in Avon towels, and she was laughing, blood trickling down her chin. Oona said the giggling was on account of the gas.

'Your mum not in?' Dad asks as I get into the car.

'She's had some of her womb taken out today. She's still down the General,' I explain, clipping myself in. 'What are we up to tonight, then?'

Dad stares straight ahead at the council estate like it's a dartboard and he's aiming for the bull's eye. After a while he says, 'Let's go to the Spread Eagle. I could do with a sun-downer.'

At the village pub we sit in our usual spots in the snug, the only room where children are allowed come the evenings. There's a Galaxy 200 jukebox in the corner; I override the Willie Nelson song playing quietly in the background by choosing two tracks – one by Blondie and the other by Barry Manilow – in a bid to cheer Dad up. While I'm there, Dad goes to the bar to refill our glasses and gets talking to the barman. I decide that now's a good time to go and visit the ladies' so Dad can spill his heart all over the soggy beermats.

A new machine has been screwed to the wall in the toilets: it sells coloured condoms, tampons and sanitary towels all at 20p apiece. Periods and pregnancy protection must get expensive. If you were to add up how much you must spend over your bleeding and anti-breeding life, then I bet it would cost hundreds of pounds: maybe that's why Mum's decided to have her womb out?

Back in the snug, the barman's asking Dad, 'What's your poison, then. A Bloody Mary?'

Dad lifts his head to square with him. 'Not funny. Another lager, please. Make it a pint.'

That Saturday morning, I'm up before Dad. There isn't a clean bowl in the kitchen, so I eat my Cornflakes out of a lidless Tupperware pot with a knife: it makes breakfast last a long time, but even after that there's still no sound of Dad being awake upstairs. Heavy rain is falling, so I go back to bed with *The Almanac of Spooky Happenings*. I read about a boy who was born with water where his brain should be, a woman who sat on a bone from a three-inch pork chop but she was that fat that she didn't notice so it grew into her bum-flesh, and the one about a Muslim man who found the symbol of Allah in an aubergine.

All this gets me thinking about what happens in life that they don't teach you at school.

It's one thing being taught about the Romans, shipwrecks, or even the facts of life. But what about the facts of death? What will happen to Kit's body when he dies? Nobody cross-sections that in any book. There are precautions you should take like condoms to make sure you don't get pregnant, but what precautions should you take to make sure you don't die?

> *What did Kit do so wrong that he got cancer?*
> *What did Kit do so wrong that he got cancer?*
> *What did Kit do so wrong that he got cancer?*
> *What did Kit do so wrong that he got cancer?*

This is the question that's stuck like a stylus on the scratched seven-inch of my mind.

If her brain isn't full of water this morning, Mrs Curtis might have some answers. After all, she's been around so long that all her friends and relations, bar me and her long-lost son, have now settled six feet underground. I find her at her dining-room table, labelling glass jars with her spidery handwriting: *1988 Gooseberry Jam. Longer Kept the Better.* The air's fat with fried butter. Green and blue damp blooms on the faded wallpaper like week-old bruises.

'Harper!' she wheezes as I push the rain-swollen front door closed behind me.

'How's your mother?' she asks.

'Fine,' I say, sitting on a dining chair with a sagging rattan seat. 'She's got a boyfriend, but he's dying from cancer.'

'It doesn't catch,' she says. 'They say it does, but it doesn't...'

I hadn't even thought that Mum or me might catch it off him.

'...That's how the best of them go nowadays, love,' she continues.

'Why do people get it?' I ask.

Mrs Curtis sinks back into her chair as if she's a turtle and the chair's her shell. She doesn't say anything for a long time while her brain bubbles. I start to sort through the large colander of gooseberries on the table, dividing them into those which are hard, tart bullets and those which are bulging and soft with faint white stretch marks. Mrs Curtis's mantelpiece clock chimes two o'clock, a full four and a half hours ahead of itself; she keeps it running for company rather than time-keeping.

Eventually she cranes forward and says, 'Death is part of living, you know. Your mum probably won't know how to cope again. She manages to stay on the surface most of the time, but she runs deep.'

Now I'm the one with a colander for a brain; I've no idea what she's talking about or what Mum's surfaces have to do with anything. But it sounds very wise, so I shall try to remember that Mum runs deep and that she probably won't cope well.

'What are these for?' I ask, pointing to the jam jars.

'Raffle prizes. We're fundraising for a new graveyard bench.'

I picture the broken bench that's opposite Heaven Called a Little Child's grave. Weighed down by too many heavy hearts and lonely souls, I suppose. Not even good for firewood.

I stay to help finish sorting the colander of gooseberries. When Mrs Curtis rises from her armchair to put her gramophone on, I offer to do it instead and I give the Italian 78 a good polish before I set the needle down on the ancient vinyl. It plays without getting stuck. I bite into a raw gooseberry. The bittersweet seeds explode in my mouth. *Ma l'amore no.*

Back at home, Dad has shaved the stubble that was crawling across his face. I eye him up and down and wonder where we're going, and if he's about to spray himself with perfume à la peanut.

'There's a Lone Rangers fête at midday in Coventry,' Dad says. 'If you fancy it?'

The timing's perfect: my CND T-shirt that I sent off for arrived just this week and not only that, I remembered to pack it for my Dad weekend. Plus I can palm off the jar of gooseberry jam that Mrs Curtis just gave me at the tombola stall or some other lame fundraising game.

'There's going to be a sponsored baked-bean bath,' he says as I turn to run upstairs and get changed. 'I'm taking all of those.' Dad looks at the five cardboard boxes full of out-of-date baked beans which are stacked by the front door. As I said, I'm not religious, but that doesn't mean I can't whisper a prayer of thanks to God now and then.

twenty-eight

▼▼▼▼▼

Ten weeks is a long time for Craig to take to reply to my divorced-
kid quiz, but I'm sure there's one of Dad's 'rational explanations'
for his delay in writing back. Strikes me that adults aren't always
rational. For instance, sitting in a bathtub while 120 tins of
out-of-date baked beans are being poured in to raise £27.16 for
a single-parent club does not seem rational. I leave Dad to get
repetitive strain injury with his tin opener while he fills up the
bath with pulses. Another one of the bearded single dads sits in
the tub in just his Y-fronts, already up to his waist in beans.

At the other end of the church hall there's a table where you
can try out and buy executive desk toys like Rubik's cubes, kinetic
polo players, cat's cradles and pinscreens which show your fea-
tures in three dimensions. Of course, Dad and I are a quarter of an
hour early so nobody else is waiting for a go. It's while I'm pressing my hand into a screen of blunt pins that Louise comes over.

'Harper,' she says. 'Here with your dad?'

'And five boxes of beans.'

'Right.'

She sets the cat's cradle ticking: click-*clack*-click-*clack*-click-*clack*.

I refuse to break the ice, and press my hand deeper into the pins.

'How is he?' she asks.

'Why don't you see for yourself?' I say, nodding towards Dad, who's standing by the bathtub, still furiously operating the tin opener. I hope she apologizes for leading Dad on. If she doesn't, I'll pin-art her face when she's least expecting it.

This seems like a good moment to confess something about my hands. Ever since Mum bundled me into the Mini when I was five, having shovelled into the boot her suitcases, high heels, her share of the baked beans, plus her unopened books and a belief in a better life, warts have been growing on my fingers. For the first couple of years it was just one, on my right-hand Peter Pointer, but since I turned eight, they've started to multiply like mushrooms in rain.

There are several ways of removing warts. First, Mum tried painting them with ointment that, when I smelt it, frazzled my nostril hairs. When that didn't work, we went to the doctor, who brought out a canister of dry ice with a wand attached. The doctor tried to reassure me by saying he was using the same stuff that *Top of the Pops* pump on to the stage to add atmosphere as he pressed the cold wand down dead hard on each of the warts for a minute to burn them to their roots. Next, they're supposed to turn black and fall off. The turning black bit happened. But then the warts went white again and didn't disappear.

Strikes me it's funny that we spend a lot of our lives trying to keep things secret: false teeth, warts, periods, who we fancy, who our parents are, what we're really thinking, who we truly are. As I'm inspecting my handprint, the church hall door opens and in walks Craig.

'Stay cool, Harper. Don't blush.' I whisper to myself under my breath. 'Think about cold things: hands in the shapes of icicles. A cola-flavoured Mr Frosty. Vanilla ice-cream. Orange lollies. Orange lolly ice kisses. Oh God...'

'All right,' Craig says.

'All right,' I say. I decide to wear my question on my CND T-shirt sleeve, straight up. 'Did you get my letter?'

'Letter?'

'Well, it was more of a quiz, actually...'

'No,' he replies.

'I definitely put a stamp on it. You're at number one Vicarage Crescent?'

'Number five.'

'Who's at number one?' I ask.

'The vicar. Who told you I lived there?'

'The girl with tight jeans and lipstick,' I say.

'Mandy? My ex-stepsister?'

'That sounds complicated.'

'She's got a chip the size of a brick on her shoulder: my mum left her dad. What did the letter say?'

'I just needed some advice. It doesn't matter now.'

'Nice T-shirt,' he says. Just as Craig's going in for a kiss, Dad comes over.

'Fancy apple bobbing?' he asks cheerily, his arms akimbo with tomato sauce up to his elbows. At least he doesn't look heartbroken.

Apple bobbing is one of those games that seems fun when some-one else is doing it, but if you're trying to look cool in front of a potential boyfriend, then sticking your face in pins is probably a better bet. Dad's manning a low table where a bucket of water sits in which several Granny Smith apples are afloat. Craig, me and a nine-year-old boy are picked as the first contestants. Louise places our hands around our backs then ties a pair of laddered tights around them, hopefully not hers. Then Dad blows a whistle and we plunge our faces into the freezing water. At least this helps to cool my flushed face.

The apples are slippery like wax against my teeth. I gnash my jaws, but the apples bob away from my mouth. Craig gives me a wink as he edges closer to me. The third boy is a woodpecker, seems he's determined to win. Just as I'm about to bite the green-est apple in the bucket, Craig sneaks a quick kiss on my cheek which puts me off, and then he manages to plunge his teeth into an apple. Dripping, his head rises from the bucket, apple in mouth.

Louise unties our hands, gives us a towel to wipe our faces with, then presents Craig with his prize: a jar of Mrs Curtis's gooseberry jam. As runners up, the nine-year-old and I are given booby prizes of an apple each.

'If you put it under your pillow, you'll dream of your future husband,' Louise says, nudging me.

I smile sweetly, and give her back my booby prize. I suggest she eats all of it, even the core; apple pips have arsenic in them.

Craig and I retreat to the back of the hall, where he finds a dark corner to lose the jam in.

'Now you know my address,' he says, having poked the jar behind a stack of plastic chairs with a dustpan brush, 'will you write again?'

'Of course,' I smile.

171

'I don't even know where you live.'

'Blackbrake.'

'Cool. There's an anti-nuclear protest there coming up soon. I'm going on the bus with my half-brother, Atom. Fancy coming?'

Protests are something I've only done at the dinner table about boil-in-the-bag cod with parsley sauce. I'm not sure what an anti-nuclear one will involve, but I guess I'd mostly be waving flags and shouting down metal cones. There was one the other Saturday along the High Street to do with making water private. It seemed bonkers to me because of course water isn't private: nobody owns the clouds that rain falls out of. I say this to Craig to make it look like I know the score.

It's the right thing to say, it seems, as he leans across and says, 'Right on, Harper,' and he kisses me bang on the lips.

twenty-nine

▼▼▼▼▼

The moment I dump my weekend bag at the bottom of the stairs on Sunday I know something's not right: the house is the cleanest I've ever seen it. Even the dado rails and the skirting boards are cobweb-free. Not to mention the carpet, which is two shades of yellow brighter: from English mustard to Bird's custard. Cigarette-smoke stains that once collected in the corners of the walls and ceilings have been attacked with a coat of magnolia.

In the lounge, Mum's hammocked on the sofa, her feet higher than her head. She's fast asleep.

I find Kit diluting condensed mushroom soup on the hob. He's wearing a silver glitter wig. At least someone's back to normal.

'What's with all the cleaning?' I ask.

'Don't tell your mum – she hasn't noticed yet – but while she was down the General, the estate agent came round with a professional cleaner. Getting the house ready for viewings.'

'But they haven't given us a second chance to buy it!'

'Don't worry. I'm sure Mary'll find a way to get a mortgage. I'm going to do all I can to help.'

So as not to disturb Mum's vacated body, we eat the soup at the small kitchen table next to Freddie Mercury. On Freddie's door, Kit has spelt out in magnetic letters, 'WELCOME TO THIRTEEN KENDAL ROAD HOME TO THOSE BODY PARTS LIGHTER'.

'Did you know Mum has falsies?' I ask.

Kit throws his head back and laughs, silver hair raining down his back.

'Of course!' he says.

'Don't you think it's a bit weird?'

'It's what's inside that counts.'

'But what if what's inside is taken out?' I ask.

'Don't take things so bleeding literal, Harper,' he says. 'I mean, it's who you are inside that matters most. Remember that, won't you, when I'm toast?'

'When does your radiation start?' I ask.

'They haven't even bothered this time, H. The doctors give up on you when it's in your bones,' he says and sips on a spoonful of mushroom soup. It goes down the wrong way and Kit has a coughing episode at the table, one so bad he has to spit the soup out on to the closest thing at hand, an old grey tea towel. I glimpse specks of red blood on it.

Freddie Mercury shudders. Inside the fridge, two glass milk bottles chink and kiss.

The womb doctor said Mum would need lots of bed rest after her operation, but she's up at seven o'clock the next Monday morning to get ready for her nine o'clock appointment with Mike Hyde. Having her womb removed seems to make Mum more

174

determined than ever to get a mortgage.

It isn't just Derek who wears clothes and bags like armour. I swear Mum adds four inches to her height with her shiny heels, shoulder pads and hairspray.

'You're dressed to kill,' Kit says as Mum totters down the door-step. I trail behind dressed in ripped jeans, my CND T-shirt and my denim jacket.

We have time to murder even with an extra twenty minutes to allow for Mum walking in heels, so we take the back route through the council estate to the bank. As we pass the compound I hear small wheels running across tarmac: school-skivers like me, only they get to throw shapes on skateboards rather than be an accessory for credit. Mum's stiletto heels click on the pavement like a ticking bomb; her chin points skywards. I'm carrying a black case that contains as many bank statements as Mum can find in her filing system, one which is ordered by the number of coffee halos on brown envelopes.

Inside the bank there's a hospital hush, but instead of beeping monitors and nurses in white gowns charting heartbeats, coins are rattling through counting machines and men in black suits discuss base-rate rises in low voices. I notice all this because we're left sitting in the reception for half an hour with a cut-out life-size yellow dragon for company. I count Mum zigzag her legs thirty times as if she could knit them into Mike's office.

Finally, a bubble-permed receptionist calls out, 'Mrs Smith?'

'Ms,' Mum hisses.

We're led into an office marked PRIVATE: FOR CUSTOMER CONSULTATIONS ONLY.

'She staying in?' the receptionist asks, over my head.

Mum nods.

'Would you like a tea or coffee?'

'Coffee, please. But only if it's filtered. Milk, three and a half sugars.'

The receptionist turns to me and skewers her electric-green eyes into me. 'CND's your favourite pop group, then?'

'It stands for the Campaign for Nuclear Disarmament,' I say. 'And mine's a glass of milk. Thanks.'

This gets rid of the bubble-perm double-quick. Mum paints me her biggest fire-engine-red grin and we sit down on the hard seats opposite a desk which is bare save a packet of antiseptic wipes and a paperweight with a scorpion frozen in glass. Mike's voice, smooth as engine oil, pours down the corridor. He's ordering an espresso with an extra shot. I glance at Mum, who cocks her head even higher as if she's a puppet and her string's being pulled.

'Mary. Harper. Great to see you again,' Mike says, as he oozes into the office, smelling of tea tree oil; maybe he disinfects himself in between customers. His mean black tie, as thin as a runner bean, dangles down his crisp pink shirt. If his tie were a runner bean, it would be grown on a factory farm and injected with water: fast-growing, but tasteless.

'Thanks for finding time in your schedule,' Mum says.

'How's school, Harper? Got on to long division yet?' Mike asks, turning to me.

I shake my head, mumble that I prefer English.

'Ah, but being in the numbers game is where the money's at.' Mike rubs a forefinger and thumb together as if cash were as easy to make as pastry.

Bubble-perm knocks and then bums open the door, setting down the tray of drinks on the desk.

'That'll be all, Henrietta,' Mike says.

'We're here about a mortgage,' Mum says, opening her black file of papers.

'Right, you'd like to get down to business, then?' Mike says, and launches into a speech about deposits, interest rates and application forms. It's enough to make my heartbeat slow to a dangerous pace. I block up my listening chimneys and look around the echoey consultation room. The walls shake when doors are opened and closed, like those in the homes on Ramsay Street in *Neighbours*. I tune into the conversation on the other side of the cardboard wall, where a man is telling someone on the other end of the line that their application for a loan has been rejected.

Mum knits her legs for the umpteenth time.

I tune in to what Mike's saying.

'...and I don't see evidence of any savings. Nor a wedding ring.'

'I'm applying on the basis of my sole income,' Mum says, gritting her falsies.

'Which is?'

'Five thousand pounds a year.'

'We'll have to credit check you. Again. Hopefully you haven't been melting plastic...'

Mum smiles to hide the fact that she's turned six Tupperware lids liquid in the past month alone.

'Don't call us,' Mike says, getting up.

'Mike,' Mum says. 'If there's anything you can do to speed up the application...'

'Leave it with me,' Mike says. 'I'll see what I can do.'

Mum gets to her feet now, shaking his hand. Then he shakes mine.

'Can I take one of those?' I ask, looking at the antiseptic wipes.

When we're back on the High Street I wipe the hand Mike shook twice over.

'You can't catch anything from shaking hands with someone!' Mum says, laughing.

'Not even cancer?'

Mum stops dead on the street and turns to me. 'Whoever gave you that idea?'

'Mrs Curtis.'

'Harper, Mrs Curtis is senile. More than that, she's venomous. Don't listen to her, OK?'

'Like a scorpion?' I ask.

'Sorry?'

'Venomous like a scorpion?'

'Venomous like a tired old hag who has nothing better to do but stir up other people's lives to no good,' Mum says.

I know better than to quiz her when she's in one of these credit-induced moods, but it would seem that there's more to Mrs Curtis than I've realized. There's also more to *me* than meets the eye: Mike Hyde's paperweight is the first thing I've ever stolen. While he was holding open the door for Mum, I swiped it from his desk. It's smooth as an egg. I clasp my hand around the cool glass in my denim jacket pocket. One day I will smash the glass to smithereens and see if the scorpion still has a sting in its tail. For now, though, I'll hide it in between my crop tops in my chest of drawers.

Mum sugar-coats the bank episode with a doughnut each. On the walk to the school gates we have a competition to see who can eat hers without licking lips.

I win.

thirty

▼▼▼▼▼

Cassie's allowed to call for me on the way to school now that Mrs Pope has agreed that finally, aged thirteen, she's old enough to cross the Greytown Road on her own. On the way to school, we eat the chocolate bars out of our packed lunch boxes and Cassie spills more grief about living with Lisa.

'You'd think her UCCA form is the most important thing in the galaxy.'

'What's one of those?' I ask.

'It gets you into university,' Cassie explains. 'She wants to study philosophy.'

'You can get a degree in how to think?'

'You can get a degree in anything.' Cassie shrugs and snaps off a portion of fruit and nut chocolate for me.

Our topic for the last two weeks of July is energy; it's the kind of thing that the government flyer called 'Implications of the Great Education Reform Bill: New National Curriculum Standardized Education for All' the school sent home says we will be doing come September. Today, we're going on our end-of-term summer trip to a farm on the outskirts of Blackbrake to see where meat and milk come from. If it's energy we're talking about, I'd rather be going to visit a nuclear power plant and putting placards up outside it.

My teacher, Mrs Morrison, stands by the coach ticking our names off the register. The driver is asleep at the steering wheel, his eyes hidden behind sunglasses. Drizzle falls. Wipers scream across the windscreen. The further back I go into the coach, the stronger the smell of undiluted bleach, so I park myself on an orange and brown seat halfway back where Cassie joins me. I check the armrest ashtray for forgotten fag ends but it's stuck together with bubblegum.

Once the coach has filled up with the rest of the class, Mrs Morrison uses a buzzing microphone to say something about smashing windows with hammers, and then pokes the driver with it so that he jolts awake. Underfoot the engine roars as he turns the key in the ignition. Blue-grey smoke chugs out of the exhaust and wraps itself around the coach like a toxic fog.

The floor is toasty warm by the time we're sitting at lights opposite Blackbrake brewery. A yeasty smell pours through the air vents on the coach. It reminds me of the one time Dad and I experimented with baking bread. We left the dough in a bowl on top of the warm oven covered with a damp tea towel, but then we were distracted by a game of battleships. By the time we went back to check on the dough, it was erupting over the side of the bowl like lava and was oozing over the electric hob rings.

As we leave the centre of Blackbrake and heave up the hill, the buildings change from shops to factories, from red-brick terraces to concrete council houses and then there's a sprawl of detached houses with large front gardens and two cars in the driveway. Rich people tend to live on the west side of towns because of the direction smoke blows, according to my geography teacher. We must be heading west, because by the time we reach the town limits the houses are so big you can't even see them: you only know they're there because there's a high wooden gate, a doorbell, and a sign saying 'Beware of the Dog'.

Twenty minutes later we arrive at Peabody Farm, which is surrounded by vast fields, the odd hedge interrupting acres of green. I don't know what I expected of a farm, but what I find shocks me. What I find shocks me enough to go off spaghetti bolognese for life.

We crocodile in twos out of the coach towards a shed with a metallic, crinkle-cut roof. Inside, the farmer explains how the cows are kept there from the day they're born until the day they turn one year old. There are small pens dividing up the large stable where hustling cows struggle to reach the mangers. Raw cowpat covers the floor. One cow looks up at me and moos in a long, low voice.

'How often do they go outside?' I ask the farmer.

'Never,' he says.

At the other end of the shed, where the one-year-old cattle nudge up against a barrier dividing them from fields, squats a large metal plate. It's hooked up to a socket and a red button. This, explains the farmer, is where the cows are placed and then electrocuted on their first birthday.

Mrs Morrison hands us a worksheet to colour in, of a calf suckling a cow's udder.

'We'll visit the milk vats after sandwiches,' she says, inching around a black, oily puddle in her beige pumps.

Luckily, I've made my own packed lunch today, so aside from the chocolate bar I've already eaten, I've got crisps and a grated Red Leicester cheese sandwich. I don't think I could stomach anything meaty. Cassie sits next to me on the picnic bench. She munches a semi-circle out of her roast beef and pickle bap. An extra-terrestrial moan drifts over from the cowshed. I close my lunch box again, my hunger vanished.

I find Mrs Morrison and ask if I can just sit out the rest of the school trip in the coach. The driver is asleep again, this time with his feet on the dashboard and his head covered by a newspaper. I'm not sure being on a coach which smells like a cleaned toilet bowl is the best place when feeling queasy, but I've seen enough of where food energy comes from for one day.

In my rucksack, I've packed a copy of the CND newsletter that the man with the clipboard posted me. I try to concentrate on words like 'democracy' and 'reactor vessel' but it's not long before I drift off and fall fast asleep too.

When I wake up, we're back outside the school gates and rain is falling in sheets from the sky as if being emptied from buckets. I'm last off the coach. Drenched through, I drip my way home and the first thing I see as I open the front door is Mum at the cooker stirring a jam pan of bolognese. Smells of mince turning grey in burning butter waft towards me. I peel layers of soggy uniform off, now two shades of grey darker, and pad into the kitchen in my vest and knickers. Mum's nosing beef around the pan with a wooden spoon; I peer over the edge of it. Strings of mince are breaking off into maggot-sized chunks.

At the kitchen table sits Oona, her back leaning against a

182

rattling Freddie Mercury. She sips a cup of hot water with a slice of lemon. 'What you going to eat with that, then?' she asks Mum as I sit down at the table.

'Parmesan. Spaghetti. Wine.'

Oona sighs.

'It can't be good for you, starving yourself every other day...' Mum says.

'I lost four and a half pounds last week.'

Mum adds a slurry of chopped tomato into the pan and grinds black pepper, adds a pinch of salt.

'Don't want to lose your marbles with it, though,' Mum says.

'I won't be happy until you can peel a potato on my collar bone and play my ribcage like a xylophone.'

'Mum?' I interrupt.

'Yes?'

'I'm becoming a vegetarian.'

'Doesn't surprise me,' Mum says.

How Mum knew I was going to turn vegetarian, I can't work out – especially as I've always been dead against people who don't eat meat. Oona takes another tiny sip of hot water. As I close the kitchen door behind me, Mum says, 'Off to her first protest at the weekend.'

'I bet you don't know where she gets it from!' I hear Oona say, and then they burst out laughing.

thirty-one

▼▼▼▼▼

'It's nuclear chic, Harper.'

Craig hands me a luminous yellow all-in-one outfit coupled with a black hood and a heavy, black gas mask to wear over my dungarees. It's the day of the Blackbrake CND march and all twelve protestors are wearing them. I step into the large suit, roll up the tough, plastic material at my ankles and wrists where it's dangling; it's like wearing an oversized Marigold glove. Craig and I both put on our gas masks. Sweat instantly trickles down my face.

We huddle together in a scrum so Craig's half-brother Atom can talk us through the plan, including the back-up procedure if we're bothered by the police. I listen carefully, keeping my lips stuck together with nuclear glue.

'Take this end of the banner. *Sch-tuck*,' Craig says, handing me a beanpole. Taped to it is a flapping bed sheet on which he's written in black marker pen: 'CND: Creating New Democracy.' There's that long word again. I'll just have to blag it if anyone happens to ask what the point is. At least wearing this mask means nobody will recognize me, or hear what I'm saying.

Opposite us, policemen in black helmets begin to group together, watching us like we're terrorists; a couple bang batons in their palms as if pummelling dough.

I inch behind Craig.

'Don't let them give you the heebie-jeebies. *Sch-tuck*,' he says.

A whistle blowing cuts through the air.

A drum thunders.

'What do we want?'

'Nuclear Disarmament!'

'When do we want it?'

'Now!' goes the chorus that we chant three times, then set off in a march through the Black Knight shopping centre and then up the High Street.

Atom skirts the edge of the luminous yellow herd, peeling off to collect the odd signature from women weighed down with a Saturday spent haemorrhaging cash, their shoulders as low as their boobs with bags full of cheap clothes. A group of kids from my year eating skinny fries and anorexic burgers on a metal bench ignore us as we pass.

Our finishing point is the top of the High Street, opposite the World of Three-Piece Suites. Or, as Mum prefers to call it, Credit Upholstered Heaven.

'*Sch-tuck*. Time for some direct action,' Atom says.

For a crazy minute, I think we're going to go in.

We do.

A gangly lad in a suit starts to approach us, then walks backwards when he realizes there's a dozen of us. His many spots seem to glow redder as he slinks off to find the manager, a man who wears mayonnaise brackets either side of his thin mouth.

'Sorry to interrupt your lunch,' Atom says, taking off his mask. Behind it is a pale face with a grey half-moon under each eye.

'How can I help you?' the manager asks, slightly too politely, I think.

We all sit down on settees, sofas and pouffes with tags dangling that shout '0%! Interest! Free! Credit!'

Sch-tuck.

Sch-tuck.

Sch-tuck.

'Our intelligence tells us that you're an investor in Nuclear Armament,' Atom begins.

'Your intelligence?'

'It tells us that you're happy to see nuclear take the place of traditional energy forms—'

'Isn't coal a little short in supply these days?' the manager says, then adds. 'As well as your intelligence?'

Somebody whistles through their teeth.

'Uranium may be plentiful. But it's toxic...' Atom replies.

'Need help, boss?' says a voice so low it makes the pouffe I'm sitting on vibrate. I crane round to see that it's coming from a security guard who makes a midget of Atom. I should have warned him about security guards and plain-clothed policemen; they're trained to pop up when you least expect it.

Atom seems to have run out of steam.

The *sch-tuck* sound stops as we all hold our breath.

Craig squeezes my arm.

'We just wanted to deliver this,' Atom says to the security guard, handing him a brown envelope. 'It's a petition, signed by our forty-seven local members calling for research into nuclear arms to be, well, disarmed.'

'Says 'ere it's 'azardous,' vibrates the security guard, taking the letter. 'Better dispose of it in the appropriate manner, then,' he says, ripping it into shreds fit for gerbil bedding.

Craig lifts my elbow to steer me out of the shop. Atom is last out, his under-eye half-moons looking greyer. 'I guess you can't win them all,' he says. 'But let's be encouraged by the four new sign-ups we got outside Our Price.'

There's a long blast on a horn behind us: it's coming from a vehicle double-yellowed across the delivery bay. Its bonnet is spray-painted with CND COVENTRY. I take off my outfit and hand it to Craig, who congratulates me on my first bit of direct action.

'Didn't do very much,' I say, as we walk towards the minibus, which is more mini than bus.

'It's about standing up for what you believe in,' he says. 'By the way, did you notice the pouffe we were sitting on vibrate?'

'What was that about?' I ask.

'That's how they make them nowadays: vibrating. Some sofas come with heated pads. I tell you, settees'll be making you a cup of tea before you know it!'

'Won't happen, *sch-tuck*,' says another protestor, who's struggling to get off his gas mask.

'That's the brave new world we're entering, Harper: 1984!'

'But that's the past, not the future!' I shout as Craig clambers on to the minibus. The rusted orange door slides shut with a slam.

He clambers to the back of the bus and then scrawls on a scrap of paper in black marker pen three words which he then pastes against the rear window of the minibus. It says: 'Read George Orwell.'

A black bullet of smoke escapes the exhaust pipe as the engine fires and the minibus snails out of the loading bay. Looming opposite, the security guard beefs up his chest. I leg it to the number fourteen bus stop that'll take me home. Home to look up 'democracy', and see if any books by George Orwell might be lurking between the creased, pink spines of *Uniforms, Underwear and Ulrika* and *Hot Flash for Frances*.

I don't get to scour the bookshelves as soon as I get home though, because Mum's having one of her moments. She's in the lounge, leafing through holiday catalogues. The covers show pictures of slim women lounging on beaches in gold bikinis and couples in orange sarongs sipping cocktails at pool-side bars.

This is not a good sign.

'All right, Mum?'

'Paradise!' she says. 'That's what they promise! A little slice of paradise. I'd take a crumb.'

'Is everything OK?'

'Everything is not OK.'

I sit down beside her on the sofa, and Mum passes me a letter from the bank. 'Mike fast-tracked my application all right,' she says.

I scan the paragraphs and the word 'rejected' jumps out. These eight letters alone explain my mum's dark mood.

'I want to take a holiday from my life,' Mum says, deadpan.

'Can I come?'

'Course you can, sweetness,' she sighs, and gives me a squeeze.

The big, bad world might seem to be against us right now, but I know Mum is brave enough to face it head-on. And I intend to face it with her, come what may.

thirty-two

▼▼▼▼▼

Kit'll get paid a heavy pound coin per eyelid for dying; not that heaven takes cash, I imagine. Dead souls barter using good deeds they stocked up while still alive – things like telling someone they've got mayonnaise around their mouth, like keeping a crispy old woman company while sorting gooseberries, or trying to make sure your Lone Rangers parents don't get their lonely hearts broken. I have to say I'd never thought about when people buy their coffins. I kind of assumed Kit's would arrive when his pulse stops.

Turns out, I kind of assumed wrong.

'Easy does it!' A deliveryman in brown overalls is trying to get a parcel twice the size of him through the front door. It has the same unmistakable shape as a coffin.

'Not gonna fit, Brian!' calls another man from inside the house. 'It'll have to go in through the window.'

Mum is sucking hard on a cigarette from the pavement where she stands a couple of coffin-lengths away from the action.

'What's going on?' I ask. When I left to visit Mr Power's, all was normal at number thirteen: Mum was swearing at her Amstrad while Kit was watching afternoon quiz shows with the sound muted and Teletext subtitles on. He was drinking from a can of Blackbrake lager every time there was a spelling mistake.

'Ask Kit,' Mum says, then glues the white tip of an unlit cigarette on to the glowing stub of the one in her mouth.

On the other side of the window, Kit's thin hand slides the yellowed net curtain back and then he pushes the window right up.

'All right,' he says.

I peer in at him and squint. 'You don't *look* very dead,' I say.

'Thanks very much.'

The coffin box is steered through the open jaw of the window. I watch as it's placed upright next to the fireplace. The deliverymen take Kit's signature and exit through the front door.

As soon as they've gone, Kit takes a penknife to the thick cardboard and cuts through the first layer. The coffin is wrapped in umpteen layers of bubble wrap as if it's a present in pass-the-parcel; but even with those layers taken off, the coffin still seems huge. It is the same walnutty colour of one of Mum's strong coffees. Kit measures his head against the closed lid, which stands upright.

'It'll fit perfect,' he says.

It's when Kit goes to open it as if he's about to climb in that I get the willies. Only, he can't get in on account of there being six empty bookshelves inside. Kit doesn't seem surprised by this; in fact, as soon as he has opened the lid, he starts to fill the shelves with stuff from all over the house. I perch on the edge of the sofa and watch as he arranges on the shelves:

a shrivelled cactus;

a metronome;

the pot containing the aborted sunflower seed which I gave
  to Kit and which never grew;

a candlestick with a half-melted candle;

his Queen cassettes;

a stopped clock;

the mantelpiece make-up mirror;

Kit's horse-racing binoculars;

Mum's Premium Bonds jar;

a can of Blackbrake lager...

Mum comes into the lounge to join me on the sofa. Kit carries on, not paying us any attention:

his penknife;

a box of teabags;

the top-shelf copy of *Hot Flash for Frances*;

a tin of anchovies and one of rice pudding;

lemon jelly squares;

my Princess Di 'n' Prince Charles breakfast bowl, which I
  sent off for with cut-out tokens from a cereal packet;

Mum's Wedgwood vase (she doesn't dare complain);

the upper and lower plaster cast of Mum's rotten teeth;

my hairbrush;

the box of Grecian 2000;

an empty pint bottle of milk...

When he has finished, Kit stands back as if looking at a painting he's been so close to that he can't see where it's beautiful and where it isn't.

'There. That's full, isn't it?' he says.

I don't know what to say, and neither does Mum. So we just say: yes.

The coffin fades into the wallpaper over the days that follow. Now and again, I have to remind myself where my hairbrush is, or where to find the Premium Bonds jar if I need to nick 5p. I'm always careful to put back whatever I take exactly where I found it (save the cash, course). Not that Kit says I mustn't touch the mental display, but it's just I get the feeling it's important to him that the coffin's full. One time I spy him through the crinkle-glass door as he feather-dusts everything. A few days later I notice he's added a new book to the shelf with the cover facing outwards, a copy of *Creative Ways to Kick the Bucket*.

Mum bites the bullet one evening. Kit's shaking salt over his chips, then he presses a button on his 'hip flask' – a light blue box the size of a pencil case attached to a drip that feeds morphine into his thigh. A Marie Curie nurse comes to visit regularly to check his vitals and pain-relief levels.

'Anything good on telly tonight?' I ask, dipping a chip into tomato ketchup.

'Not that I could see,' Mum says. 'When you're finished with the salt, Kit...'

'Don't have to worry about a coronary now...' he says.

'...And the tartare sauce...' Mum adds.

'...I could eat chips for breakfast, lunch and dinner if I wanted,' he says.

'Why,' Mum says, banging her fist down on the table so hard my mushy peas wobble, 'do you have to make so many God-awful jokes about dying?'

'Do you think it's easy for me?' Kit says.

'Of course not. But it's not easy for us either, to watch you fading away.'

'Have you ever thought about how you'd like to go?' he asks.

'I haven't,' Mum says in a quiet voice.

'You should.'

Kit jumps up out of his chair and goes to grab *Creative Ways to Kick the Bucket* from the coffin-shelf.

'Says here...'

'While we're eating? Really?' Mum sighs.

'It's a part of life, dying,' Kit says. 'No good ignoring it.'

'Quite,' Mum says, looking towards the coffin, which is blocking her view of the television.

'I'm opting for a home death,' he says, flicking through the pages. 'There's a chapter on it here, somewhere...'

'Home death?' Mum says.

'You've heard of home births? I want the opposite. You leave your dignity at the door in those hospitals and hospices. Look.' Kit thrusts the book beneath Mum's nose.

Mum reads aloud a passage that Kit has underlined in red: '"Accustom your loved ones to your imminent passing by making your coffin a part of the furniture. Why not pre-order one so that before the point of departure, it can double up as a bookshelf, larder, linen cupboard. Or even a bed?" A bed? Blinking heck!'

'I thought the General was for dying and having babies,' I say.

'You were a home birth,' Mum says.

'No I wasn't.'

'You were born at home just after midnight. They transferred us to hospital because I wouldn't stop bleeding. Nearly died of a haemorrhage, I did,' Mum says, straightening herself up in her chair.

'A home birth...' I repeat.

'Born on the bathroom floor of Ivy Cottage only one hour after my waters broke,' Mum continues.

'Bloody hell,' Kit says.

'It was,' Mum continues. 'I went through ten towels. The midwife arrived half an hour after you were born.'

'Was Dad there?' I ask.

'In body. Not in spirit.' Mum shudders as if she's got cold all of a sudden. 'He held a torch between his teeth, so he could have his hands free to help...' Mum pauses. 'He hid behind them.'

'You had no drugs, then?' Kit asks, cradling his syringe driver of morphine as if Mum might snatch it off him.

'Nothing. Not even paracetamol. No time.'

'You doing a Ben Jonson?'

'None. I swear.'

'Bloody hell.'

'You're repeating yourself,' Mum points out. 'And please would you be so kind as to pass the ketchup?'

'It's worth saying twice,' Kit says, as he passes the bottle. Mum holds it upside down over her battered cod and wallops the bottom of the glass bottle. Kit takes a sip of his milky Earl Grey tea. He looks the same colour as it.

'Always bloody stealing my thunder,' he mumbles.

I was born on the bathroom floor by torchlight! Imagine the scene: Mum, screaming. Me, poking my purple head out of her vagina, not yet alive, but somehow a person already. I wonder when my life began. From my first breath or long before, in Mum's ovaries? Doesn't tell you that in the *Facts of Life*. I thumb Kit's copy of *Creative Ways* and wonder if it talks about when the point of actual death is. Will it be when Kit stops breathing, or long after that? It's not like he'll just stop working, like a broken electronic keyboard. People aren't machines. Though you could argue that a coffin for a person is like a skip for a reject toy. Except a coffin has a lid. Plus you don't have chimney dust and sand bags for company. However, that is what you can end up as: dust. Some people choose to be cremated, see. So when Kit says he wants to die at home, I suppose he means my home. Maybe on Mum's bed? Or perhaps on the three-piece suite? Mum'll have to cover it with extra plastic on account of it being bought on the never-never...

'Harper! Please can you pass the vinegar!' Mum says, shaking me and the Boggle box of my deathly thoughts.

'You OK?' Kit says.

'Just wondering what it feels like to die,' I say.

'Well, if it's anything like what it feels like to give birth,' Mum says, 'it feels amazing.'

Kit rolls his eyes.

'Think positive, remember,' Mum says.

The telephone ringing cuts the brewing air in half.

I jump up to get it.

Dave the estate agent barks down the other end, demanding to speak to Mum. I hold my hand across the handset and pull a face like I've just sprinkled the vinegar into my eyes by mistake. Mum whispers, 'Tell whichever prick it is that I'm not here!'

'I'm sorry,' I say, speaking as if I have an avocado stone in my mouth like Mum does down the advertising agency. 'She's engaged.'

Mum gives me the thumbs-up.

'I'll be sure to pass on the message,' I say.

'Mr Slick the bank manager, or Mr Slippery the estate agent?' Kit asks.

'Mr Slippery. Something about a delay in the house going on to the market,' I lie. Telling Mum there are four viewings booked a week Saturday will just crack her vase completely. Best get her out of the house, and see to those viewings myself, I decide as I sit back at the table and nibble a cold chip. I'll do a far better job of being the worst possible saleswoman. I'll be just as good at exterminating potential house buyers as stepdads. Plus, the coffin should put people off – bar perhaps any romantic Goths. I'll have them out of the house quicker than you can say 'base-rate rise'.

thirty-three

▼▼▼▼▼

I didn't realize Kit was religious; I don't think he did either until his cancer came along. It's recommended in *Creative Ways* that, if you are sitting on the kerb-edge waiting to hitch your one-way lift down life's cul-de-sac, then you should not only 'make amends with long-lost friends and bury hatchets with estranged family', but also consider the Bigger Picture and your place in the universe.

It seems a bit shallow to me to suddenly find spirituality in the bottom of your teacup, but that's what Kit takes to: reading tealeaves and finding religious messages in every brew. Not only that, but he starts drinking infusions. I suppose if you can find the symbol of Allah in an aubergine, then why not your higher purpose in a cup of green tea?

When the doorbell rings one afternoon, Kit's looking up the symbolism of his latest cuppa in his book; it predicts an 'imminent confrontation or celebration'.

'If it's my mum, tell her I'm already dead,' Kit says as Mum goes to get the door.

I pray to Five Star that it's not the estate agent come round for a pre-viewing visit. My prayer is answered, but I should have been more careful in choosing what to wish for.

'You've a visitor,' Mum says to Kit, as she walks back into the lounge.

It's Melanie-I'm-sorry-I-don't-have-a-brain-cell. And she's not selling insulated glass. I watch Kit's face as it turns kaleidoscope-quickly into a smile.

'Hello, Christopher.'

'Melanie!' Kit says. He presses his drug box and winches himself out of the sofa.

'Say hello to Melanie,' Mum says to me.

'Hello,' I exterminate.

'I was just wondering how you were both doing?' she says. 'But maybe now isn't a good time?'

Mum pulls at my sleeve. 'We'll go into the kitchen. Give you some time with Chris.'

'Do you know who she is?' I hiss.

Mum shuts the lounge door behind us. 'It's a long story.'

Mum brews a pot of tea and we sit at the kitchen table. Telling white lies, Mum explains, is something adults do when the truth is too difficult to understand for children. But at some point kids grow up and then they're big enough to see the full picture. I ask if it's a bit like adding a net curtain to a window so you can't see right into someone's lounge, and only see the shadowy outline? Mum nods her head. She starts to cry.

I peg it to fetch the plastic bags of loo roll I stashed in Cupboard Love. Mum asks me what it has been doing in there all this time. I guess keeping secrets is a way of telling white lies, too; I tell her that they're from the twelve rolls of toilet paper I unrolled so Bangers and Mash could gnaw on the cardboard. Mum laughs – a little – and blows her nose.

Many years before Melanie started selling double glazing, Mum says, she used to be a mental-health nurse down the Hopkin Wynne.

'So how do you both know her, then? Did Kit sell chocolate to the crazy patients?' I laugh.

Mum shakes her head and then the truth sinks into me, as heavy as the *Mary Rose* hitting a rocky bottom.

'Kit was a patient, wasn't he?' I ask.

Mum nods. 'He's what they like to label a manic-depressive,' she says, 'which means he swings between high and low moods. Sometimes the moods are too much for him, and then he needs to be looked after.'

'Is that why he came to live with us?' I ask.

'I didn't want him to go back into the Hopkin Wynne. It looked like he was on the edge of one of his manic episodes just before he moved in with us.'

'Why didn't you want him to go in? What's wrong with the Hopkin Wynne? They have a gym and everything...'

Mum shakes her head and looks at me with a muted face. 'Social services were going to take you away from me after I got out. Dad had to fight tooth and nail for me to keep you.'

'Got out? What are you talking about?'

'The Hopkin Wynne hospital,' Mum says.

'I don't understand.'

'Dad knew that the best possible thing was for you to be with me, despite my illness,' she says. 'It was just a bit of undiagnosed post-natal depression that turned into something bigger, surfaced a lot of demons. I was at the hospital for four months. I was twenty-three.'

For once, it's me who is lost for words.

Mum pours a mug of tea each, shovels three teaspoons of sugar into both and stirs them with my Di 'n' Charles teaspoon. 'Where was I? When you were in hospital, I mean?'

'You lived with your dad mostly, apart from the odd weekend that he took you halfway to Brighton, where you'd spend time with your grandma to give him a break. You were three.'

'That explains the *déjà vu* at the Little Chef,' I say. 'So, a couple of years after you got out, you got divorced?'

'Your dad did an amazing job of proving that I was sane enough to look after you. He believed in me as a mother, even if he could no longer love me as a wife – I was impossible. I still am. We tried to live together again, but it was hopeless. Everybody in Hardingstone shunned me after I'd been away, especially Mrs Curtis.' Mum dabs the tears away with her loo roll. 'Your dad really loves you, Harper, you know. He just struggles to show it sometimes.'

These are quite a lot of net curtains to suddenly rip from my window. Maybe her spell at the Hopkin Wynne explains why Mum always sits on the top deck of the number fourteen bus: it's not to spy on three-piece suites, but to steer clear of her mental friends on the bottom deck. Her illness might also explain why Mrs Pope kept Cassie at a nuclear distance from me at first: she needed to make sure that I was sane, even if my mum wasn't.

In my head, I rewind what I overheard the day I crumpeted myself between the radiator and the sofa just before I jammed my fingers into my ears:

Dad: 'You got Harper.'

Mum: *'You didn't want her.'*

Dad: *'Now, Mary...'*

Dad having to take care of me explains why he had to give up his teaching job. But why didn't he go back to being a history teacher afterwards?

'How did you meet Dad?' I ask Mum. 'Was it over a photocopier?' I don't know what or who to believe any more.

Mum fills in the picture of how she met Dad: she was Dad's student at college where he taught history. Their affair, she says, came to light in her last few weeks while she was on study leave for her A-level exams. Patrick, he of the Photographic Palace, was an art teacher in the same college.

'Did Patrick take a photo of you and Dad outside school on the day of your last exam?' I ask.

'I don't remember,' she says, staring into her mug of tea which she hasn't touched. 'It's all a blur now. There was such a hoo-ha. Your dad was fired. I flunked my exams. No university would have me.'

'What about Kit? Did you split up with Dad because you fell in love with him at the Hopkin Wynne?' I ask.

Mum shakes her head.

'Do you know that Kit has been two-timing you with Melanie?' I ask.

'Darling, Kit and I aren't and never were in love. We're just good friends, kindred spirits. And as for Melanie and Kit, they did go out for a short while after he was discharged years ago, but she's married to someone else now.'

'But, can you kiss someone when you're not going out with them?' I ask.

Mum cranes forward as if she's about to whisper something

in my ear, and instead she kisses me. 'Of course you can,' she says.

I take a swig of sugary tea; it's that sweet it makes my eyes water.

'But if you're not in love with Kit, then why did you get engaged?'

'The idea of us getting married was purely a convenience thing. He was doing me a financial favour.' She waves her hand as if her relationship with Kit could be brushed away as easily as a dozy fly. As I said, grown-ups act all mysterious about love.

'Why have I never met Kit before now if he was such a good friend?'

'When Kit got out of the Hopkin Wynne, just after me, he moved north to get a job where nobody would know he had a mental-health record.'

'Why did he come back?'

'He came back after his first battle with cancer and his second divorce.'

'But I thought he only just found out he was ill!' I cry.

'He was in remission. Some cancers can come back very aggressively and then you're just a ticking time bomb...'

'A ticking time bomb,' I repeat, and take another sip of tea, sponge away tears with my cardigan sleeve. 'Did you know he had cancer when you got engaged?'

'We both thought he was in the clear. No bank manager in their right mind would certify a mortgage to someone terminal.'

'We're going to lose the house, aren't we?'

'The hell we are!' Mum says.

Since Mum is confessing all these truths I decide to own up

that there are four house viewings booked a week on Saturday. 'I was going to put them off while you and Kit went shopping,' I said.

'We'll put them off, love,' she says. 'Don't worry. If we could just buy a bit more time...'

I let the sugary tears fall without stopping. My boggled brain doesn't stop rattling until Mum finds a fondant fancy for me in the bottom of the bread bin.

That evening, Kit cooks us reconstituted meat-free sausage granules for tea.

'Tastes like corrugated cardboard,' Kit says, as we sit around the dining-room table chewing the crumbling protein.

Mum says in one of her fake-happy tones of voice, 'Harper, while I remember – we're out tonight. Derek's babysitting.'

'Oh?' I don't look up from my plate.

'Group therapy.'

I wonder if Mum told me other white lies when I was littler. All those babysitters that came round so she could go to 'slimming groups' and 'life-long learning' – maybe she was going to group therapy then?

Thank my lucky soya beans Derek doesn't bring his hairdressing scissors when he comes round later that evening.

'Hello *in loco parentis*!' Mum says to Derek, and then she calls over her shoulder to Kit: 'Come on, you cadaver, we'll be late for dissection!'

'Has she swallowed a dictionary or what?' Derek asks as he comes into the lounge.

'That and a bottle of red wine,' I reply.

The door slams, the house now two lunatics lighter.

'Nice bookcase,' Derek says as he walks into the lounge and heads towards Kit's hatbox of wigs.

I collapse on to the sofa.

'Bad day?' Derek asks, from beneath the fringe of Kit's silver glitter wig.

'Mum's been telling me about her depression. Plus, she said Kit was never really her boyfriend. And he's dying.'

'Well, I could have guessed that about your mum,' Derek says. 'But that's bad news about Kit.'

Derek tries on a ginger wig for size which puts me in mind of Cilla Black.

'I know!' I say, sitting ECT-upright, 'I've got a *certifiable* idea!'

Over a multipack of pickled-onion Space Invaders, Derek and I do lonely open heart surgery for Mum: we write out the prescription for my new potential stepdad. Derek manages to write the Lonely Hearts ad so that it makes Mum look mysterious, but not mad:

Eccentric and lovable woman – early thirties, blonde,
bookish & with a great stiletto collection – would like to
love a new well-heeled man in her life. Bank managers
need not apply.

The last sentence is my idea.

Derek writes it out in his best handwriting on the form from the back page of the newspaper and I include two pounds, Sellotaped to a bit of cardboard. Once I've sealed the brown envelope addressed to the *Gazette*, I give it a kiss of good luck like a superstitious shipbuilder smashing a champagne bottle against a new steel hull.

thirty-four

▼▼▼▼▼

That weekend I'm at Dad's where the toxic village gossip is about Mrs Curtis's son coming back from the *Dallas* dead; they say it's because Gregory can smell his inheritance. Mrs Curtis has taken a turn for the worse; a second, larger stroke hit her while she was reducing a pan of lemon curd. It was Dad who found her on the floor in her kitchen. The smell of burning lemons made him suspect something was wrong.

News on the treacle-covered streets is that Mrs Curtis is going into the Blackbrake General to have her heart and mental state monitored, and to get her drips and things. Even the mobile librarian knows all about it already, despite being half-deaf. She discusses the ins and outs of Mrs Curtis's stroke while a woman who's dressed head to toe in tartan checks out three Delia Smith recipe books.

'She won't be back,' the librarian says, reaching for her gold-rimmed spectacles which she wears on a slight chain around her neck.

'Good riddance,' the woman says.

'Look out for the black forest gateau recipe; it's *sensational*,' the librarian says as she hands the Delia books back.

This alone tells me that the librarian's got cotton wool for brains; if she thinks black forest gateau is worth cracking eggs for, then she clearly has the IQ of a yeast culture.

I hand her the book I've chosen.

'Come back when you're sixteen for this,' she says, casting her eyes over the cover of Judy Blume's *Forever*.

I cannot believe it. I'm pretty sure this is censorship. As I'm boiling over, on the verge of reading a paragraph from the Freedom of Reading Act, the father of Richard – he of the blue balloon gun – climbs into the library bus to return a book. I sneak a peek at the title: *Make it Big After Bankruptcy*.

'Any good?' the librarian asks, slipping the pink card back into the book.

'Would've been if there was a chapter on avoiding having your house repossessed,' he says.

He doesn't notice me as he turns on his heel and leaves. Guess he thinks girls of twelve don't know the meaning of house repossession.

'There's a much better selection down Blackbrake library,' I say to the librarian as I leave the bus. She pretends not to hear me on account of her hearing aid, one which looks like a prawn-shaped sweet is stuck somewhere it isn't meant to be. Before slamming the door shut behind me, I shout, 'And they'll definitely let me borrow *Forever!*'

The librarian turns the key and revs the engine unnecessarily before she pulls away from the kerb. There may well be a waiting list for *Forever* down Blackbrake library, but I'll get to the top of it one day. It was Cassie's turn last week; she's been under bed arrest after school, reading about Katherine Danziger's love life ever since.

At least there are some matters I can take into my own hands – such as deciding which single man will get the direct dial to my mum's lonely heart. In order to get the results from our classified advert, I have to call up the *Gazette*'s office. The Sunday evening when I get back from Dad's, I go round Derek's as, like Cassie, he's lucky enough to have a telephone in his room. We press our ears against the beige receiver.

'You have four private callers,' a woman's recorded voice says. 'Press or dial one to delete. Two to save.'

Contestant number one is called Steve. He's from Corby: '...Um. Divorced. Two kids. Like, er, snooker and telly.'

I press one to delete before Derek can say 'snooker-loopy'.

Number two: 'Hi. I saw your ad and was intrigued because I used to be a bank manager, but now I trade bonds...'

I delete Bond Man dead in his tracks.

Derek chuckles.

I tell him to shush.

'I'm six foot tall, blond and below forty,' number three begins; I swear I can hear him wink. 'Work in insurance. But in my time off I like to skydive. My last wife was an instructor, actually. But she fell for a customer – no pun intended – and we divorced last year. She's moved just round the corner from me, but I'm over her now...'

Derek interrupts, 'Clearly on the re-bound.'

'You what?' I ask, over number three as he starts to detail the terms of his divorce.

'He's not over his ex. Delete!'

Which leaves just one more potential stepdad.

'My name's Ryan. I'm an English teacher in a secondary school in town. I've never been married.'

'Ah,' Derek sighs.

'...I love visiting the theatre and, when I can afford it, I go to Stratford-upon-Avon to watch Shakespeare. I've had my ups and downs, but at thirty-five, I think I know what I want out of life.'

I ask Derek what we do next with this lonely heart.

'You should vet him first down the pub,' Derek says. 'I'll come along. It'll be fun!'

thirty-five

▼▼▼▼▼

I don my dungarees to visit Mrs Curtis down the General the second week of the summer holidays. She's been transferred to a private room with a view of the car park. It's not quite as exciting as being behind the locked doors of the Hopkin Wynne where electric shocks and neon drugs are doled out, but I'm hoping I might get to taste some free hospital pudding if I time my visit right. Mum said she wouldn't touch Mrs Curtis with a Zimmer frame so I've come on my own. And I've come at lunchtime. Even though Mrs Curtis may be an ill, bitter woman with a gooseberry fetish and, now, the memory span of a goldfish, she was the only one from the village who talked to me after the divorce.

At the nursing station, one of the nurses looks up from her desk and I explain I'm here to see Mrs Curtis.

'She's got a visitor already,' she says, pointing her chewed HB in the direction of a closed door.

I can't imagine who else would visit Mrs Curtis; she's the Hardingstone village stalemate: surrounded by people but visited by none. But sure enough, there's a man by sitting by her bedside where Mrs Curtis is perched half-upright, fast asleep.

'Hello,' he says, closing a puzzle book.

'All right.'

'I'm Gregory,' he says, smoothing down the lapels of his black blazer.

'Harper,' I say.

I hover at the end of Mrs Curtis's bed. Her hair, as white and brittle as desiccated coconut, is peppered across her speckled scalp. One side of her face droops like a cockerel cheek and her shoulder is slumped into the pillow. 'Has she had lunch?'

Gregory nods and sits back down. 'How do you know mother dearest, then?'

'I live next door...' I say, '...every other weekend.'

'Oh my God, of course,' Gregory says like I'm some kind of hologram he's just figured out. 'You're the spit of Mary. How's she doing?'

'Been better,' I say, wondering how well he knows my mum. I try to checkmate him – show that I know more about him than I should, too. 'Have you won any trophies recently?'

Gregory screws up his nose.

'Cricket trophies, I mean.' The story I was spun was that Gregory lame-ducked to London seven years ago after his divorce to be paid to play cricket in the capital.

Gregory lets out a laugh so loud Mrs Curtis's arm twitches. 'I may live near the Oval but I'm not bowling for England or anything. Far from it, in fact.'

'You do live in London then?'

He nods. At least some of my intelligence is correct.

'As a stylist.'

A blur of white and blue swooshes past me as a couple of nurses whisk in to check Mrs Curtis's pulse. Her arm, which is hooked up to a drip, is as veiny and purple as a beetroot leaf. The nurse checks the upside-down watch attached to her blue dress, and notes Mrs Curtis's pulse on the clipboard at the end of her bed. I wonder how they measure illness at the General – how sick you have to be to get a room with a view. Did Mum get a private room down the Hopkin Wynne when she went post-natal nuts? Maybe she and Kit were neighbours, chatting like they do now after group therapy, when they fix the jigsaw of what's known as their subconscious over cheap red wine.

'Relative or friend?' the other nurse asks as she rearranges Mrs Curtis's pillows.

'Friend,' I say, and then correct myself: 'Well, friend-ish.'

'She may not recognize you at all, and even if she does, you won't be able to understand her speech. Her stroke was very severe,' she says. And with that, they're off.

Gregory paces in front of the window. 'They built this place to last,' he says, more to the plastic pot plant on the windowsill than to me.

'I guess there'll always be sick and dying people,' I say.

'You're philosophical for your age. What are you? Thirteen?'

'Nearly,' I say.

Orange tan makes people look older than they probably are, and also vaguely nuclear: so says Derek.

'Guess you're about thirty-eight?' I say.

'You're good!' Gregory says.

He pats the chair next to his and I take a seat next to Mrs Curtis's shrivelled body.

'What do you want to be when you grow up, then, Harper?'

211

'Wish I knew,' I say. 'Derek – he's my best friend next door, he's sixteen – he's known all his life that he wants to be a hairdresser.'

'Reputable career.'

'Mum thinks I should be a writer on account of my using my *Chambers* dictionary as a pillow.'

Gregory laughs.

I change tactics. 'So, what do you have to do to get ECT round here, then?' I once tried to get a shock by touching an electric fence around the pony enclosure in Hardingstone; all I got was a warm feeling in my hand.

'Don't think they use that for strokes,' Gregory says.

I take Mrs Curtis's hand and stroke it gently. It's only then that I become a human SodaStream. Gregory finds some blue tissue paper for me to mop up my tears while I sit there holding her hand. It won't be the same visiting Dad and not being able to pop next door to eat lemon curd straight from the jar or listen to a scratched Italian LP. Hell, I'd even eat her gooseberry jam if you paid me. She's my *in loco grandparentis*; the only grandparent I have left still living tempts skin cancer on a much hotter island on the other side of the world.

'There, there,' Gregory says, taking a clump of wet blue tissue from me.

'My mum's mad,' I sniffle once I've managed to come up for air long enough to get a whole sentence out.

'So's mine,' Gregory says. 'Only now she's mad *and* a cabbage.'

'You don't seem to like your mum so much.'

'Perceptive and philosophical,' Gregory says. 'She's a homophobe,' he says. 'Which is unfortunate when her only son comes out as gay.'

'Weren't you married?'

'I was. But not just to the wrong woman, to a person of the wrong gender,' he says. 'It was your mum who encouraged me to up sticks and start afresh in London. I owe her my life.'

thirty-six

▼▼▼▼▼

The Spoon in the Moon on Greytown Road is famous for serving under-eighteens. Derek's is a pint of snakebite and black while I stick to cherryade and a packet of Space Invaders; even with what's left of my hair in a pineapple up-do, there's no escaping the fact that I'm not yet a teenager.

Derek had the brainwave of writing to private caller Ryan via the *Gazette* PO Box to arrange the blind date, which solved the problem of how I was going to sound thirty-two on the telephone. Thank my lucky cartridge pen, Derek can do calligraphy, and he wrote a dead neat letter. He said that Mum would be wearing a red flower in her hair, so both Derek and I have tucked a carnation behind our ears. Next door, in the no-kids-allowed-lounge, a man is shouting out questions over rowdy chat; people taking part in the pub quiz spill into the bar where Derek and I are sitting, ready with our own questions.

'Music and film round! Pens at the ready! Question one: who was top to toe in tail lights last winter?'

Thick cigarette smoke cyclones above a team of four orange-skinned women with crimped hair sitting in the bay window.

I glance down at my own list of questions. My first one is: *How much did you earn last year, after tax?* I turn to Derek, 'Do you think that's too direct to start with?'

'You want to be able to buy the house, don't you?'

I glance up at the clock above the bar. Ryan's due any minute. On the cuckoo nose of seven o'clock, a man wearing green corduroy trousers and a matching jacket enters.

The heads of the fake-tan team pop up like burnt crumpets in a toaster but sink back down when he throws them a nervous smile; looking at his hair as he comes closer to us now, I can see why. I thought Derek's dependency on hair product was a matter of concern, but Ryan's hair is that slick it's dripping in product. It throws me off my act of being a thirty-two-year-old chain-smoking single mum with a yoga habit and a mortgage deposit to find pronto. Thankfully, Derek spots I'm distracted and he begins the script we've written.

'Ryan. Pleased to meet you. I'm afraid Mary can't make it tonight, but she's sent us in her place.'

'...' Ryan's eyebrows take off to find a new home under his greasy centre parting.

'I'm Harper,' I say, finding my voice now, looking directly at Ryan's chickenpox scar in between his eyebrows, which have landed again.

'Well...' Ryan says, his corduroy jacket half-on and half-off as if he can't decide whether to bolt or buy a round. 'Are you named after anyone in particular? Harper: it's not a common name.'

'I'm named after the author of a novel Mum read the blurb of when she was pregnant with me,' I say.

215

'*To Kill a Mockingbird*,' Ryan says, taking off his coat. 'Harper Lee.'

'I know,' Derek says, coming over all dead intelligent, 'As in: "It's not over until the fat mockingbird sings."'

I don't give Ryan a chance to reply. 'Have you read *Nineteen Eighty-Four*?' I ask. 'Or *Forever*?'

'Yes. And no,' Ryan says, sitting down opposite me. 'Those are grown-up books for someone so young...'

Don't you start, I think, but I give him what Kit calls the benefit of the doubt, and allow him one last shot.

'I'm afraid we've spent our pocket money on this round.' I glance at our empties.

'I'll get it,' Ryan says. 'Another snakebite and half of cherryade?'

While Ryan's at the bar Derek leans across the sticky table and hisses, '*That's not a hair-do, that's a hair-don't.*'

I ignore him, and watch Ryan as he takes out his wallet from his back pocket; it looks pretty fat. I'm not sure what kind of wage English teachers get, but it might be better than Kit's commission off chocolate. Plus, teachers get long holidays and maybe Ryan would be able to coach Mum through her OU course and even help me get a GCSE or two. So far, the scorecard is looking pretty healthy: *Brains: 10; Looks: 3.*

Next door, the quizmaster is asking who the 'young man in the twenty-second row' is. I've no idea what the answer is; however, the other evening, over Quorn spag bol, Mum said having an Emotional Quotient is more important than an Intellectual one and that my EQ was probably the best in the world. She said that I had a good instinct, that it would serve me well in life. I'll have to trust that she's right when I'm trying to decide later this evening which man to give the golden ticket to a snorkelling holiday in Majorca, I think, as I clutch my pink purse close to my chest. It might well be empty now, but perhaps one day people will think that EQ is more important than IQ and I'll get a good job and be on more than five grand per annum for typing and taking tea orders.

'Penny for them?' Derek says.

'They're worth a pound,' I bullet back.

Ryan's clutching the three glasses together as he weaves between the tables back to where we're sitting. I tune into my inner Cilla and flick through the Rolodex of questions Derek and I have rehearsed.

'Cheers,' I say. 'So, your wallet's pretty fat...'

I've pedalled the gerbil wheel of broken dreams for long enough to know when my luck is changing. And that evening, I leave the Spoon in the Moon a pint of cherryade heavier and with the sinking feeling that Ryan isn't quite right. While he was nice and clearly has plenty of tenners, I'm not sure that he has enough pizzazz for Mum; he may well be able to quote Shakespearean sonnets and lines from plays by Harold Pinter, but I wasn't, well, *dazzled*.

Derek and I make our way back through the council estate to Kendal Road.

'You've got to stay positive,' Derek says.

I kick an empty can of drink into the gutter.

'It's not like you to lose hope,' he continues.

'Maybe I should give up,' I say. 'Maybe Mum is better off alone.'

Derek squares up to me, puts a hand on each of my shoulders.

'If I gave up on my dreams and decided that I'd spend the rest of my life in this backwater doing purple rinses for the over six-ties, what would you say?'

'That you should make like Vidal Sassoon: cut and run.'

'Exactly! And you'll find your Vidal Sassoon if you keep looking.'

'Is that one of your mum's pointless positive affirmations?' I ask.

'What? No!' Derek laughs.

'You should write a book of them. You'd probably make a fortune.'

'There you go, see,' Derek says. 'You're thinking like a winner again.'

'*Thinking like a winner?*'

'Now, that one is actually tattooed to my mum's eyeballs. But seriously, Harper: things will get better. I promise.'

And although things get worse before they get better, things do improve.

thirty-seven

▼▼▼▼▼

A book I got from Dad for my twelfth birthday, *How Things Are Built*, says Birmingham's Gravelly Hill interchange became better known as Spaghetti Junction on account of how complicated the pattern of tarmac is when you see it from a bird's-eye view. If I could float above our lounge the next day, I would say it looks like a pile-up on Spaghetti Junction. A pile-up where my mum's past, present and future come together in a head-on collision.

I chance upon Gregory in Mr Power's corner shop where I'm taking a pit stop for a packet of sherbet Dip Dabs between doing a CND leaflet drop within a two-mile radius of our house. Gregory's buying a dusty box of Milk Tray when I spot him at the counter.

'Great to see you again!' he says. 'Actually, these are for your mum,' he says, of the chocolates. 'I was on my way over now; I asked your dad where you live.'

I'm not sure how Mum is going to react to Gregory rocking up on the doorstep, but I guess that if it really is true that she encouraged Gregory to pull a Dick Whittington, then she'll be pleased to see how it has all worked out so well for him in the Oval.

What I don't account for is that she'll already have visitors.

I press the doorbell, which plays its tinny version of 'Für Elise'.

As he approaches, I make out Derek's outline through the glass in the front door and – for a moment – think we've called on the wrong house.

'All right?' he says brightly as he opens the door, but then he pulls it to behind him and as he comes down the pebbledash steps the white moon of his face clouds over.

'We've got a bit of a situation, Harper,' he says.

'Hello,' Gregory says to Derek. 'Pleased to meet you.'

'Derek, this is Gregory.' I struggle to find the right words to introduce him: 'He's my mum's ex-next-door-neighbour's son?'

'Not your mum's only ex round here, then,' Derek says.

I frown.

'First of all that English teacher, Ryan, arrived about half an hour ago. I saw him pull up in his car, and I pegged it across the road to explain to your mum before he could get in first. I knew she was in because my mum came round earlier with one of her pans of cabbage soup. While I was explaining, the doorbell rang and it wasn't just Ryan at the door. Mary's bank-manager ex was standing there too with some urgent form for her to fill in.'

'How did she react to the Lonely Hearts ad?' I ask.

'She said it was spot on, actually.'

'Is Kit in?'

'He's doing a cancerous commentary.'

I turn to Gregory; rather than offering to come back later, he says he's in for some light entertainment, so we file into the house.

Mum doesn't glance up as we go in, and she certainly doesn't notice Gregory sneak in with me; she's too involved in playing umpire between Ryan and Mike Hyde as they sit at her desk and match-make. She looks like she's either been at her blusher or the red wine. Kit's horizontal on the HP sofa, nursing his morphine pack.

'Welcome to Wimbledon,' he says, perching up on one elbow and swinging his legs round to make room for us. 'Come and take your front-row seats.' Gregory sits down in between Kit and Derek, while I sit cross-legged on the floor.

At the dining-room table, Ryan has unearthed Mum's OU coursebook which had been calcifying under several strata of unopened novels, and he's asking Mum which Shakespeare play she is studying. Mike is excavating the contents of the brown envelopes, many of them now written in red ink.

'Haven't got on to Wills, yet,' Mum says.

'Shall I compare thee to a summer's day...?' Ryan says.

'Fifteen–love,' whispers Kit.

Mike Hyde says something about interest rates reaching 20 per cent if things follow the trajectory they're heading in. 'It'll be eye-watering,' he says, bedoomed.

'Where's Oona?' I whisper to Kit.

'Mixing gin.'

'Is that a tasselled jacket I see before me?' Gregory hisses, nodding in the direction of Mike Hyde.

Derek nods.

'Trumps the V-neck, who could do with a complete hair re-style,' Gregory replies.

'Fifteen all,' Kit grins, as he presses for pain relief.

'You had forty-five days to move out or buy this house, according to this letter,' Mike says, reading one of the letters, which had been screaming *URGENT* on Mum's desk for some time.

'Which letter?' Mum asks, snatching it out of his hands.

'One from the estate agency. But, given that it was sent a fort-night ago...' he continues while reaching for the tiny diary which sucks fun out of everything that he says and does, '...by my cal-culations, you'll be evicted four weeks from today.'

'The weasel!' Mum shrieks, snatching the letter. Just then, Oona comes in carrying a tray with a jug of gin and tonic, glasses and a plate of bourbon biscuits. 'Half time!' she announces.

Mum gets up to pour herself a half pint of gin and tonic; it's while she's knocking it back that she notices that Gregory and I are sitting there.

'Greg?' she says, coming over. 'Bloody hell, you look different.'

'That'll be the Calvin Klein,' Gregory says.

'Who were those two losers?' Gregory asks Mum, once Mike and Ryan have made their excuses and near as damn it made splin-tered glass of the front door.

'Courtiers,' Oona says, sipping gin. 'Wooing a fair maiden.'

'And what's all this about being evicted?'

Kit explains, 'Mary's screwed if she can't buy the house. We were going to marry so that she could actually get a mortgage certified. But I don't think she fancies marrying a corpse.'

A centre-court hush washes over the lounge.

'My divorce papers came through a few years ago, Mary.' Greg-ory serves an ace-winning line.

Oona, of course, is the person bold enough to ask the question that's on all our minds. 'What are you getting at?'

'If you need to marry someone, you could marry me.'

'But have you got a dowry?' Oona asks, topping up her gin.

'Bloody hell, are we in a Brontë novel or something?' Kit guffaws into his green tea.

'If it weren't for Mary,' Gregory says, 'I'd still be in some dead-end village batting first in the order, scrutinizing profit-and-loss sheets and living a lie.'

'What do you do now, then?' Oona asks.

'He's a stylist,' I say.

'Hair stylist?' Derek pricks up.

'Not quite. I earn about ten times as much as one of those.'

'Bloody hell,' Kit says.

'You're repeating yourself,' I say.

'Somebody's got to yuppify the interiors of suburban houses for a living.'

'If you get married,' Derek says to Mum. 'Can I do your hair?'

This wedding sounds more like a bank transaction than a proposal. If I'm supposed to be baking the wedding cake, it's going to have a Monopoly board iced on top of it. Seems Mum has just pulled the pink card out of the community chest that takes her directly past *Go!* pocketing a fat Mike Hyde profit and a house on Kendal Road dead end, no leather jacket tassels attached.

thirty-eight

▼▼▼▼▼

I have the brainwave to open the box of Grecian 2000. Ten minutes before Mr Slippery is due on the day of the viewings, I anti-dust the bookshelves by sprinkling muesli on them and then empty the contents of the vacuum cleaner bag back on to the floor. It's while I'm doing this that I spot the hair dye on the coffin-shelf. Careful to wear the disposable gloves, I upend the bottle into the kitchen sink. An acidic smell drives me back, but not before I manage to add what's close at hand – half a bottle of malt vinegar, the contents of a green bottle marked 'toxic' from underneath the sink and some leftover spaghetti from the night before.

In the lounge, I let Bangers and Mash out of their cages to leave small gerbil-sized poo presents on the carpet. If they never come back, I won't be upset; I'd rather spend my pocket money on a subscription to the *Socialist Worker* magazine than on sawdust and sunflower seeds. I've also gone off the idea of getting a cat. In fact, I'm plotting to sneak all the leather and suede products out of the house and take them to the charity shop.

If you become a vegan, you refuse to eat, drink, or even wear animal product. And having a pet gets a big thumbs-down. So that would mean no more patent leather Mary Janes from Gordon Benét's – instead I'd be in jelly shoes. But, I wouldn't be able to actually *eat* jelly because it contains the ground-up bones of animals. And ice-cream would be banned, for sure. Wine is known to contain fish scales, and Bovril's made of beef.

As I list the food items that contain animal product on our way to the High Street once we've left the house in chaos, Mum occasionally says '*Really?*' but I feel like she's tuning out of my airwaves.

We've left Kit in the Zedbed upstairs where he says he'll look morbid. Before leaving Kendal Road, we also called on Derek and asked him if he'd play his Adam Ant LPs at top-decibel level.

The humming engine and exploding exhaust of Mr Slippery's scraping-tarmac sports car echoes against the concrete council block we're walking past.

'What an utter plonker,' Mum says.

Mum wanted me to have an extra Dad weekend this weekend, but Dad's gone on his Lone Rangers holiday to Skegness, dragging Patrick along with him. As a result, I get to go along to Mum's first date with her husband-to-be – as of yesterday – over lunch at the Harvester, the most sophisticated restaurant in Blackbrake.

We're fifteen minutes early, which gives me plenty of time to dissect the menu for animal protein. Turns out, if you want to go vegan and eat out, then your options are pretty much limited to: salad (but without the thousand-island dressing or bacon bits) pizza (minus the cheese); chips (checking first they're not deep fried in animal fat); a butter-less jacket potato and baked beans – or a bowl of beans. Being that I've already squeezed a life's worth of baked beans into twelve and three-quarter years, becoming a vegan isn't looking quite so likely – at least not today – so when the waitress comes over I order a Harvester brunch but without the sausages and bacon. I also ask for the fried egg to be as cooked as possible because then at least it's as far away as possible from being a potential hen.

Mum asks for a strong, white filter coffee with three and a half sugars; she's too nervous to eat.

I watch her closely as she chain-lights a cigarette. She sucks on the orange filter as if it's her only oxygen in an airless room. Then she brushes back her blonde fringe and casts her steel-blue eyes over her red nails which Oona touched up last night. No amount of war paint can hide the fact that Mum has been fighting a losing battle these past few months: her skin, usually as smooth as a Wedgwood glaze, is patchy and dry with a new map of tiny red veins trickling across her cheeks. Not even Avon concealer can hide the dark circles under her eyes which are as brown as a spool of camera film. She runs her forefingers under them, as if she could wipe away the tiredness.

'Harper, I just want you to know that I try my best.'

She gets up before I can reply to go to the loo and comes back with a new coat of make-up. I wolf down my brunch and bolt before Gregory arrives: I may like preserving gooseberries, but I don't actually want to be one. Mum just tells me not to go home until teatime so I don't disturb Mr Slippery.

When Derek and I were waiting for our lonely heart to arrive down the Spoon and the Moon the other night, there was a quiz round on famous last words. According to the quizmaster, L. Frank Baum who wrote *The Wonderful Wizard of Oz*, said on his deathbed, 'Now we can cross the shifting sands.' It got me thinking about our first and final words. According to Mum, my first words were 'Daddy's Noo-ars', which was my way of asking to sit on Dad's shoulders. I guess from up there I could see things better, look directly into grown-ups' eyes.

That afternoon, I visit Blackbrake's very own magical Land of Oz: the public library. It's on the shelves there that I find my equivalent of Dorothy's sparkling red slippers: *Nineteen Eighty-Four* by George Orwell. The book has been well-read, and some naughty borrower has underlined sections in pencil and scribbled notes in the margins alongside parts which are, apparently, '*Ironic!*'

None other than Hopkin Wynne's statue is on a raised plinth overlooking the reception desk where I check it out. I'm not allowed to take out adult fiction on my library card, but I lifted Mum's card from the credit-card section of her wallet while she was in the ladies' applying her war paint. I fib to the librarian, and tell her Mum's waiting with the car running outside and that she's asked me to pop in to get the Orwell out for her OU reading list.

'OK, pet,' she says. 'Good on your mum for doing some life-long learning.' Seems this librarian isn't missing the sympathy gene.

I try my luck. 'Can I check the status of my Judy Blume reservation while I'm at it, please?'

She flicks, with some difficulty owing to her nail extensions, through the red file of index cards on which reserved books are stored. Eventually, she pulls the set of cards for *Blume, Judy*.

'Which book is it, m'duck?

I lean over the counter. '*Forever*,' I whisper.

'Your name?'

'Harper May Richardson,' I say.

'It was returned this morning, but went straight back out again. You're next but one. You'll have it by the end of August,' she says, shuffling the index cards back together.

I find myself a cosy seat in the sandstone alcove of the church in the centre of town and read *Nineteen Eighty-Four* from cover to cover that afternoon. A lot of it is beyond me, especially the political parts, but that doesn't mean that I don't feel something when I read it. And what I feel is despair, but also hope.

Despair because George Orwell apparently wrote the book in the mirror year of 1948 and a lot of what he describes has come true. Just think of the plain-clothed policemen! And the Dalek-like security camera which follows you around the singles section in Boots the Chemist. Not to mention the television sets that have crept into every front room blasting out advertisements selling people products they don't need.

But I also feel hope because it wasn't as bad as Orwell thought it would be in 1984. After all, 1984 was the year that Torvill and Dean Bolero'd their way to the gold medal in the Winter Olympics by playing dead fishes on an ice rink floor in purple floaty costumes. In Orwell's 1984, art, history, news: everything is censored. Not so in Sarajevo. That winter, ice skaters were allowed to dance without Big Brother censoring the sport or a bomb falling unannounced from the sky. In Blackbrake, claxons blare at midday to signal lunch hour down the shoe factory, not to warn of nuclear attack. Cats here have four legs, not seven.

There is still one thing, though, that not even my mum, the law, or a belief in the healing properties of green tea can protect you against, and that's dying. Next time I visit the library, I'll check if there is a book about the facts of death. And if there isn't, then I've spotted a definite gap in the market and I'll write it myself under my new pen name: Harper O'Croaks.

thirty-nine

▼▼▼▼▼

The viewings of thirteen Kendal Road were as successful as my mum's attempts at cooking with an avocado: she once tried baking the green flesh in a crumble and serving it with custard. Ever since the failed viewings, Mr Slippery has been on the answering machine leaving messages for Mum which should be bleeped over they contain that many swearwords. Meanwhile, Mike Hyde has been hand-delivering the application forms for Gregory and Mum to fill in for their mortgage. It doesn't take an IQ of over 150 to spot that Mike Hyde has still got the hots for Mum. Gregory has been trying to persuade Mum to go on a date with the walking pound sign. I reckon he's as interesting as watching cricket-match score updates on Teletext; Mum couldn't agree more.

It takes a bit of double-think to get your head around Gregory marrying Mum when he's only interested in men. Luckily, council officials don't appear to be bothered about this. The Blackbrake Council Offices for the Registration of Births, Deaths and Marriages is where Mum and Gregory will be brought together for something only half-holy but totally legal. And there's a bonus prize in Mum choosing the register office: Joanna recently won the PR contract for the county council. She not only did a deal for the wedding venue – Mum and Gregory have the annexe at 50 per cent off for the after-party, all inclusive – but the council have also fast-tracked their marriage licence.

When Mum announces the plan to Kit, he stares into his green tea and says, 'Maybe you'll be there to register two things in as many months.'

The morning of the wedding, Derek spends an hour backcombing Mum's bouffant. I swear, if anyone lit a cigarette, the lounge would go up in a flaming ball of Elnett. But seeing as Mum's wearing a coat of lip gloss which she doesn't want to spoil, she's not smoking. Instead, she sips gin and tonic through one of the prototype toys she's written about: an orange straw which you wear like glasses; the gin double-helixes around her eyes. In between sips, she says that it was her favourite gadget to write the copy for, and practise using.

I've dug out the envelope where Mum and Kit wrote the agenda for the Mark One wedding, plus Mum's reporter's notebook with the minutes. Since that meeting, a few more lists have spawned under headings such as 'Calorie Intake', 'Premium Bonds: Profit and Loss', and 'Electricity Meter Readings'. Under 'Sun Salutations' she's also chalked up the number she's done as a prisoner would days he's been locked up: with four lines slashed through with a horizontal one, like badly made prison bars.

While Mum's hair is being stiffened into the shape of what I can only describe as a cathedral nave, I remind her that we need to discuss points 8.ii and 8.iii: what my surname will become, and what happens in case of divorce.

'Harper May Richardson-Curtis doesn't sound too bad,' she says.

'HMRC would be my initials...'

'Her Majesty's Revenue and Customs?' Kit guffaws into his third brew. 'Your man Mike Hyde would approve.'

Mum's hair is finished now. Derek stands back – I'm not sure whether this is to avoid the chemical mist or to admire his combustible hair sculpture. Talking about revenue reminds me that we still have to bulk-buy some Panda Pops.

'Yes, yes...' Mum says, when I ask her for some cash. She seems distracted as she gives me some coins from her purse, then she asks after the wedding cake.

'I haven't forgotten, Mum,' I say. 'It's keeping the fridge company.'

'Well done, Harper,' she says, and sucks at her alcoholic glasses.

As I'm leaving the room to get changed, I turn to Mum and ask, 'What *will* happen when you get divorced?'

'We've both signed a pre-nup. It's over there.' Mum nods her solid noggin towards the top shelf of the coffin. In between the lemon jelly and a tin of anchovies is an envelope on to which someone, probably Kit, has scrawled, 'Legal Procedures in case of Death, Divorce or Derangement'.

As all three of those things are likely to happen within the next few months, I'm glad Mum's made it legal.

Mrs Pope chaperones Cassie round to my house that morning; Cassie's dressed in what I suspect is a Laura Ashley hand-me-down from her privatized sister. She rolls her eyes at me as her mum hands over a Tupperware box.

'Melting moments,' Mrs Pope says. 'It's a Delia recipe. I've never tried it before.'

Cassie comes indoors and heads through to the lounge. Mrs Pope cranes to see past me, her eyes narrowing behind her X-ray spectacles. I know she wants to be invited in, but this would melt my mum's moment altogether. Laughter floods down the corridor towards us.

'How is Christopher doing?' she asks.

'So-so.'

'Will he get down the aisle all right?' she asks.

'There won't be any aisle,' I say.

'Register office?' she X-rays.

I nod. 'And Mum's not marrying Kit, she's marrying Gregory.'

Mrs Pope frowns. 'Gregory?'

'He's Mum's ex-next-door-neighbour's son. He's thirty-eight and he's gay. He's an interiors stylist. Thanks for the biscuits, Mrs Pope,' I say, then I push the glass door closed in her shocked face. Mrs Pope's mouth is frozen in the shape of an O, like Mum's when she puffs out halos of cigarette smoke.

In the lounge, Oona is untying the paisley sash at Cassie's back. 'Looks like it might have a corset,' she says.

'Have you got some clothes I can borrow, H?' Cassie exhales as she clasps the undone dress to her chest.

Thank her lucky heated car seats, my matching pair of pastel-pink trousers are just back from their weekly visit to the Full Cycle.

'Don't worry, Cassie!' Mum shouts as we climb the stairs to my bedroom. 'All public offices have to have fire extinguishers by law!'

*

To crucify the time before we have to leave for the register office, Cassie and I visit Mr Power's shop where we liquidate my assets into penny sweets. We park our flammable bottoms on the broken wall opposite the corner shop.

'I'm sitting the entrance exam at the Blackbrake School for Girls over the summer holidays...' Cassie's sentence fades out like a felt tip that's run out of ink.

'*What?*' I spit out my cola Frostie. Cassie swore on Madonna's grave that she'd never go dry-clean only. 'I hope you're too thick to get in.'

'So do I,' Cassie says, winding a strawberry bootlace around her fingers. 'Lisa has to wear tracksuit bottoms *and* a pleated skirt to play netball.'

I don't think it's just IQ that they measure at private schools; I reckon it also depends on whether your mum's bank statements are printed in red or black ink – though sometimes if the ink's red, but you're dead intelligent, then you can still get in on a charity stamp. If it's just intelligence that they meter, I think the chance of Cassie getting in to Blackbrake School for Girls will be as slim as a French woman on a lettuce-only diet. Although in some private schools, it helps if you do extra-curricular activities like twizzling batons or being able to do a perfect back flip. I don't think knowing about tampon application counts.

forty

▼▼▼▼▼

It's one thing having Hopkin Wynne's marble eyes peering over your shoulder down the library as you flick through Judy Blumes to get to the thumb-greasy best bits, but it's another thing having his portrait peering over us down the register office. His eyes follow us around the room as if the loony poet is checking out just how mad the marriage is, while the registrar ties the knot between Mum and Gregory. A knot just tight enough that it can be loosened as soon as they've bought a terraced house together.

In between vows, Mum's boss Joanna fields calls in the atrium from her mobile telephone briefcase. Designer Spike sits on the back row smoking a cigarette through his fringe, next to Melanie who's on her double-glazing lunch break. Kit, who's sitting in a wheelchair next to me, injects himself with more and more drugs throughout the ceremony. By the time the registrar presses play on the cassette tape of classical music to signal the end of the demi-semi-religious bit, Kit's out cold. Not even the whiff of warm food wakes him up as I wheel him into the glass annexe.

Cassie and I take up goal-attack positions next to the melon balls as soon as the cling film is unwrapped. There are also bowls of some brown shrivelled food product – I'm not sure if it's cold cocktail sausages or dried dates, but either way, I steer clear of those along with the garlic chicken kievs.

As a waitress stirs a bowl of prawns in Marie Rose sauce, I ask her if there are any Quorn alternatives.

'I didn't realize this was a Quaker booking!' she says.

'Oh, God, I'm not religious or anything. Just vegan,' I explain.

'She only goes to church when the Brownies let her hold the flagpole,' Cassie says, to back me up.

'Vegan?' the waitress says, her eyes quizzing me as if I'm straight out of Star Trek. 'Try the vol-au-vents?' she suggests.

Cassie and I head over to the other side of the glass annexe with the plate of mushroom vol-au-vents, where Derek is plucking his pointy eyebrows with a pair of tweezers, using a silver wine cooler as a mirror. Oona stands next to him, filling her glass to the brim with white wine.

'The chicken kiev's still pink,' Derek says.

'So's your over-plucked skin,' Oona says, and then turns to me. 'Did you know, there are only eighty-five calories in a small serving of wine?' she says before knocking half of it back. Changing the subject she asks, 'What did you think of the ceremony, Harper?'

I open my mouth to reply, but no words come out. Nobody has asked me before what I actually *think* about Mum marrying a gay man to get a mortgage. Luckily, I don't have to reply as at that moment, Gregory taps his knife against the fake crystal glasses out of which he's drinking duty-free champagne-alternative.

236

'Ladies and gentlemen, it is time to cut the cake. Lights, please!'

Somebody dims the lights while Derek draws the burgundy curtains closed around the annexe; the only light now comes from the sizzling sparklers I bought down It's a Gift, which I've stuck into the top tier of the wedding cake. The three round sponges are propped up in tiers with red Lego bricks. I decorated each round with white icing sugar, which I mixed to be as thick as plaster of Paris. I've also raided the Monopoly box to decorate the top tier; there's a replica of Kendal Road on it made from the red hotels and green houses. Six small pieces from the game also keep a £500 note from the bank in place: the battered boot, wheelbarrow, old-fashioned iron, top hat, destroyer boat and the Scottish terrier.

Oona sets to slicing up the rounds. Due to it being vegan and made with powdered egg substitute, grated carrot, sultanas, sugar, flour and sunflower oil, the cake rather crumbles to the touch. Cassie and I scoop up our portions on to a plate and head out through the annexe to the small garden.

'What presents are your mum and Gregory getting, then?' Cassie asks, then sprinkles cake into her mouth.

'I'd guess another paua shell product from Grandma Kiwi, cut-glass carafes for whisky Mum doesn't like and a vegetable steamer, probably from Oona. Weddings are for dummies, Cassie. I'm going to go to university instead of getting married.'

'What'll you study?'

'English Literature. You?'

'I don't know whether I'll go to university. But I definitely don't want to sell Tupperware or make-up for a living.'

Derek comes out on to the veranda. 'Cassie, Harper, we've just had some bad news.'

'Yazz and the Plastic Population are still at number one?' I say.

'Your mum's officially a size twenty?' Cassie takes a punt.

'Mrs Curtis has had a heart attack. She's dead, Harper.'

forty-one

▼▼▼▼▼

Mrs Curtis's funeral is scheduled for Saturday 6 August. On the family calendar, that Saturday is coloured in blue highlighter. It's a D-day. I suggest to Mum that I should bunk off school the day before so I can go to Hardingstone early to help Dad get things ready; he has offered to hold the wake in Ivy Cottage.

Dad spills the out-of-date beans about his Lone Rangers weekend on the drive back to Hardingstone. 'Patrick has met someone.'

'Really?'

'She calls the numbers at the bingo in Skegness. Legs eleven, you know.'

'Legs eleven?'

'He's closing up shop. Moving there,' Dad says as he pulls up outside Ivy Cottage.

'Ah, Dad, I'm sorry,' I say, and I really mean it; I know he'll miss Patrick. Now the heat really is on to get Patrick to help me see what's on the film reel before he disappears.

'I'm quite OK about it.'

While Dad seems to be looking on the sunny side of life, I summon up the courage to tell him that Mum has got hitched.

'She's married Gregory, Mrs Curtis's son,' I say. Dad takes his glasses off to look at me square-on, but I keep my gaze on my reflection in the car wing-mirror.

'Well I never! It's all change, isn't it?'

'I suppose so.' I glance at Dad to see how he's taking it. Now he's polishing his glasses with his shirtsleeve. When he puts his spectacles back on, he strains his eyes at the straight road ahead as if it hurts to see the world.

'Are you upset?' I ask.

'No, no, not at all. In fact, I've got more good news. I've been rather inspired by Patrick. And now by your mum...'

Please God, don't say he's going out with Louise again, I think.

'...I've been made redundant.'

'I'm sorry,' I say, but Dad is smiling.

'I was going to leave my job at the end of the summer anyway, to go travelling. I've got to get my mojo back, Harper.'

'They sell those down the newsagents'—'

'I've been hanging around since your mum left me,' Dad interrupts. 'Waiting for her to have a change of heart.'

'Dad, I know about Mum. That she went to the Hopkin Wynne when I was little. That you took care of me for those months while she was away.'

Dad's chat is single-track; he doesn't tune into what I'm saying. He carries on, 'She's always been unconventional, Harper. It's my time to do something different, too. I'm going to rent out this cottage and see the world.' Dad gestures towards his overgrown front garden as if Tutankhamun might be buried under the weedy flowerbeds.

240

'That's radical, Dad.'

'Radical? Yes, I suppose it is unusual.'

'Don't take things so *literal*, Dad. I mean it's cool! Will you send me a postcard?'

'Of course. That reminds me.' Dad reaches into his black jacket pocket. 'A letter arrived for you last week via the Lone Rangers fundraising committee.'

I snatch it out of his hand faster than you can say 'one-way ticket' and peg it inside. Up in my room, I dive under the covers and tear the letter open. It's written on the back of a Scrabble score sheet:

Dolgellau Police Station

Middle of a Mountainside

Snowdonia

Wales

Saturday 30 July, 1988

Hey daydreamer,

I'm waiting to be interviewed about taking part in a protest Atom organized. We were at the gates of a nuclear-powered energy station at Trawsfynydd. While I'm waiting, I've been playing Scrabble in Welsh with a lad called Twm. The scores are astronomical!

Do you fancy catching a film down the Optimum in Blackbrake with me sometime? I'm on Coventry 76921.

Craig x

He hasn't forgotten about me! I kiss the letter back, fold it up and think about what I should wear to my first ever date. If I ask Derek for compensation out of his Headlines wages on account of losing Mash I might be able to scrape together enough for a shell suit. Now that would make me look *super* radical.

That evening, Patrick arrives with a four-pack of Blackbrake lager to share with Dad. Luckily for me, Dad's out buying Friday night Reduced for Quick Sale goods to share at the wake. Since swapping the dark room for Skegness, the CMYK reference for Patrick's skin is heavier on the magenta than yellow. Fact is, he's glowing.

'Dad'll be back in a bit,' I say. 'Do come in.'

'Thanks, Harper, I can't stay long,' he says.

'Actually, there is something I need your help with, Patrick,' I say, closing the door behind me, and then quietly sliding the chain across so that if Dad comes back, I'll hear him struggle to open the door.

'Oh yes?' he says, setting down the cans on the table.

'I found this Super 8 reel of film in my nursery,' I say.

'This sounds like a game of Cluedo!' Patrick laughs. 'It was me! In the nursery! With the film reel!'

'Patrick, this is deadly serious,' I say. 'Have you got a projector in your hearse that would be able to show it?'

'I might have. There's all kinds of junk in there.'

'Please go and look.'

Patrick, who stares at me warily as he walks backwards to the front door, nearly knocks himself out when he then opens it, on account of the chain being strung across.

'Are you OK if I undo this?' he asks. I nod, and he opens the door.

I twitch the curtains and watch through the window as Patrick rifles through the many cardboard boxes which are strewn across the back seat and then as he searches in the boot. At last he finds a small machine with two large wheels, one higher than the other, where I suppose the spools of film go.

'Do you have a plain white sheet?' he asks as he sets it down on the table. 'We'll need to erect some kind of screen.'

I leg it upstairs and whip the sheet off my bed. I stand on the dining chairs so I can tie it to the hooks that are still hammered into the black beams; they're left over from the olden days when people used to hang and cure ham indoors.

'I haven't seen one of these for years,' Patrick says of the reel. 'It doesn't look like this one's got a magnetic soundtrack.' He loops the film around the two small wheels.

I tug the curtains tight and close the door into the kitchen so that we're thrown into darkness. A single shot of white light pierces out from the projector on to the bed sheet, picking up all the dust which whirlpools around the room. A fan starts to whirr.

The image is flickering and fuzzy to begin with until Patrick fiddles with the focus so that Hardingstone church spire, before its wonkiness was corrected, comes into view, then we swing down from the steeple to the gravelly path. Next we pan over the many gravestones. I catch a glimpse of Heaven Called a Little Child's, just as weather-beaten as it is now. A cluster of people are standing at the door to the church in the far distance. The camera moves towards them, and I spot Dad's bushy beard; he's wringing his hands and checking his watch beneath the long sleeves of his smartest suit.

'Jesus Christ! It's your dad's wedding!' Patrick says, and he starts to fumble with the projector to make it stop.

'*Don't*,' I say, shooting him a look as sharp as an arrow.

Patrick eases himself back down on to the dining-room chair, as if into a paddling pool of freezing cold water.

Next we cut to the visitors all waiting inside the church, heads down, reading the orders of service. Cut again to the guests milling around and talking, Dad at the altar with his back to the camera staring up towards Jesus on his crucifix.

'Your mum was an hour late,' Patrick says. 'But your dad refused to give up waiting.'

Next, we're outside and the camera is pointed directly towards the sun so that when Mum's silhouette comes into view, it's as if she's walking straight out of heaven. Her image jumps closer towards the screen as the old film warps. She's a Russian doll, getting larger and larger. Once she is in full view I can see her floor-length dress, if dress is the word: it looks more like a large sheet with a hole in the neck that gathers around her chest and then triangles downwards from there without touching her body again.

'I never knew she used to be so *fat*!' I say.

'She wasn't fat. She was pregnant.' It's Dad, who has crept in the front door. I forgot to chain it again after Patrick fetched the projector.

'But I wasn't born until three years after you got married,' I say, turning to him. 'I'm not really fifteen am I?'

Dad shakes his head.

'I don't understand.'

'She was pregnant with your sister, Sylvia,' Dad says.

'Sister? Where is she?' I look around, as if she might be lurking in the lounge, about to introduce herself.

'She was stillborn.'

244

Sylvia. My big sister. The sibling who would've halved the weight of my jar of unanswered questions.

The projector starts to overheat and the film churns up between the two spools. Patrick busies himself with stopping the projector from chewing up the film any more. Dad wrenches the curtains open.

Numb, I climb the stairs up to my bedroom.

I take *The Almanac of Spooky Happenings* and hold it tight across my chest. I never imagined I'd bust a real ghost, let alone a big sister.

Mum must have got pregnant when she was just seventeen.

Dad's already up and dressed in his black suit when I go downstairs the morning of the funeral; I fell asleep fully dressed in my black CND T-shirt and black jeans and on top of my duvet.

'What's for breakfast?' I ask Dad in the kitchen.

'This,' Dad says, handing me a bowl of Twiglets. I take a fistful. It's as if last night never happened.

The church clock tolls half ten. Mrs Curtis's funeral is at half past eleven with the wake an hour later. Dad's not expecting any villagers to come, so it'll probably just be the vicar, me, Patrick, Dad, Mum, Gregory and Kit, if he's well enough. This will be the first time since I quit Hardingstone that our nuclear family will be Sellotaped back together in the village. Only now I know it's always been one family member short.

I head to the church early, scattering the Twiglets on the village green for the birds. As I reach the black gates and walk up the path, I picture Mum walking up the same one just a few years older than me – pregnant, a drop-out, all wide eyes and big heart. A heart big enough to try again, to get pregnant with me, but a mind unable to hold it together. No wonder she got post-natal depression.

I push the church door open into the vault of coldness. One vase of lilies stands by the lectern, their stamens a shocking orange against the pure white petals. The church organist practises some sad sonata. I go up to the lectern and breathe in the fresh scent of the lilies.

Perhaps one day I'll be able to understand who my parents were before I was born. Maybe church isn't a bad place from which to start trying to understand. It's while I'm kneeling on a rock-hard cushion the size of *Chambers* that Mum sneaks in next to me.

'Mind if I join you?' she whispers.

I shake my head.

'Have you found Jesus?' she says.

I shake my head again. 'Not even written in tealeaves or an aubergine,' I whisper back.

'Dad told me that you saw our wedding film...' she says. 'I'm sorry you had to find out that way.'

I return my head to the crux of my hands, fake prayer.

'Is Sylvia buried here?' I ask, wondering if my sister's grave may have been here all this time.

'No, she was cremated,' Mum replies. 'We just scattered her ashes in the wind.'

I take a deep breath.

Mum puts an arm around my cold shoulder.

'I'm surprised they'd have you in here...' I say, out of the side of my mouth.

Mum bursts out into laughter. From a dark church corner, someone tells us to shush.

'...and what was with that dress?' I say.

Mum wraps her arms around me, smothers her giggling in my armpit. I lasso my arms around her.

My mum may be sad sometimes, starting to wrinkle and have a forty-a-day habit. She's been through hell and back, but despite all this she still manages to be the best mum on earth who buys me all the fresh cream cake products I like. And I bloody love her.

Mum spends the funeral service chugging on Silk Cut by the church's compost heap of mown grass. Sitting in between Dad and Gregory, I'm the smoking gunpowder between each end of a spent Christmas cracker: my two dads.

The service is over in just fifteen minutes.

Nobody cries.

There's just one guest that I didn't expect: the travelling librarian who refused me *Forever*. I walk back to Dad's cottage after the burial with Mum and Kit, who she's pushing along in his wheelchair; Kit's batteries are running low on energy today, he says. While the librarian is out of earshot, I tell them both about the episode on the book bus.

'What a numpty,' Mum says as she battles with the wheelchair up the weedy garden path. Gregory is standing by the front door to greet mourners, his eyes behind dark glasses like a pop star camouflaging eye-cysts.

'Another one bites the dust,' Kit says.

'Kit! There's a time and a place for your Freddie Mercuryisms,' Mum says, but Gregory laughs.

Patrick and Dad are already in the kitchen, preparing peach melba. In the lounge, Mum sits next to the librarian in front of a plate of home-made crumpets and Battenberg cake that she brought with her. Kit is stationed alongside the cake products.

'Will you be cremated or buried?' Kit asks the librarian, straight up. I spit out the crumpet I've just nibbled. Mum giggles.

The librarian adjusts her hearing aid, pretends not to hear; it lets out a piercing screech. 'Crumpet, please,' she says.

I quickly lick the one I was eating and pass her mine.

'Thank you,' she says.

Mum smiles sweetly at Kit. 'How about you?' she asks.

'Cremation.'

I offer him the plate of crumpets.

Kit narrows his eyes.

I say: 'Foam with a hint of polyester.'

'Then I shall politely decline,' he says.

If only declining death were as easy.

forty-two

▼▼▼▼▼

When the *Mary Rose* tall ship was salvaged just off the coast of Portsmouth a few years ago, what was left of the wooden frame looked like a cross-section of an enormous rib cage – a rib cage with all the vital organs nibbled and rotten. From the seabed, the divers excavated sailors' skeletons, ancient cannons, oak longbows and tarnished pieces of eight, even the remains of leather shoes with rusting eyelets. All that time, the ship had been aground just a stone's throw from thousands of people but the deep, dark Channel had kept the wreckage secret for centuries.

It's possible to hide who you are beneath depths of pretending, whether you're Gregory faking love for a woman, Kit acting as if he's not scared about dying, or my parents hiding from me that I had a big sister.

I, however, choose not to hide anything. I am not a pretender.

I'd rather, when the time comes for me to reach those pearly turn-stiles, that people back on earth sum me up in their obituaries, cry into their stale crumpets and remember me, *as the person I really was.*

So when Mum says one afternoon soon after Mrs Curtis's funeral that she can afford to send me to Blackbrake School for Girls on account of Gregory's inheritance, some of which he's giving to us, I say that I will sit the entrance exam, but on one condition. My condition is this: if I get in, I'm not going to wear a dry-clean-only coat on the grounds that it's dead expensive to wash and comes from John Lewis, which only posh people shop at. I will wear my acid-washed denim one instead.

I have to break the news to Cassie that I'm crossing the streams too, but I've vowed that I'm not going to go if Cassie doesn't get in as well. I tell her over vegan Chinese food – boiled rice and spring vegetables – with Mrs Pope. If anyone is going to be pleased about me stepping on to the bottom rung of the oily ladder that is privatized education, it will be her.

'Why, Harper, that's marvellous,' she says, then adds, 'You do know that they measure your IQ?'

'Mum has been taping *Mastermind* each week for years in preparation for my entrance exam,' Cassie explains. 'Lisa didn't have to watch it.'

'Lisa didn't need to watch it,' Mrs Pope says. 'Would you like to join Cassie's study group, Harper?' Cassie pleads with her eyes; I'd rather stick chopsticks in mine.

'Thanks, Mrs P, but I've been swotting up down the public library.'

I have discovered that, if you take them one at a time, then the Judy Blume back catalogue can fit quite neatly in between the pages of an encyclopaedia; I find this is the best way to revise the important facts that everyone needs to know, like how to practise snogging on a pillow, shave your armpits or squeeze zits.

Even Mum has caught the study-bug; she just scraped a pass in her first year and her second-year reading list has arrived through the post. Mum vows not to leave things so last minute this time around, and that she'll get ahead with the reading. Mum joins me one day after work at the library and borrows four of the six novels she's supposed to have finished by mid-September. She reads them while soaking in the bath for hours at a time. The electricity bill goes through the roof, but for once we don't have to worry. Worst of all, Mum tapes *Hamlet* over *Annie* when it's shown late one night, before the brassy National Anthem has played and whoever's last up in England makes cocoa then turns off the lights.

A few days after Mrs Curtis's funeral, the GP visits while Kit and I are watching an episode of *Neighbours* over a lunch of triple-decker peanut butter sandwiches.

'How are you, Christopher?' the doctor asks while he straps a blood-pressure monitor around Kit's thin, grey arm.

'Been better,' Kit wheezes, hitching himself up the sofa. He starts to cough; it sounds like a rattling abacus is inside his chest. Once he's stopped, the doctor hands him a device that tests lung capacity.

'Can I have a go on something?' I ask.

'Here,' the GP hands me his metal stethoscope. I put the plastic plugs into my ears and place the cold, metal disc against my chest. I listen to my heart boom in between my ears while Kit breathes out into the plastic tube. The effort drains what little colour was left from Kit's cheeks; he folds back into the sofa, like a book softly closing. I take the stethoscope out of my ears to hear what the doctor is saying.

'...to go on oxygen, I'm afraid.'

'Is it portable?' Kit says, with his eyes closed.

'To a degree, but I'm recommending that you move to hospital to get it around the clock.'

Kit shakes his head. 'I'm not ready to go in yet.'

'They'll also be able to monitor your pain levels better and give you even better pain relief.'

At this, Kit opens his eyes and takes a shallow breath. 'OK,' he whispers.

Kit never owned very much stuff. That afternoon Kit directs me from the sofa and I divide his possessions into two piles in front of him: one for things to take with him, the other for things to give away. He leaves behind a large box of sample chocolate bars, his wigs, and I inherit his ten-year's-service gold fountain pen. There's one item that's too big to pack.

'I'll be back for that,' he says, of the coffin.

'I thought you wanted a home death,' I say, as I fold up his shirts and place them in his half-empty suitcase.

'Just think of it as a little journey I'm going on, kiddo,' he says, then adds, 'a one-way journey. I'm taking *all* that heavy baggage I've been lugging around these past forty-odd years and should have dumped a lot earlier. Luggage you shouldn't bother carrying in life, Harper.' He takes a shallow breath: 'Envy, fear, regret. When I go, all that rubbish will disappear with me. And what good has it done me or anyone around me? Harper, you mustn't fear anything, regret your decisions, envy anyone. These feelings are toxic.' He punches his chest. His breath heaves as if he's just surfaced from being underwater for too long.

'Is that what gave you the cancer?'

'That,' he says, between breaths, 'was because of those.' He

252

points towards a packet of Mum's Silk Cut on the coffee table.

'Aren't you afraid now?' I ask. 'Of dying, I mean.'

'We're all going to die,' Kit says. 'I'm just getting an upgraded, fast-tracked exit.'

To stop myself from crying, I laugh instead at Kit's deathly humour. 'Is there anything I should do?' I ask.

'Read books. Get a good education. Don't self-flagellate. Love deeply. And don't let your mum settle down with a jerk.'

I listen carefully, and chalk these up on my mental blackboard.

That night, I wake up with a start as if from a nightmare. I press my talking alarm clock which says in its electronic voice that it's four a.m. I creep downstairs and fetch our pint of milk from the doorstep. In the kitchen, I pour myself a small glass and sit at the table, leaning back against Freddie.

I down the milk in one.

It's so cold it's as if a knife is slicing down my throat. My eyes sting and I close them to stop the tears from falling. Freddie sighs, as if he can tell how I'm feeling. Before I go back up to bed, I pick up the packet of cigarettes that Mum's left by the kitchen sink and hide it in the back of Freddie's freezer compartment.

When I wake up the next morning, Kit has already left.

forty-three

▼▼▼▼▼

The entrance exams are to be held in the Grand Hall of the Black-brake School for Girls. Cassie and I wait in the foyer outside the hall with half a dozen other girls, a couple of whom are cramming last-minute facts from index cards highlighted in a rainbow of neon colours. Mum needs to be at the office, so Mrs Pope has brought us. She's trying to make Cassie feel better by saying dumb things like 'It doesn't matter if you don't get in.' I'm keeping my head down, concentrating instead on the herringbone pattern of the polished parquet floor.

I peer through the bolted doors of the Grand Hall. Inside, there are six windows on either side which I swear are as high as our house and the desks are set out like desert islands with yards between each. 'NO Calculators, Books or Notes allowed', warns a large sign which hangs from the invigilator's desk.

I've never done anything like this before, and I'm starting to feel a little bit underprepared. In fact, the only preparation I've done – aside from reading Judy Blume's complete works – is to barter with a market stallholder to get a shell suit worth a fiver for £3.99; I'm wearing it now for good luck.

The invigilator arrives after a few minutes. It's Ryan, but I don't recognize him right away as he's got some dress sense and had a haircut.

'Harper!' he says, adjusting the smart brass cufflinks on his shirtsleeves. 'How's your mum?'

'She's fine, thanks.' And then my EQ kicks in and I realize that the question he really wants to ask is whether she got hitched. 'She married Gregory,' I say.

'The Calvin Klein guy?' he asks, while unlocking the door with one of several large keys hanging from a key ring.

I nod. He deflates like a bouncy castle when the party's over.

Between fascinating questions such as how many minutes it would take Paul to drive to Coventry to visit Jane if Paul averaged twenty miles an hour and Coventry were fifty-two miles away, I look up at Ryan, whose head is almost lying on the desk on top of the books I guess he's meant to be reading.

After the wall clock has circled round the sixty minutes that we are given to complete the test on what mostly seems to be about visiting friends in the Midlands, I go up to hand Ryan my paper. 'Gregory's gay,' I whisper, as I put it on the pile. 'It won't last.'

This seems to pump Ryan up a bit.

'Plus, if I get into dry-clean-only school, Mum'll do the school run.'

He may not be my first choice of potential stepdads (who aren't gay or terminal) but Ryan would be able to teach me about dead poets and help me get into university. But I'm getting a bit ahead of myself. First of all, I have my own date with Craig to think about.

*

Mum's in the dining room, knee-deep in printouts of the final proofs for the Christmas catalogue so she doesn't notice when I sneak upstairs with her can of Elnett and mascara wand. I've watched Oona apply mascara enough times to know how to do it. I don't bother with blusher because wearing a shell suit is like being wrapped in an electric blanket. Now that my hair has grown out of the scarecrow phase of being short, it is possible to slap it down with gel on a side parting and firm it into place with hairspray.

It is twelve o'clock on Saturday.

It is time for my first ever date.

And I wish Judy Blume was my mum.

'Doing something special, are we?' Mum looks up from her desk as I sneak into the lounge to get some coins out of the Premium Bonds jar from the coffin.

'No,' I fib. 'Just going round Cassie's.'

'Uh-huh,' she says. 'Well, be bad!'

I grab an extra fistful of coins as she jabs her earplugs back in. As I walk along the Greytown Road towards the Optimum, I get wolf-whistled by a boy across the road who's hanging out in the midday shade of the Spar. That usually happens to my mum, not me. I must be looking good, I think, as I slacken my pace and try to look cool, but trip over a kerb.

There's a queue of people snaking outside the cinema; it's not the usual Saturday afternoon crowd of kids – these are adults, reading the weekend papers and smoking openly while they wait to be let in. In the foyer, salt and sweet popcorn hardens under bright lights and spilt cola browns the carpet. An unlit gateway to the screens where the 15 and 18 films are shown is guarded by Barbara, the gatekeeper of 'Swearing and Explicit Scenes'. Her face is criss-crossed by the chicken wire which she sits behind, playing Ticket God to those of us under fifteen. If Barbara spots you're underage, you cannot worship the lives of those far more exciting American teenagers who French kiss, get naked and have sex.

'It's *A Summer Story* this afternoon, me duck,' Barbara says when I get to the counter, magicking a pen out of her white hair bun. 'Don't forget your tissues.'

'I've already got you a ticket,' Craig says, creeping up behind me. 'Mum recommended it. She saw it in Coventry last week.'

We sit on the back row, of course, on the red velvet swinging seats which are singed with cigarette burns. I'd been looking forward to snogging Craig and eating a trough of salted popcorn, but I can't keep my eyes off the screen. The film, which is set at the beginning of the century, is about a lawyer called Mr Ashton who's hiking through the moors with his friend in Devon when he sprains his ankle and has to stay at a farmhouse while it heals. He falls in love with a beautiful young girl called Megan who lives on the farm, but Mr Ashton breaks her heart when he travels back to the big city. Twenty years later, he returns with his posh wife to visit the farm and discovers that Megan had a child – which was his – and that she died in childbirth. In the final scene, he glimpses his son shepherding sheep across a country lane with a shotgun.

The credits roll. Craig stands up, stretches and says, 'Well, that wasn't exactly *The Terminator*!'

I dab at my tears with my jumper sleeve to try to hide them from Craig. 'I can see why your mum loved it,' I sniff.

'So can I,' he says. 'Shall we go and get milkshakes?' he says.

'I'm vegan now,' I say, recovering myself. 'So…Maybe a lemonade?'

'Right ON, Harper!' Craig says and he kisses me bang on.

Craig takes me to Wimpy's which is that upmarket that they even set out cutlery, plus there's table service. Craig asks the waitress for two lemonades and a plate of chips for two.

'You seem quiet,' he says.

'My mum's sort-of-ex is dying. He's only forty-one,' I say, scrunching up a paper napkin.

'Cancer?' Craig asks.

I nod.

'We just have to "watch and wait",' I say. 'I went to visit him twice yesterday. He was fast asleep, totally out of it. Mum says he's just given up, that he doesn't want to live any more.'

'I'm sure he knows you're there when you visit, Harper,' Craig says, reaching for my hands, warts and all. 'I'm sure he loves you very much.'

forty-four

▼▼▼▼▼

You could be forgiven for thinking that Derek was packing a suitcase for two months, not two weeks. I'm round at his house as he's preparing to go to London for work experience that Gregory's organized for him in a hairdressing salon on Sloane Street during the final fortnight of the summer holidays. All the surfaces in Derek's bedroom are covered with clothes which have been ironed, folded and placed in piles according to colour. I'm lying on his bed, surrounded by an array of hairspray, mousse and leave-in conditioner.

'According to Gregory, pop stars come into the salon all the time,' he says. 'Their scalps get really dehydrated because of all the product they use,' he giggles. 'Not that I'll be allowed to cut their hair, or even wash it. I'll probably just be sweeping up their split ends.'

'If Madonna or Kylie come in, will you bring theirs back for me in a jar?' I ask.

'Course,' Derek says. 'Though I'd want to keep half. Now,

which of these fabulous jackets do you think I should pack?'

Meanwhile back at home, signing the dead pledge paperwork and being a homeowner seems to rattle Mum into action. She finishes her final set of Christmas catalogue proofs an hour before her deadline. Apparently the catalogue needs to be printed immediately so it can be dropped through letterboxes in early September for those people already thinking about what plastic crap they're going to stuff in their stockings.

Once she's delivered the hundred-page document to Joanna at five o'clock on Friday evening, Mum opens the final bottle of imitation champagne left over from the wedding.

She's on her second glass when Dad calls to pick me up for my last weekend with him before he goes on holiday.

'Have you got two minutes to come in for a drink?' she asks.

'I have if it's alcoholic,' Dad says, and he takes off his shoes.

As soon as Mum owned thirteen Kendal Road, she put up a sign on the front door saying 'Welcome to our SHOES OFF house'.

'Where are your gerbils?' Dad asks me, as he comes into the lounge.

'They're feral now,' I say. Last week, I loved Bangers and Mash enough to set them free in the shrubbery surrounding the compound.

'Better to be feral than behind bars,' Dad says, taking a glass of bubbly from Mum. 'Congratulations,' he says.

'I hear you're leaving Hardingstone for a while,' Mum replies, chinking his glass. 'Not before time.'

They both knock their drinks back in one gulp. Then the bubbles must truly go to their heads, as they hug each other. I can't remember the last time I saw them touch each other. While they're at it, I take a quick swig from the bottle myself.

If anyone looked through the net curtain at this exact moment, I wonder what they'd think – aside from me having a pre-teen alcohol problem. Perhaps that my parents had just got re-engaged to be remarried? For one second, I close my eyes and allow myself that fantasy. Mum asking Dad what we're up to that weekend shatters my daydream.

'We're doing a car boot sale to get rid of my junk,' Dad says. 'We need to be in Coventry to set up by six o'clock tomorrow morning.'

When we get back to Dad's, I help him clean Ivy Cottage ready for the renters who are going to caretake the crumbling cottage while he's away. I start by sorting through the kitchen cupboards.

I pull out fistfuls of out-of-date banana Angel Delight packets and vanilla blancmange mixes. Dad may well say tinned food doesn't go off, but I discover that some of the tins of oxtail soup and Ambrosia creamed rice he owns are over ten years old; I reckon that the metal could probably have leaked into them. I chuck the tins into the bin. I don't even try to scrape out the chip pan of hardened yellow fat, I just throw away the heavy pan – fat, sieve and all. The jar of freeze-dried coffee that has gone rock-solid goes to recycling; the potatoes silently budding in the bottom cupboard, compost; the eggs which, when I crack them, ooze brown liquid, down the plughole. We replace the see-through bed sheets and the pink air-fresheners shrivelled to the size of shrimps and do away with the worn-down doormat.

But I do rescue a jar of Mrs Curtis's home-made gooseberry jam that I find, unopened, in the back of Dad's fridge. I tie a white ribbon around the neck of the glass jar and, at some ungodly pre-dawn hour on Saturday morning, slip out of the cottage to the churchyard to Mrs Curtis's plot, which is right above her husband's.

The brown mound of earth is still settling. I place the jar on the granite plinth then go over to Heaven Called a Little Child's headstone which I polish with my bandana. I whisper to her that I won't be gone long; come March next year, I'll visit again.

forty-five

▼▼▼▼▼

When the letter from the girls' school arrives in the fifth week of the summer holidays, I'm still in my pyjamas, looking up in the *London A–Z* street atlas the address of the salon where Derek's working. The letter announces that I shall be student number 10,573 at Blackbrake School for Girls. I've never known anyone who has signed up for the army, but I imagine that when you do, you receive a kit and uniform list like the one I've got to buy by the beginning of term. And, of course, there is the issue of the wool coat.

I telephone Cassie as soon as I open the letter.

'Did you get in?'

'Yes!' Cassie squeals. 'My folks don't know yet – they've taken Lisa down the annual Midlands MENSA Challenge.'

'Lisa's going to be furious!' I say. 'Let's conspire and celebrate. Where shall we go?'

'I've got the best idea,' Cassie whispers down the line. 'Meet me in an hour down the playground.'

I arrive first and sit on the swings, watching as workmen erect a two-metre-high fence around the demolished wing of the Hopkin Wynne. Construction has begun today. Soon there will be a new rash of executive houses with paper-thin walls and box-sized rooms, just like every other house on the Old Marshes. Yellow earth-eating machines are digging deep trenches and gaping craters, scraping away layers of old hospital rubble and mud, ready to lay foundations. The soil Cassie and I scoured for signs of madness and poetry will soon be consumed by concrete, crazy paving and carports except for the gardens, which will be surrounded by fences six feet high.

'I bet they didn't get an archaeologist on site,' Cassie says, joining me on the swings.

'It's a site of historical interest. It must be illegal,' I say.

'Come on, Harper. Follow me!' Cassie says.

I can't put the needle on the record to explain why, but seeing that scrap land being built upon makes me feel bulldozed. Even though it wasn't exactly a nature reserve, it was an open space, somewhere we could roam and run free without a grown-up trying to make it fun for us by building climbing frames or fencing off a 'play area'.

Turns out, Cassie has the best antidote to my sadness.

When she opens her front door, Cassie makes me put my hands over my eyes then she pushes me up the stairs and steers me along the landing. 'Surprise!' she says.

On the antiseptic bathroom floor, she has laid out bowls of vegan food. 'I went on a little shopping spree down the God Squad wholefood shop,' she says.

'Wholefood?' I ask. To be as frank as Anne, I'm not sure

whether I'm going to like it from the look of what's on offer. I guess my mum's more of a half-food kind of cook.

Cassie and I sit on the floor, leaning our backs against the bath. First course is a bowl of surprisingly tasty houmous, which we dip into with batons of carrot and cucumber. The main course is a bowl each of crunchy apostrophes called quinoa and pudding is carob bars and fruit leathers, which I sniff first for the scent of animal hide.

'I'm never going to wear a wool coat,' Cassie says, tearing a strip off her fruit leather.

'We promised, right?' I say.

'Just like we did to eat a meal in here,' Cassie says.

'Cassie,' I say, trying not to well up. 'You're the best. I feel like I don't have to explain myself to you...'

'I've learnt it's easier not to ask,' she says.

'You know, I discovered that I had a sister called Sylvia, but that she was dead when she was born.'

'That's so sad,' Cassie says, nibbling a carob bar. 'I wonder what she would have been like?'

'I think about that a lot,' I say. 'Don't you ever wonder who your real parents are?'

'Of course – all the time.'

'They're probably completely mental,' I say.

'Just like yours, then?' Cassie says and we both laugh so hard I nearly choke on the carob.

'Harper! Cassie! Whatever are you doing?' Mrs Pope, back from Lisa's IQ test, throws the bathroom door open.

'Being kids,' Cassie says. 'You know, those things that you wanted so badly but you couldn't make yourself so you had to choose two out of a catalogue?'

'Cassie!' Mrs Pope looks as electroconvulsive as I feel; Cassie has never stood up to her mum before.

'This is what kids do,' Cassie continues. 'We make mess. We have fun and we forget ourselves. Why don't you try it, Mum?' she says. 'Go on. Let things dangle.'

'Dangle?' she says, creeping into the bathroom as if there might be land mines beneath the bleached white tiles.

'Here.' I offer her a fruit leather which Mrs Pope turns over in her hands.

'Is it edible?'

'Apparently so,' Cassie says, taking a bite of hers.

Mrs Pope sits down on the fluffy white toilet cover and nibbles it. 'Quite nice,' she says.

Cassie laughs. 'See?'

'Yes, I think so,' Mrs Pope says.

'Mum, I've got some good news for once,' Cassie says. She's going to spill the beans that she's got a place at private school, I bet. I'll leave them to their straight talk and fruit leathers. Besides, I haven't told my mum that I've got in yet, and if I leave now, I can just catch three o'clockses in the office.

A new secretary sits at Mum's old desk, her bright red high heels kicked off to one side. She's buffing her fingernails while gorging on gossip columns. Today, there's no magnetic power radiating from Joanna's office. Her door is open; on her desk there's a large packet of dried cranberries and a multipack of orange energy drink.

'Barbados,' says the secretary, without looking up. 'Two weeks. All right for some.'

I find Mum at her new desk, tucked away in the corner by the photocopier. There's a far-off look in her eyes, as if she's dreaming of white sand and suntans. The wrinkles on her face seem to have multiplied. She's an elastic band that's been left in the desk drawer too long: ready to snap.

'I've got some good news,' I say.

'Tell me.'

'Only if we can get cream horns to celebrate.'

Mum nods.

'I got into dry-clean-only school!' I hand her the letter. I'm not going on a charity stamp, so it'll cost £250 a term to send me, an amount which, until this summer, would have been as eye-watering as a barrel of chopped onions and nail-polish remover mixed together.

'Harper, that's wonderful,' Mum says, but her face stays weather-beaten.

'Shall we bunk off and tell Kit? It's not like your boss is even here...'

'Kit's not very well, Harper.' Mum doesn't look at me, but instead looks down at her undrunk cup of coffee.

'I know that, Mum, he's got cancer.' Something makes me stop. 'Have you got some bad news?' I ask.

'Kit's under full sedation. He's never going to wake up again.'

'But he was hoping to come home to die!'

'The thing about birth and death is that they can both take you a little by surprise. You have to be prepared for things not to work out the way you want them to.'

I dissolve into her lap. As I weep, she takes the teaspoon from her saucer and catches my tears as they roll down my cheek. Then she uses them to water her desk plant, the shy one that flinches when it's touched. The leaves shrink and curl in on themselves.

forty-six

▼▼▼▼▼

The air in the Oncology ward feels tropical, like a stuffy greenhouse where exotic orchids should grow. I follow signs to the reception desk, keeping my head down, counting the black streaks on the grey vinyl floor where patients have paced up and down so much that the soles of their shoes have left permanent signs of their pain. Far down one corridor, a melancholy cello solo plays on the radio.

'Hello, sweetpea.' The nurse at the desk has a voice like cotton wool. 'Can I help?'

'I'm Harper. Here to see Christopher Reynish.'

'Are you on your own?' she asks, as she gets up from her wheely chair and comes round to the front of the nursing station.

'Mum did offer to come with me,' I find myself explaining to her open face, 'but I wanted to pay my last rites on my own.'

She bends down so she's the same height as me, puts a hand on my shoulder; I can feel the warmth from her hand through my T-shirt instantly.

'Christopher's in a very deep and sedated sleep, but he'll still be able to hear what you say.' Her words are cushions, meant to soften how sad I feel.

'OK,' I say, not meeting her eyes.

'He's just along here,' she says, and she guides me to his room with her hand still on my shoulder.

While I'm used to one-way chat on account of Freddie Mercury, this is going to be more difficult. Kit is propped up on several blue pillows. His face, which is as pale and puffed as a grain of overcooked rice, is half-covered by a facemask where he sucks in oxygen. A drip hooks into his arm. When he breathes, it no longer sounds like a rattling abacus but like a pan of water boiling furiously.

The nurse hovers at the door. 'I'll be just down the corridor if you need me.' She closes the door softly behind her.

I didn't bring anything for him, I realize as I perch by his bed-side on the light-blue easy chair which is as hard as a graveyard bench. I should have brought him something! Grapes, chocolates. But then I see a sign above his bed that he's nil by mouth. He has decided to die.

I hold Kit's bruised hand in mine; it is damp and limp. The flesh on his hands has begun to sink between the small, delicate bones. His palm settles in mine like a leaf.

'Kit, I got into private school.'

His breathing suddenly changes, becomes more shallow and raspy.

'No! Don't worry! I'm not going to become a snob,' I say, quickly, to dampen his panicking. 'I'm not wearing a regulation wool coat.'

Kit's breathing returns to the deep and bubbly gulps again. I grasp his hand tighter.

'What else?' I say, looking around the room for inspiration. 'I had the best idea for Mum's birthday present.'

'...'

'I've booked a trip up the Dynamo Lift Tower where they test elevators. Me, Mum and Oona are going the day after next. Gregory gave me the ticket money.'

'...'

'Dynamo Elevators are diversifying. Bit like balloon rides but without the basket...'

'...'

'What else? I had my first date with Craig. We saw a film about a shepherd who never knew his father. You would've hated it. But you'd like Craig. He drinks green tea and everything...'

'...'

'I'm still vegan, but the other day I forgot and ate three packets of Bacon Fries. But then I cancelled out the badness by eating the same number of salt and vinegar crisps straight afterwards.'

'...'

I'm struggling now. 'What else? Derek's still Vidal Sassooning it in London. And I'm growing my hair out.' I lean down now to whisper into his ear. 'And do you know what? I worked out from the *London A–Z* that the only Underground station not to have the letters from the word "mackerel" in it is St John's Wood.'

I am sure I see Kit smile for a second; perhaps he's imagining that he's won the top prize of 64 million dollars.

The soft-as-cotton-wool nurse comes back in. It's time for Kit's wash and mouth care, she says. It's time for me to go. I kiss Kit on his balmy forehead. I summon up the courage to find the one word I really want to say but can barely bring myself to utter: goodbye.

A tear, which had been wanting to trickle down my cheek and which I had willed not to, so Kit would never see that I was beyond sad, falls.

forty-seven

▼▼▼▼▼

Blackbrake spells itself out in tiny lights from 400 feet up.

We're on the roof of the Dynamo Elevator Inc. testing tower which, from ground level, looks like a concrete finger is pointing straight to heaven. A wall that comes up to my shoulders topped with barbed wire wrapped like Christmas tinsel around it protects me from toppling off. Street lamps glow orange across the town. Occasional blue flashing lights jazz past as fire engines scream down streets to rescue stranded cats or people from blazing buildings. Cranes with wrecking balls swinging in the breeze blink redly to stop aeroplanes from flying into them. I try to work out where Peabody Farm would be on the saddle of the hill and imagine the cows inching towards the electrocuting plate, scan the sky for the orange hum of the M1 which leads to Craig in Coventry.

Oona rummages through the large tartan bag she's brought with her.

'It's not quite like being up the Empire State Building,' she says. 'But at least there's a view.'

'Who needs New York?' Mum says.

'That could be today's mantra!' Oona says, then Mary Poppinses two bottles of Babycham, plastic cups, and sparklers out of her bag.

Mum and Oona don't gossip like they usually do over bubbles; being 400 feet closer to heaven makes them quiet for once. Instead, they just drink in the view and down a bottle each between them. With Kit's horse-racing binoculars, I zoom in to where he's reaching the end of life's conveyor belt, close to the checkout.

Mum has said not to be shocked if the next phone call we receive is one from the undertakers.

Derek once said that the roots of a tree mirror the branches that grow above ground. I saw this for myself in the storm-damaged park in Brighton. Derek reckons this is what his hero Boy George was on about when he crooned 'Karma Chameleon': namely, the more you give, the more you get.

When Mum hands me a sizzling sparkler, I write out, in dying sparks, a little prayer to the God who Towers Over the Testing of Elevators: *May my roots run deep, may my branches reach far.* I get to the final letter just as the sparkler fizzles out.

When we get home, the light on the answering machine is flashing. Mum rewinds the cassette. It's the nurse from the hospital asking if we'll call straight back. Mum asks if I will do it; she's too teary to call.

I dial the number and picture the red telephone ringing at the nurses' station on the Oncology ward. I imagine the nurse setting down her cup of sweet tea on top of a half-solved cross-word, reaching across the desk to answer the phone. I will her not to pick up.

When Dad and I went on the pirate-ship ride in Brighton, there was a moment when, on the highest swing, I felt my body hanging, weightless, in the air: I was neither rising, nor falling. I felt as if, for that second, I was outside of myself, outside of my body. This, I think, is how it must feel when you die.

The nurse picks up. 'Hello?'

'It's Harper,' I say.

'Hello, sweetpea,' she says softly. She doesn't have to say any more. I know that Kit has gone.

forty-eight

▼▼▼▼▼

31 August 1988. The family calendar reads: 'Coffin Collection.'

Kit's funeral director could have been parachuted straight out of a Charles Dickens novel, I swear. He wears a black suit and matching shoes that look as if they've just come out of their shoebox. It's like he's dressed for a permanent funeral.

'What do you wear on your days off, then?' I ask, as the funeral director – wait for it – puts on a pair of bright white gloves and starts to remove the objects in Kit's coffin-come-bookcase and place them on the coffee table. It's like he's about to magic a bunny rabbit out of the coffin. I'm standing in the doorway, sucking on a lemon ice-lolly that I've excavated from the freeze chest.

'A shirt, tie and trousers?' He seems a little uncomfortable as he sets aside the dead cactus and a tin of anchovies.

'How do you get your shoes that shiny?' I try again, pointing my half-sucked lolly at his feet.

'Lots of polish. And they're from Gordon Benét's.'

There goes the candle, burnt to the bottom of the wick.

'Thought so. Is that part of your job then, polishing your shoes?'

'Well, no, but it's just the etiquette.'

I suck on my lolly. The coffin's now one metronome, Di 'n' Charles cereal bowl and cast of teeth lighter. 'How much do you get paid for dying?'

'Um...' Mr Dickens is starting to get hot under his cardboard-stiff collar.

'I mean, on your eyelids. When you die. And why do you put coins on the eyes? Is it to stop them falling out and freaking you out?'

'Well, nowadays, we don't use coins. We just make sure we pull the eyelids down.'

'Like, making sure you draw the curtains at night time to keep the cold out?'

'I suppose so.'

The coffin's contents are now all laid out on the table, as if we're about to play the memory game and guess which object has been taken while one of us has had our eyes shut. Before I have time to suggest a quick game, the tinny tune to 'So Long, Farewell' plays; Mr Dickens's sidekick is at the door. He's only just taller than me, but between the two of them, they heave the coffin out through the door and into the hearse without a single scuff on their shiny leather brogues.

I'm removing the three most important items from the coffee table – the pre-nup, *Uniforms, Underwear and Ulrika* and *Hot Flash for Frances* – and putting them back on top of the bookshelf when the phone rings.

It's the long-nailed librarian from Blackbrake library.

'You're at the top of the reservation list for *Forever*,' she says.

'It'll be put to one side for three days and then it'll go to the next borrower on the list.'

'I'll be there in fifteen minutes,' I say. 'While you're on the line, would you mind checking if you have a book called *The Facts of Death*, please?'

'*The Facts of Death*?' she repeats. 'Hang on a moment.'

The librarian puts me on hold and, I imagine, flicks through her index cards with her red talons.

'I'm sorry,' she says coming back on to the line. 'No such book exists.'

forty-nine

▼▼▼▼▼

'Harper! Get the door!' Mum yells from the bathroom. 'I'm bleaching my facial hair.'

It's the day of Kit's funeral and Mum has been doing beauty voodoo behind the locked bathroom door all morning. Chemical smells woke me up at eight. Since she turned the lock to Engaged Mum has been yelling out instructions for me to tidy things ready for the wake.

Melanie's at the front door, holding a large parcel wrapped in brown paper. I recognize Kit's handwriting on the front; it says 'For Harper and Mary'.

'Special Delivery!' Melanie says, handing the parcel to me.

'Mum's in the bathroom,' I say, taking it from her. 'But you can come in, if you want.'

'I won't disturb her,' Melanie says. 'How is she?'

'She's a little bit upset.'

'Call me if you need anything, OK?' Melanie says.

I take the parcel into the lounge. Mum joins me in her fake

silk dressing gown; I know better than to comment on the colour of her face, which is giving off enough wattage to power the heated rollers she'll likely plug in next.

I exhume the presents from the flurry of white polystyrene figure-of-eights.

There's a small box for Mum with a label which reads *I get the last laugh. Ha Ha*. It's a brand new pair of false teeth and a small plastic wind-up toy – a set of teeth with tiny feet. I wind it up, and the toy takes tiny milk-teeth steps across the coffee table, chattering away until its wind-up energy is spent. Mum slips in her new dentures, which fit as perfectly as Cinderella's glass slipper; Kit must have borrowed Mum's plaster cast from the coffin-shelf to get them made.

A tiny parcel, addressed to me, reads *Don't give up*, and contains a packet of sunflower seeds.

Another one for Mum, labelled *Give up*, includes nicotine patches and chewing gum.

I chew on one of the smoky gums as I read the letter for me from the *Socialist Worker* magazine, with details of my lifetime subscription. There's also a stuffed soft toy, a tortoiseshell cat with a label around its neck. Its name: Kitty Kat.

Mum starts to cry again. I scaffold myself around her, let her weep. 'It'll be OK, Mum,' I say, offering her a tissue.

'It will,' she says, smiling weakly, her new fake teeth radiating from her red, blotchy face. 'It will.'

'Mum,' I ask gently, undoing my arms. 'Do you mind if I stay at home this afternoon?'

'Really?'

I've decided that I'd rather do my own private ritual for Kit while he's being turned into eternal toast, although I have prepared a little something to go up in smoke with him. I hand an envelope to Mum.

'Will you put this in the coffin for me?'

'You look like a box of Black Magic with legs,' Oona says when she turns up to chauffeur Mum to the cremation. Mum flows down the stairs, a floor-length black dress made out of crushed velvet draping to her feet, a red bow flowering at her narrow waist. 'I should know,' Oona continues, 'I ate an entire box for breakfast.'

Since Kit died, Mum has been distributing the chocolates that he still had left over from his salesmanship. Oona seems to have been benefitting the most.

It seems that the only way Mum can stop herself from crying is to pretend that she's off to a mortgage meeting with Mike Hyde rather than to cremate Kit. She's war-painted her glowing face; her eyelids and lips are toffee-coloured, her cheeks are caked in foundation with blusher the colour of the antique rose in our back garden that has just started to turn brown around the edges. Her hair is a walnut whip on top of her head, made nougat-tough with Elnett. She slips her silver heels over her steel-grey tights, throws the chainmail strap of her black, boxy handbag over her stiff shoulders.

'We'll be back in a couple of hours,' she says.

In the kitchen, I rummage behind the jars of sugar-free hot chocolate and low-calorie powdered soup and find a packet of sandalwood incense left over from Mum's yoga habit. As if getting ready for a birthday party, I wrap a grapefruit in tin foil but instead of cheese and pineapple, I pierce the sharp ends of the incense sticks into the fruit.

I set up the shrine for Kit in the lounge where his coffin stood.
I sacrifice the two secret-mix chocolate bars that I have set aside
for the ceremony, by eating them whole. Then I read out loud a
carbon copy of the poem that I have typed, the original being in
the envelope which is joining Kit in his coffin.

Death of A Salesman

> Trail your fingernail
> on the dusty bookshelf
> and leave a hidden message
> so I know where the frail fabric
> of angel wings is kept.
>
> Leave instructions under my pillow
> so that I can teach Mum
> how to make halos from coat hangers,
> not Silk Cut smoke.
>
> Steal stars.
>
> Pinch Halley's trail
> and light our living room
> with heavenly skies at night.
>
> Make the microwave ping
> when I'm sitting watching
> daytime television so I know
> you're watching the silly adverts with me.
>
> Push pens off tables
> when Mum's got clients

round for briefings
so they leave before they bore me.

Make curtains swish on still evenings
and ward off next door's not-just-for-Christmas-Rottweiler
with ghost-like whistles and whispers.

If the doorbell rings,
check to make sure it's not an attacker –
and if it is, rattle the letterbox
so we know not to open the door.

Make sure Mum chains the door each night.
If she doesn't?
Do your thing and jangle it.

Speak to those famous people I admire who died.
Look up Sylvia and Heaven Called a Little Child
and tell them both how you survived
the fall, but not the blow.

Find out if white sheets
are uniform for the afterlife.
If so, spirit a spare one
from Mrs Pope's airing cupboard.
That would give her a fright
(serves her right).

But seriously, make sure
you don't put up with taunts
about being the new boy:

you shouldn't have to
brew green tea for eternity.

Remember, on the thirty-first of October,
to go down the Spread Eagle for a laugh.
Pour a pint of draught
over the travelling librarian
like I've always wanted to,
but have never had the guts.

Remember if you decide to go vegan:
and if product placement has reached the heavens,
that Ambrosia creamed rice would be out of the question.

Make things go bump
in the night like you used to
when a book would fall off
your chest as you slept.

Watch me as I speak about
you having checked out
of the supermarket of life.

I might smile, but it's all an act.
In fact, I'll miss you all the time.

Especially when Mum runs a bath;
you'd laugh at her turbaned hair
and mud-packed face.

Now I'll laugh for you.

Laugh with me when
I cremate another pizza
so smoke sets off the fire alarm
and I have to boff it with a broom handle.

You were always tall enough.

fifty

▼▼▼▼▼

From the *Blackbrake Gazette* obituary section, 2 September 1988:

R.I.P. KIT
24 April 1947–27 August 1988

What a way to go.

1. Be endemically positive.
2. It's who you are inside that matters most.
3. Read books.
4. Get a good education.
5. Don't self-flagellate.
6. Love deeply.
7. Don't take things so bleeding literal.

HMRC x

fifty-one

▼▼▼▼▼

Turns out, being endemically positive can have its up-sides. Though I've never been fond of Mike Hyde, I don't mind wasting my eyesight on him if he's got the house deeds between his sterilized hands.

'Your mum in?' he asks, checking his watch.

'She's bleaching her face.' Although this isn't strictly true, it's currently number one in my top ten of Mum's excuses.

'Suppose that's more original than washing her hair,' he says. 'Could you just give her these, then, please?'

'Sure,' I yawn.

'How's school?' The desperado can't even think of an original question to ask.

'Fine,' I say. 'Sorry, I think I may have left a Tupperware lid on top of the hob by mistake. Might you excuse me?' I don't wait for a reply, but close the door and walk down the hallway from where I spy on Mike as his shadow retreats from the pebbledash doorstep. I had actually just been sorting through Mum's Tupperware collection as I'm storing Harper's Bazaar stock in it while the shop is temporarily closed for business. Now that I'm a fully fledged subscriber to the *Socialist Worker*, I've got some serious petitioning and picket-lining to be getting on with.

When Mum breezes in later, back from the Black Knight shopping centre, she's four John Lewis bags heavier. I eye them from the other side of the kitchen.

'I've got your entire new school uniform ready for your first day tomorrow...and I panic-bought a garlic crusher,' she says, fishing the crusher out of the bag and demonstrating its hinge.

A crumb of my old negativity slips out: 'But the only garlic we have is dehydrated and comes in a tube.' I should know; I've been struggling to make home-made houmous with the stuff ever since tasting it round Cassie's. Mr Power hadn't heard of tahini, so in its place he sold me a jar of smooth peanut butter. Another one of the ingredients – olive oil – was only available at the chemist, and the shop assistant there said it was really meant for pouring down earholes. And even bearing in mind these set-backs, houmous is the most successful thing I've cooked since going vegan.

'Well...' Mum thinks on her high heels, 'we'll have to start buying garlic from the market. It's a fresh start, Harper.'

'A fresh start?' I creep towards the bags, which have flumped to the floor and are still rustling under the weight of the clothes as if there's something alive in them.

'I didn't buy you a statutory coat, if that's what you're wondering,' Mum says. 'I do know you quite well.'

I feel a stone lighter when she says this. Ironic, given that's how much I bet those coats weigh.

287

'These came for you while you were out,' I say, handing her the paperwork. 'From Mike.'

'You got rid of him. Did you?' Mum says, looking around as if he might be hiding behind the door.

'Is the whole point of advent calendars getting twenty-four chocolates?'

'Given that I know you slide out the tray from the advent calendar, eat the entire lot and then tape it up again before the first of December, I'll take that as a yes.'

I guess there are some secrets you can never keep to yourself.

Mum toasts the arrival of the deeds with the last of the alcohol from Kit's wake yesterday, inviting Oona round to share the platter of leftover sausage rolls and jam roly-polys. In a move that shocks me more than an electric fence, Oona refuses the food on offer, and boils herself a pan of brown rice which she eats with a thimble-sized knob of butter. She doesn't even melt when Mum whips out another chocolate box.

It's while I'm holed up with the guide to the top tier of the chocolates in my room (I figure that if nobody is watching you eating dairy then it doesn't count) that the second post comes rattling through the letterbox. Since Mum and Oona are marinating themselves in orange plonk while playing Dolly Parton's single 'Jolene' at thirty-three rpm instead of forty-five, they don't hear the letterbox. Slowing down Dolly has the same effect on their gossip per minute. When I spy through the lounge window, I can see they're horizontal on the HP sofa sharing a cigarette between them.

I'm expecting a letter from Craig, so it's disappointing to find there's just the usual brown envelopes with OVERDUE written on them along with a heap of junk mail. It's when I'm about to chuck the lot in the kitchen bin that the strapline on a red and green catalogue catches my eye:

Inspirations: for Incredible Christmas Gift Ideas! It's Mum's equivalent of a nineteenth-century novel. She says the catalogues are even going to be posted in sections, like story instalments from Charles Dickens, with the one posted at the end of November being like a 'Best of' the plastic crap. Before showing Mum, I take it up to my bedroom to read some product descriptions that she sweated, cried and bled over for months.

Sunglasses with windscreen wipers on:
Perfect for a picnic with an unexpected serving of precipitation.

A tea towel with a map of the UK shipping forecast areas printed on it:
Hold this up and listen to the shipping forecast for a complete audiovisual experience.

A snow globe which rains pound signs over a man in a black suit:
It's raining sterling! The ideal executive desk toy.

A sign for hanging on doors that reads 'Do disturb. Geniuses hate work':
A special gift to adorn any teenager's bedroom door.

Three porcelain pigs with wings to hang on your wall:
For those everyday miracles: pigs CAN fly!

fifty-two

▼▼▼▼▼

Ryan is on duty outside my new school the first day of the autumn term. He's supervising the privatized girls as they pass through the gates with the same air as an usher at a funeral: his hands grasped behind his back and a slight grimace on his face. But when he spots Mum, his mouth breaks into a smile, and his cheeks turn pink – not that Mum notices, she's that focused on not tripping up on the cobbles in her high heels.

I still can't believe Cassie and I are going to Blackbrake School for Girls. I hope we'll always be different in denim, even if we do learn Latin and Greek. Never shall I leave the tap running when cleaning my teeth, nor shall I parade my hockey stick down the Black Knight.

I reach into my jacket pocket where I've tucked away my lucky charm: the paperweight scorpion. I've decided not to shatter the paperweight just yet. Bottom line is this: maybe you're just not ready to understand some things until you're regularly bleeding every twenty-eight days, have a mortgage and receive urgent correspondence. For now, I'm quite happy as an A-cup, sending love letters to my boyfriend in Coventry and the occasional one to the editor of the *Socialist Worker*. I've got a way to go yet before I see if there's a sting in any tail.

'Beautiful day,' Ryan says to Mum, his cheeks returning to the colour of marzipan.

'Isn't it just?' Mum smiles in reply.

'Does the Great Education Reform Bill apply here?' I ask Ryan.

'The only gerbils here are the school pets,' Ryan says.

As I go through the gates and wave goodbye to Mum, it's not a pop lyric but a line from *Nineteen Eighty-Four* that flicks to the front of my Rolodex-like mind: 'Perhaps a lunatic was simply a minority of one.'

It must have come to me for a reason, so I shall tattoo that to my eyeballs, I think, as I hang my denim jacket on to the coat hook marked Harper.

THE FRESH START

What a Way to Go

Mum: Mary Curtis *née* Smith *pre-decree nisi* Richardson
Dad: Peter Richardson
Daughter: Harper May Richardson-Curtis
Potential Stepdads: Christopher *KitKat* Reynish; Gregory Curtis;
Ryan Stockwell; Mike Hyde
Best Friend: Cassie Pope
Best Friend's Mother: Mrs Pope
Mental-Health Nurse & Double Glazing Specialist:
Melanie de Burgh
Avon Vendor: Oona Williams
Hairdresser: Derek Williams
Boyfriend: Craig Arrowsmith
Square: Lisa Pope
Senior: Mrs Curtis
Bangers and Mash: As themselves
Fridge: Freddie Mercury
Extras: The village people
God: Barbara the cinema vendor

Author: Harper May Richardson-Curtis
Producer, Director, Executive of Everything:
Harper May Richardson-Curtis

PA to the Author, Producer, Director, Executive of Everything:
Cassie Pope
Accountants: Mike Hyde Associates
Hair and Make-Up Executive Designer: Derek Williams
Interiors: Gregory Curtis
Story Consultant: Judy Blume
Director of Funerals: Charles Dickens

Floor 27, 13 Kendal Road, Blackbrake, BKI 3JF, England,
The Universe, The Solar System.
MCMLXXXVIII

Acknowledgements

As once the winged energy of delight
carried you over childhood's dark abysses,
now beyond your own life build the great
arch of unimagined bridges.*

Harper's fortune cookie message contains two lines from the first stanza of this poem by Rainer Maria Rilke which was pinned above my writing desk throughout the composition of this book. Writing *What a Way to Go* would not have been possible without the energy and enthusiasm of many individuals and organizations.

This novel was born and bred in Wales. The idea came to me while on a course at Tŷ Newydd Writers' Centre in Llanystumdwy in Gwynedd. A Literature Wales Writer's Bursary in 2011 then enabled me to get the writing under way, for which I am very grateful. I also wrote sections of this book at The Hideaway in Gorfanc, Carno, and at Gladstone's Library in Flintshire. *New Welsh Review* published an extract of an early draft of the novel in the September 2012 issue of the magazine (issue 97).

Thank you for the support: Amie Andrews, Diane Bailey and Geoff Young at Pen'rallt bookshop in Machynlleth, Retta Bowen, Susannah Clark, Philip Cowell, Gwen Davies, Cate Hall, Jo Haward, Alice Hendy, Machynlleth Writers' Group, Angharad

* 'As Once the Winged Energy of Delight', translation copyright © 1982 by Stephen Mitchell; from *Selected Poetry of Rainer Maria Rilke* by Rainer Maria Rilke, translated by Stephen Mitchell. Used by permission of Random House, an imprint of Penguin Random House LLC. All rights reserved.

Penrhyn Jones, Petra Sluka, Shirley Stewart, Katherine Symonds, Janet Thomas and Yemaya Wood. I'd also like to acknowledge the support I have had from all my family, especially my parents Sue Merriman and John Forster, my stepfather John Merriman and also my late and very dear grandfather, Ken Forster.

Colossal thanks also go to Sophie Lambert at Conville & Walsh literary agency and to Margaret Stead and the terrific team at Atlantic Books.

I would also like to thank Tom Crompton for joining me up on this wild and windy ridge. And thank you, Mattie and Jonah, for helping me to look at the view from a magical angle.

Books which were helpful:

The Best of the Fortean Times: The Journal of Strange Phenomena, selected and edited by Adam Sisman (Futura, 1991) This journal was the inspiration for *The Almanac of Spooky Happenings* in the novel.

There's No Such Thing as Society, Andy McSmith (Constable & Robinson Ltd, 2011)

Growing Up: Usborne Facts of Life – Adolescence, body changes and sex, edited by Robyn Gee and Cheryl Evans (Usborne Publishing, 1985). I refer to two sentences from this book on page 138; Harper re-names the book the *Puberty Bible*.

Julia Forster was born and raised in the Midlands. She studied Philosophy and Literature at the University of Warwick and has a Master's in Creative Writing from St Andrew's University. While at the University of Warwick, she was awarded the Derek Walcott prize for creative writing. She works in publishing, but has also been a magician's assistant in Brooklyn, a nanny in Milan and a waitress in Chartres. Julia now lives in mid-Wales with her husband and two young children.